"Good morning," Aisha sang.

Her twin, Felicia, glared at her. "It's not a good morning," she practically growled.

"Oh, oh! What's wrong with you, girl?"

" 'Work them hips,' " Felicia muttered, mimicking her sister's lover. Aisha burst out laughing. "It's not funny, 'Isha!"

"I'm sorry. I didn't mean for you to hear us. These walls are too thin."

"This is the third time this month that you didn't mean for me to hear you. I haven't had a good night's sleep in like forever," Felicia complained. "I can barely concentrate at work. I've turned into a freaking zombie."

Aisha picked at her toast. "What are we gonna do? I don't want to give up my men, but I don't want you pissed off at me every morning either."

"I don't want you to give up your men but so far this year, you've dated two men named Patrick, three Derricks, four Larrys, three Michaels, two Roberts, one Lorenzo, three Phillips and two Miguels."

"I guess I like variety," Aisha laughed.

"I don't think so. It means that your ass slept with half of Atlanta," Felicia retorted.

The twins were quiet as they ate their breakfast. Felicia broke the silence. "You know, I think we should get separate places."

Aisha's fork dropped to her plate with a loud clanking sound.

ALSO BY DESIREE DAY

Crazy Love

Cruising

One
G-String
Short of
Crazy

Desiree Day

POCKET BOOKS

New York   London   Toronto   Sydney

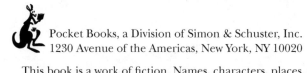

Pocket Books, a Division of Simon & Schuster, Inc.
1230 Avenue of the Americas, New York, NY 10020

First Pocket Books trade paperback edition October 2007

POCKET and colophon are registered trademarks of
Simon & Schuster, Inc.

For information regarding special discounts for bulk purchases, please contact Simon & Schuster Special Sales at 1-800-456-6798 or business@simonandschuster.com

Designed by Jamie Kerner-Scott

Manufactured in the United States of America

10 9 8 7 6 5 4 3 2

Library of Congress Cataloging-in-Publication Data is available

ISBN-13: 978-1-4165-4316-9
ISBN-10:   1-4165-4316-3

To the love of my life, Hamilton.

Acknowledgments

A million thanks to my editor, Megan McKeever. I truly value your input; you're very insightful.

A special thank-you to my agent, Bob DiForio, for his continued support.

Thank you, Sarah Wright, for your awesome copyediting skills.

XOXO's to my family and friends. I am truly grateful for your constant encouragement.

And lastly my readers, thanks y'all. I've written the same thing in the last two acknowledgments and I still believe it. You guys are phenomenal!!!

Enjoy!!!

Chapter 1

"Oh shit!"

"Oh, Miguel!"

"Work those hips, girl!"

"They're working overtime for you, baby."

"I'ma slap that ass!"

"Slap it *hard*!"

"Ooh, make it bounce, baby!"

"Nu-uh. *You* make it bounce for *me*!"

"I'm bouncing, baby! I'm bouncing!"

The sounds snatched Felicia Goodman out of a deep sleep. Her eyes snapped open as though unhinged. Anger built and worked its way up her spine with every grunt, moan and groan that seeped into her room until she went as rigid as a pole. The paper-thin walls muffled nothing. "Not again," she sighed before pulling her pillow over her head. But the sounds trickled through her down pillow and into her ears. Cursing, she tossed the pillow to the floor and glanced at the alarm clock.

"Two o'clock in the morning. Damn her! I'm going to kick her ass," she vowed, before burrowing her head under the covers, then clamping her hands over her ears. Thirty minutes later she drifted off into a restless sleep.

The next morning Felicia dragged herself into the kitchen. Circles the color of rotten apples stained the area under her eyes. The lack of sleep made her look like a half-dead raccoon.

Her fraternal twin sister, her business partner, her roommate of twenty-eight years and her best friend, Aisha, was already at the table picking at two slabs of burnt toast and looking like she had just spent a weekend at a spa. Her creamy chocolate-hued skin glowed and her eyes sparkled. "Good morning," Aisha sang.

Felicia glared at her, then, "It's not a good morning. As a matter of fact, it's a horrible morning," she practically growled.

"Uh-oh! What's wrong with you, girl?"

" 'Work them hips. . . . I'ma slap that ass,' " Felicia muttered, mimicking her sister's lover. Aisha burst out laughing. "It's not funny, 'Isha!"

"I'm sorry. I didn't mean for you to hear us. I thought we were being quiet. I did!" she insisted at seeing her sister shaking her head with disgust. "These walls are too thin."

Felicia regarded her sister. All their friends had teasingly dubbed them the Goodman Siamese twins, because they were always together, and if they weren't in the same room they were on the phone with each other. They had the same body shape, the one all the Goodman women had. Barely seeing five foot one and with enough curves to make Tyra Banks jealous.

Felicia's shoulder-length hair was pulled into a haphazard ponytail and Aisha's hair was a tousled mess on her head, reminding Felicia of a bird's nest. Felicia was the color of toasted white bread and Aisha was the color of lush dark chocolate. "This is the third time this month that you *didn't mean* for me to hear you. You know the walls are about as thin as a Kotex pad," Felicia finally answered. "How come you never go over to Miguel's place?"

Even when they were freshmen at Howard, Aisha had more men parading in and out their room than a casting director for a hip-hop video. And that behavior had carried over to every apartment they'd shared.

"I guess I could go over to his place, but he said that he liked my bed."

"Yeah, because your ass is in it," Felicia snorted. She went to the refrigerator and pulled out a carton of eggs, cheese, chopped ham, tomatoes, mushrooms and green onions. "Where is he anyway?" She stood on tiptoes as she peered into the cabinet for a bowl, and when she found one big enough she placed it on the table. Aisha glanced at her rock-hard toast, then hungrily eyed the items.

"He left. He grumbled something about working out."

"He still needs a workout?" Felicia asked, her voice rising with incredulity. "It sounded like he worked out four times last night." She reached under the sink for a skillet, quickly cleaned it before coating it with oil, set it on the stove, then turned the burner on low.

"I wish. It was only three," Aisha corrected her sister.

"Whatevah, girl! This is bananas. I haven't had a good night's sleep in like forever," Felicia complained as she cracked four eggs into the bowl and began whipping them until they were as fluffy as clouds. "I can barely concentrate at work. I've turned into a freaking zombie."

"Stop exaggerating. It's not that bad."

"Yeah, it is," Felicia argued. "I was catering a job yesterday and I was so tired that I was tempted to use my red velvet cake as a pillow. I love you, girl, and we've been hugged up together since we were in Momma's stomach, but this can't continue." She poured the egg mixture into the pan, then tilted it until the egg mixture firmed before expertly flipping it. As soon as the batter looked like a yellow Frisbee, she sprinkled on the tomatoes, green onions, ham, mushrooms and cheese, then she folded the eggs, nestling the goodies inside. Aisha's stomach growled and her mouth watered as the aroma wafted through the kitchen. Felicia slid the omelet onto her plate.

"I know. I'm sorry." Aisha picked over her toast. "What are we gonna do? I don't want to give up my men but I don't want you pissed off at me every morning either."

Felicia eyed her sister's breakfast and burst out laughing. "What the hell are you eating? It looks like slices of leather. Here take this," she said feeling sorry for her sister. She cut the omelet in half and passed it to her.

"Thanks, girl," Aisha said, grateful for the food. She immediately stuck a forkful in her mouth. "I think the toaster's broke," Aisha mumbled around a mouthful of eggs.

"It worked fine for me yesterday. I think it's more of a case of operator error," Felicia answered. "I don't want you to give up your men. But *you know* that's something to think about," Felicia started, and Aisha groaned. Whenever her sister said "you know" some shit wasn't too far behind.

"So far this year you've dated two men named Patrick, three Derricks, four Larrys, three Michaels, two Roberts, one Lorenzo, three Phillips and two Miguels."

"I guess I like variety," Aisha laughed.

"I don't think so. It means that your ass slept with half of Atlanta," Felicia retorted. They were quiet as they ate their breakfast. Aisha shot her sister a grateful glance. If it wasn't for Felicia she wouldn't have anything decent to eat. Her skills in the kitchen were just as bad as Tammy Faye Bakker's skills were in the makeup area. Just as Aisha stuck some of her breakfast into her mouth, Felicia broke the silence. "You know," she started, and Aisha rolled her eyes. "I think we should get separate places," she announced.

Aisha's fork dropped to her plate and made a loud clanking sound.

Chapter 2

Derrick Tolbert handed the valet the keys to his BMW along with an extra ten dollars to make sure he'd park it far away from other cars. The last thing he needed was some dings on his baby. Like a parent eyeing his child being led away by a kindergarten teacher on his first day of school, Derrick watched as the attendant carefully drove off with his car. He waited a moment to listen for the squeal of tires. When he didn't hear the telltale sign of abuse, he strolled off, whistling. A Mercedes is next, he thought.

In Chicago, where there were more Michael Jordan clones running around per capita than in any other city, Derrick had his own flavor and he made heads turn. Just half an inch over six three, two hundred fifteen pounds, with more muscles than a World Wrestling Entertainment wrestler and the color of a ripened mango, Derrick was gorgeous.

He sauntered into his favorite restaurant and the maître d' immediately escorted him across the room to his table. En route Derrick waved and smiled at more people than a campaigning politician. Chicago's African-American lawyer population was sizeable, but he knew most of them, and it looked like they all were eating at the restaurant tonight.

Halfway across the restaurant he could see Darla, his girlfriend, sitting stiffly as though she had a pole for a spine. He slowed his steps, not looking forward to what he had to do. He nervously tugged at his collar and glanced longingly at the bar. "Man up," Derrick ordered himself, causing the anxiety to disappear just as quickly as it came. As soon as Derrick made it to the table Darla's stance immediately relaxed.

"Hey," she gushed, then hopped up, threw her arms around him and kissed him so hard that he was sure she had bruised his lips.

"Umm, hi, baby," he said, pulling away. "Thanks for the enthusiastic welcome." He rubbed his hand across his mouth.

"Did I hurt you? I'm sorry. Let me make it better," Darla murmured as she inched closer to Derrick's mouth.

"I'll be okay," Derrick assured her as he moved his lips out of kissing range and pecked her on the forehead before landing into his seat. "What a day," he moaned as he signaled the waiter and ordered a martini.

"Bad day, baby?" Darla asked, and Derrick shook his head.

"Quite the opposite—it's been a phenomenal day. One that'll go down in the Derrick Tolbert Hall of Fame."

Darla's eyes widened and she fixed a pointed gaze on him. "Wow. That sounds exciting! What happened?"

"I got the job."

Darla pursed her mouth in concentration. "At Steinbeck and Holmes? That'll be nice since it's downtown."

"Not that one."

"Oh, then the one in Houston?"

"No, not that one," Derrick answered slowly.

"Whew. I was afraid that we were moving. Which one then?"

"Atlanta, baby! I'll be lawyering in Atlanta!"

"I love Atlanta! The weather is a thousand times better. And I might run into that fine Michael Vick. So when are we moving?" Darla asked, grinning up at Derrick expectantly. His jaw dropped so far down that he couldn't pick it up. Darla's eyes widened with disbelief. "You're not going to take me with you?" she asked, her voice quavering with hurt.

Derrick began squirming in his seat as though he was on the witness stand. "You have your job and I know how much you love it."

"It's only a job, and I can find another one in Georgia. It shouldn't be too hard to find a job as a software engineer. So many companies are headquartered there—Coca-Cola, UPS and Home Depot. And there are tons of smaller companies."

"I wouldn't want you to do that—not for me," Derrick said, his brows furrowed with irritation. "Besides, all your family is here."

"They would love to visit me in Atlanta, especially Momma. Atlanta has the best shopping. And Daddy would love to see the Falcons play, Nathan could check out Morehouse, he's thinking about becoming a doctor, and—"

"I don't think you should come with me," Derrick blurted out.

"You don't think I should come with you?" Darla repeated. "You're breaking up with me?"

"Well, no . . ."

"Oh, so we're gonna try the long-distance thing?" she asked, relieved.

"Well, no, I won't have time for that. I'll need to focus on my job. I'll need to figure out my next step."

"So you *are* breaking up with me?"

Derrick began fiddling with his drink, then: "I guess I am."

"I love you, Derrick," she said quietly, her words ringing with desperation.

"I love you too, baby," he insisted.

"So why are you leaving me?" Darla tearfully asked as their two-year relationship was becoming another piece of black history.

"Don't cry," he softly pleaded. "This opportunity is too good for me to pass up. My salary will be doubled, the company is gonna give me a—"

"I don't care what you're going to get," Darla hissed, her tears gone and her eyes as cold as a Chicago winter day. "Answer my question. Why are you leaving me? I thought we were going to get married. We even looked at rings."

"*You* looked at rings," Derrick said, exasperated, then blew out a stream of air. "Listen, let's not have this conversation here. Let's go back to my place and talk in private. We can get our dinner to—"

Darla vigorously shook her head. "I want to talk about it *now*. Why-are-you-leaving-me?" she bluntly asked.

Derrick shifted nervously in his seat. *Tell the whole truth and nothing but the truth,* rang in his ears. *But not if it hurts someone.* "I'm not leaving you. I'm leaving Chicago." There, he thought, satisfied. But his smugness was short-lived.

"Why, Derrick?" Darla asked, the tears returning. "Just tell me the truth. Is it the sex? Is it the way I drool at night? Is it the way I look?" She looked him squarely in the eyes, then asked, "Is it someone else?" Derrick shook his head. "Then what?"

Derrick silently regarded the woman who had been at his side for the past two years. She was gorgeous, almost flawless, but she reminded him of vanilla pudding. Together they had as much spark as a waterlogged Eveready battery. "Because I'm not *in* love with you," Derrick admitted. Darla let out a strangled wail. "Shit! Darla, I'm sorry."

"All those times, you told me . . . and you just told me ten minutes ago that you loved me. I don't believe it," she whispered, too dazed to cry. "So it was all fake? Us?" she said, pointing to Derrick, then to herself. "So we weren't real?"

"We were real!" Derrick insisted. "And I do love you . . . but not the way you want me to love you. Not in the way you deserve to be loved."

"So why drag it out for two years, Derrick? Why couldn't you have told me six months into it? Hell, a year into it? You've wasted my fucking time!" she spat.

"I'm sorry," Derrick whispered helplessly.

Darla stood up on wobbly legs, planted her hands on the table and looked directly into Derrick's eyes. "I'm sure you've heard the saying: What goes around comes around," she continued without waiting for his response. "Well, life is gonna sucker punch you so hard that it's gonna turn you inside out."

Chapter 3

"This is perfect. Just perfect!" Aisha gushed as she ran through the empty apartment, gazing into every room as though it was the Taj Mahal. "I love it. It's bright, it's roomy, and it's close to downtown. It's like a freaking castle. You've done good, girl." Felicia's decision to have separate apartments was beginning to sound better.

"I know," Felicia replied smugly. She knew her sister's taste was exactly like hers. The one-bedroom apartment boasted hardwood floors that were so shiny they looked like miniature ice skating rinks. Large windows gave a breathtaking view of Atlanta's skyline. The bedroom was large enough to hold a five-piece bedroom suite with a king-size bed and still had enough room to lay out a mat and do Pilates.

"Do you think I can afford it?" Aisha nervously asked while eyeing the apartment for the tenth time. The rent on an apartment this size could easily break a sister. Aisha did her calculations and came up with one thousand dollars a month, double what she was paying with Felicia. "The rent might end up being more than a mortgage payment."

"I don't think it's going to be that high. I told Tarik we were on a budget," Felicia answered, thinking of her best friend of twenty-plus years. They had fought over colored chalk in kindergarten, ate lunch together in middle school and battled each other for class president in high school, all the while remaining friends. Their friendship had since matured like a fine wine.

"Cool. Tarik will definitely hook us up."

"Don't be so sure. He's still all about the dollar. Just because he's my friend doesn't mean he's gonna do us any favors," she said.

"He will," Aisha replied confidently.

Felicia slanted a look at her sister. "Why do you say that?"

"You guys may have learned how to ride bicycles together, but I bet he'd probably give us the building if you would've slept with him. I still don't believe after all these years nothing ever happened between you two."

"'Isha! I am not feeling him like that. He's like a big brother to me. Besides, he's not even thinking about me, he's going to marry Tara."

Aisha scrunched her face, looking like a Cabbage Patch doll. "I can't believe he's marrying that fake-bougie-vanillafied-ho. Why're you letting him do it?"

Felicia pointed to herself. "Me! I don't have any say in who he marries."

"Yeah, right! And Bobby Brown and Whitney Houston weren't voted the craziest couple of 2005. That man respects your opinion."

"He does. But he's in love. And a man in love is thinking

with his dick . . . not his head. Besides, he's going to marry whomever he wants, regardless of what I have to say."

"Well, if it was me, I'd tell him that he's about to make the biggest mistake of his life."

"No you wouldn't. Neither one of us are clairvoyant, so we don't know what's going to happen. They might end up getting married and staying together for the next fifty years."

"Yeah, in marital hell," Aisha mumbled.

Felicia ignored her sister. "Anyway, Miss Kiss Ass. Every time you see Tara, you're always trying to get her to invite you to a Jack and Jill meeting."

"Yeah, a sister gotta make business contacts. I want FAACS to be the biggest accounting management company in the world. I want mo' paper than Oprah," she said while laughing. FAACS, which stood for Felicia and Aisha Consulting Services, was their three-year-old fledgling company. It was Aisha's *baby*. She came up with the concept after working for a boss who treated her as if she had about as much sense as a forty-year-old crackhead. Felicia quickly joined her sister after she discovered her bachelor's degree in art was more of a decorative piece than something of value in the real world.

FAACS served as a boutique for financial services, their clients ranging from individuals to small mom-and-pop operations. With her BA in accounting and MBA in finance and being a CPA, Aisha did all the financial consulting, marketing and sales. Felicia did all the prospecting while picking up the pieces when needed.

"Do you think we should continue the partnership?" Felicia blurted, then studied her sister for her reaction.

"Yeah, we should. Hey, where did that question come from?" Aisha asked her, eyes wide with panic.

Felicia averted her gaze. "Just asking," she murmured.

"Don't you ever scare me like that again, girl. I don't think I could stand losing you as my roommate *and* business partner." Aisha grabbed her sister's hand. "This will be the first time in twenty-eight years that we'll be living apart," she said sadly.

Felicia nodded. "I know, we've either shared a bedroom or lived together."

"Remember how we cried when Momma gave us separate rooms when we were teenagers?"

Felicia laughed. "She thought it was what we wanted."

"We did argue a lot. So I could see how she would think that. She probably thought we would end up killing each other."

"But the separate room thing lasted for a day. After that we were back to being roommates."

"Yeah. Momma thought we were crazy." She paused for a heartbeat then: "I miss her so much." Aisha's voice went soft and her eyes glassy. She was one blink away from a major tear fest.

Felicia's eyes glistened. In the six years since their mother passed away after battling cancer, there wasn't a day that went by that she didn't think about her. "Me too, 'Isha, me too. Just remember that she's out of pain now and is with Daddy. I bet they're both watching us now."

"You're right," Aisha answered, her voice thick with tears. Then: "Hi, Mom, hey, Daddy. The Goodman Siamese twins are finally gonna be separated, can you believe it?"

Felicia burst out laughing and Aisha quickly joined in. "Thanks, girl. I needed that. I know they're both watching us and I know they wouldn't want us to be sad."

"You're right," Aisha agreed, then quickly changed the subject. "Remember living together at Howard?"

"I do. Those were crazy times . . . crazy times," Felicia said. "And we've been bouncing around together for the last six years."

Aisha's eyes misted. "It'll be interesting not being able to holla at my sis when I want to. Maybe . . ."

"Maybe what?" Felicia asked while studying her sister.

"Maybe we shouldn't move out, maybe we should stay roomies," Aisha suggested. "Keep everything the same. I'll be quiet. I'll stop dating."

Felicia snorted, then shook her head. "Yeah, right. You stop dating? That's like saying President Bush is gonna stop making stupid comments."

Aisha narrowed her eyes at her sister. "Don't be getting tart with me just because I'm realistic about dating and you got the whole fairy princess thing going on. Haven't you read the fairy tales? There aren't any black princesses."

"Ah, I guess you forget from where we descended, from kings and queens of Africa. We don't need to read any fairy tales to know that we're royalty," Felicia answered. Years before their mother had died she'd had their family tree done and had discovered that a couple of their ancestors were royalty. "My prince will come for me," she muttered, but louder: "But I think it's necessary . . . us living separately. We need to grow. It's almost like—"

"What?" Aisha prodded, trying hard not to cry. She wasn't successful.

Felicia took a deep breath, then: "It's almost like our roots are becoming tangled. Like we're becoming one. It's scary."

"I know," Aisha agreed. There were many times when she

found herself doing something while wondering if it was the path her sister would take. "But we almost started off as one."

Felicia laughed. "Yeah, it's a good thing we're fraternal and not identical twins. I don't know what I would do if we were *exactly* alike," she teased.

"We're pretty close." Aisha opened her arms to her sister and Felicia stepped into them. Here is my other half, she thought. "I'm going to miss you so much." She hugged her sister. "So where are you gonna live?"

Felicia's expression mirrored her sister's. "Across the hall," she revealed.

"Across the hall!" Aisha barked. "Across the hall? I thought you were living somewhere else."

Felicia sheepishly shook her head. "I'll be living right across from you."

"Well, why didn't you tell me? I was so scared," Aisha said as she wiped away what seemed like a handful of tears. "I thought we were really going to be separated."

"You know I can't go too far away from you!"

"Well, I'm still going to miss you."

"At least I'll be able to get some damn sleep," Felicia joked.

"Ha-ha!" Aisha retorted. She abruptly turned serious. "Do you think we can afford it? I mean it's so close to downtown," she said, glancing out to admire the view. Cloud-touching skyscrapers with logos bright enough to attract UFOs glittered in the horizon. "This place is fabulous!"

"Yeah, Nineteen Twenty Peachtree is awesome. But remember, this neighborhood is in transition, so . . ."

"Either Tarik's gonna give us a deal or he's gonna ask for a crazy amount that neither one of us can afford."

"Let's hope it's the former," Felicia said.

"And we'll have enough room for FAACS," Aisha said. "And we won't be stuck working on the dining room table. Now we have two apartments to store the paperwork." She cocked her head, studying the room to mentally lay out the furniture. Aisha moved to the bay window. "Speaking of dining room tables, we can put one right here. It'll be so nice to work in front of the window with the sunlight coming in," she said dreamily.

Felicia watched her sister's progress through the living room. "Where's Tiffany going to sit?"

"You're right," Aisha said. Their part-time secretary needed a place to work. "I'll have her set up in front of the bay window and I'll work from my bedroom. It's big enough for me to add a desk."

"Where will I work?" Felicia asked. She was used to the three of them working together in the same room.

"Well, you can use Tiffany's desk when she isn't here. Otherwise you can work from home."

"Oh!" she replied sadly. "Planning where furniture goes makes it seem so real."

"You can still change your mind."

"No," Felicia answered, nodding ruefully. "This is gonna be painful, like getting a bikini wax. So we'd better do it as quickly as possible."

"You're right. Where's your boy?" Aisha asked. Just then they heard a car honking.

Felicia raced to the window and saw a silvery gray BMW. A stocky five-foot-nine man drenched in Enyce stepped out. "He's here," she said.

"I guess we should find out how much he's going to gouge us. I just hope he isn't a slumlord."

"Would you stop it! He's not a slumlord. Tarik's a good guy. I'm sure it won't be as bad as we think. He'll take care of us."

Felicia and Aisha each crossed their fingers as they walked to the door. "Let's hope that we can afford this. If not, we'll be roomies for life."

"Yuck! That's a life sentence I don't want," Felicia joked. "I'd rather move in with Aunt Hattie than live in the Aisha Motel."

"At least you get free porn," Aisha shot back at her. Then: "Are you sure you want to continue our partnership?"

Felicia breathed deeply. "Of course I do," she answered with a tight smile.

Chapter 4

"This is so nice," Felicia murmured in her boyfriend's ear. It was Saturday night and Sambuca, the jazz club, was spilling over with people. The predominately black crowd swayed and nodded to the music as though it touched their souls. "And when we get home, Momma's gonna show her appreciation." She nibbled his earlobe. "Got any requests? Speak now or later on you're gonna be at my mercy," she said as her hand dipped below the table and landed on his lap. She grinned when she felt the hard bulge.

Lawrence Davis shivered with excitement. The last time he was at Felicia's mercy, he couldn't walk for a day. He was grateful that the jazz club was dark because he was throbbing harder than an eighty-year-old man on Viagra. "Damn, girl, my only request is that you're gentle with me, baby. . . just be gentle."

"We'll see," Felicia teased before turning her attention back to the show.

Lawrence squeezed her hand and mouthed *I love you.* Felicia closed her eyes and rested her head on his shoulder, and let out a happy sigh.

Tonight was their one-year anniversary. They had met a year ago at a fund-raiser after Aisha coerced her into participating in a bachelorette auction with her. A corporate executive had chosen Aisha, and Lawrence, an entrepreneur, had selected her. Their first date was a romantic dinner cruise on Atlanta's Lake Lanier. She never imagined that a year later they'd still be seeing each other.

She felt Lawrence shift under her. "Did you oil your hair today?" he asked. Felicia shook her head. "Last night?"

Felicia thought for a moment before answering. "I think I did. Because I watched *CSI* and then—"

"Pull up off me."

"What?"

Lawrence lifted his shoulders as though trying to throw her off. "Take your head off me," he hissed.

"What's wrong with you?"

"I don't want you messing up my clothes."

"You make it sound like I'm a big greaseball. I *lightly* oiled it."

"Well, some of that oil can still get on me."

"It's not going to get on you. Trust me," Felicia reassured him before resuming her position. Seconds later she felt Lawrence flinch. Right after that he stood up.

"I'll be right back. I need to use the bathroom." Without another word he turned and walked away.

"He's so bizarre," she muttered to herself while she watched him weave his way through the tables.

Five minutes later Lawrence returned to the table wearing a sheepish grin. "I'm sorry, baby, you know how I am about spots on my clothes."

"Yeah, I do know how you are. That's why I told you that my hair wouldn't've left a stain. You should've believed me."

"I know, baby." Lawrence leaned in to kiss her, but Felicia moved back.

"Come on, I said I was sorry."

"Yeah, but you do this all the time. And it's not just your clothes, it's your couch, your bed, your dining room chairs. I'm surprised that you don't trip over your Benz."

"I said I was sorry, can't we just move on?"

"I guess, but you need help," Felicia said. She loved Lawrence. With the exception of his fetish for cleanliness, which sometimes acted as a sexual repellent, he was the perfect boyfriend.

"Now what were you saying?"

Felicia studied Lawrence and he returned her gaze with an earnest one of his own. "We don't have to wait until we get home," Felicia whispered seductively.

"You wanna get a room at the Marriott Marquis?" Felicia shook her head no. "At the Westin Peachtree Plaza?" Lawrence scratched his head when Felicia gave a nonchalant shrug. "At the Motel Six?"

"No, baby . . . in the car." Felicia giggled when Lawrence's eyebrows shot up.

"In the car? Right outside in the parking lot?" he asked excitedly.

"Yeah, are you up for it?" She reached down and caressed his crotch. "Oh yeah, you're up."

Lawrence threw a hundred-dollar bill on the table and pulled Felicia out the restaurant.

Felicia stepped into the backseat of his Mercedes and Lawrence quickly followed her. "Thank goodness for tinted windows," Felicia murmured as she settled into the luxurious leather.

"Let's adjust these seats," Lawrence said, then turned on the car, flicked a couple of switches and the passenger and driver seats inched forward, giving them more than enough room to have fun.

"That's better," Felicia whispered. "Now we can get nasty." She lay down on the seat, spread her legs and crooked her finger at Lawrence.

He eagerly positioned himself on top of Felicia, and she whimpered with desire when she felt his hard dick pressing against her thigh.

She slipped a finger under the strap of her dress, then slid it down. She seductively rolled her shoulder and Lawrence gently ran his tongue over her soft skin. Felicia moaned softly as she cupped the back of his head, encouraging him not to stop. A surprise yelp was heard when Lawrence nipped at her skin. "I've got a better place for you to nibble," Felicia groaned.

"Where?"

"If you help me get out of these clothes, I'll show you."

Using moves that would make a circus contortionist proud, Lawrence managed to get Felicia's dress off.

Stretched out on the backseat wearing only a G-string and bra, Felicia caressed her bare skin.

"Let me do that for you, baby," Lawrence said.

"Nuh-uh, don't forget you're supposed to be nibbling."

"Nibbling what?"

"This!" Felicia arched her back and tried to pull off her panties. "I'ma need you to move. I can't lift my ass high enough to get my underwear off," she said after struggling with the delicate fabric.

"I got it, babe." Lawrence leaned back and pulled off her G-string all in one fluid motion.

"Eat me!" Felicia demanded as soon as her pussy was exposed.

Lawrence grinned down at her. "Gladly." He nestled his face between her thighs and Felicia hooked her legs over his shoulders. She arched her back when his tongue breezed over her clit.

"Oh shit," she moaned as he gently nibbled on her button. "Oh shit, shit, shit," she chanted as Lawrence increased pressure. Tears came to her eyes. Lawrence ate pussy like he was feasting on caviar. Her hips mirrored his movements, then she suddenly stopped.

Lawrence pulled up sharply and looked up at her, bewilderment marring his face. "What's up, babe?"

"I want you to suck my titties."

"Eat you, suck you. Damn you got my tongue working overtime."

"Is that a complaint?"

"Hell naw!"

"Well, do what you do," Felicia said, and Lawrence reluctantly kissed his way toward her chest.

"Damn, I love your breasts!" he yelled when he saw her globes. "Let me just help myself to these." He reached around her back to unsnap her bra, and her breasts fell into his hands.

He lowered his head to Felicia's breasts, then sighed softly. "These are heaven, baby." He lovingly cupped one of her breasts and brought her nipple to his lips, softly flecking his tongue over it, and it hardened to a small bud. He leisurely moved over to its twin, and Felicia squirmed underneath him.

Suddenly Prince's "Let's Go Crazy" blared through the car. The beat bounced off the windows, startling them both so much that they froze. Felicia moved first. She groped blindly on the floor of the car until her hand touched her purse. She scooped it up.

"What are you doing?" Lawrence gasped. "Let it go to voice mail."

"You know 'Let's Go Crazy' is Aisha's ringtone," Felicia answered as though that explained everything.

"You can talk to her when you get home." He paused, then: "Or, hell, after we're done."

"It'll only be a minute." She clicked on the phone. "Hey, girl, whassup?" Lawrence glared while Felicia chatted with her sister. This was the third time this week Aisha had interrupted their lovemaking. He leaned back against the cushions and stared out the window. Felicia flicked a glance at him. She hated it when he sulked. "I'll talk to you when I get home," Felicia finished then clicked off her phone. "Now back to you," she whispered while inching toward Lawrence's mouth, but he twisted his face away from her as though he was five years old and his mother was trying to give him cod liver oil. "What's wrong?"

"What's wrong?" Lawrence asked, then snorted. "We're getting ready to have sex, then everything is put on hold because your sister called? This is crazy."

"I just wanted to make sure she was okay," Felicia replied, her tone defensive.

"She's a grown-ass lady, I'm sure she's okay."

Felicia opened her mouth to spit off a retort, then changed her mind. She didn't want to fight. "Let's finish what you started."

"I think that'll be a challenge," Lawrence huffed. Felicia glanced down; his penis had shriveled to a pencil.

"I'm up to it," Felicia replied, then winked at him.

Lawrence felt a stirring in his dick.

Felicia cradled her breasts. They locked gazes as she tenderly caressed herself. She brought a breast up to her mouth and swiped her tongue over her nipple. And it hardened to a little topaz. She repeated it with her other nipple. Lawrence ran his tongue over his lips. "Don't you want to lick this? You were doing such a good job," Felicia said, her voice husky with desire. Lawrence nodded, then pulled Felicia's breast into his mouth.

She cupped his head, encouraging him to suck longer, and she moaned softly when his tongue flew over her nipple. "Are you hard yet, baby?" she murmured.

"As a fucking baseball bat," Lawrence boasted. "You wanna feel it?"

Felicia nodded. Her hand gripped his dick and stroked it. "Mmmm, I can't resist." Leaning down, she teased the tip of his dick with her tongue, licking it as though it was a bar of dark chocolate. "You taste sooo good," Felicia breathed as her hand slipped between his legs to caress his sack and her clit began throbbing. She wanted him in her. "Slip it in!" she begged.

Lawrence immediately opened the foil package with his teeth and slid it on his stiff penis. Felicia straddled him and hovered over him. "Am I having target practice now?"

"Yeah," Felicia murmured. "Try for a bull's-eye," she teased as she wiggled her hips. She grunted softly as his penis eased into her. He gripped her hips and slowly began moving them. "Oh, baby! You feel so good. Oh, baby! Make it bounce for me," Felicia moaned as she moved with her lover.

"What? Make it bounce?" Lawrence asked between thrusts.

"Nothing. Forget about it," Felicia said.

Suddenly Prince blared through the car and Felicia froze.

"Let it ring," Lawrence panted.

"It might be important!" Felicia reached for the phone.

Lawrence grabbed her hand and put it on his neck. "Leave it, she'll be okay."

Felicia struggled against him. "How do you know?" Lawrence sighed, released his hold on Felicia, and she hopped off him to snatch up the phone just in time before it went to voice mail. "Hey, girl, whassup?" she asked, then watched out the corner of her eye as Lawrence reached for his pants and began dressing. Catching his eye, she shook her head no. He ignored her as he zipped then buttoned his pants. Two minutes later Felicia clicked off her phone and tossed it down. "I'm sorry. I won't answer it again," she promised as she snuggled against him. "I'm still horny. Let's finish what we started."

"I'm done," Lawrence snapped.

"Come on, don't be mad," she pleaded softly while stroking his face.

"You didn't even wait until we were done. You picked up the phone midstroke Felicia—midstroke!"

"I said I was sorry," Felicia said. She reached down and snatched up her G-string. "I guess I'd better get dressed," she said, then gave him an expectant glance.

"I guess you better," he huffed before opening up the back door, rounding the car and slipping open the driver's side door and sliding behind the steering wheel.

"I'm sorry," Felicia mumbled.

"This isn't the first time it happened," Lawrence said.

"So you're keeping track of when I talk to my sister?" Felicia asked. She opened the back door and slammed it shut, then hopped into the passenger seat and slammed that door. Lawrence winced at each bang. She glared at his profile.

"No, I'm not keeping track. I think the situation is fucked up. Maybe it's just me, but I think it's a little weird that you take your sister's call while we're making love."

"It's a knee-jerk reaction," Felicia tried to explain as she stroked Lawrence's thigh. "I hear my phone ring and I have to pick it up. I love making love to you. You know that."

"I love making love to you too, baby. But you can't keep answering the phone like this. That's why they invented voice mail."

"I know but that's my sister. And she—"

"Beat up Crazy Penny for you," Lawrence finished.

"Yes."

"That's what family supposed to do, stick up for one another. But you were five years old, let it go!"

"That's the point. It doesn't matter if I'm five years old or twenty-five years old, Aisha will *always* have my back, and I hers," Felicia said passionately, and stuck her hands on her hips.

Frustrated, Lawrence drummed his fingers on the steering wheel. "Anyway, what was so important tonight that you had to take her calls."

"She umm, umm," Felicia stuttered.

"See," Lawrence said smugly. "You can't even answer. Because all you guys talked about was a bunch of BS."

"We talked about business," Felicia blurted out.

Lawrence lifted an eyebrow. "And that couldn't wait until you got home?"

"No, she was looking for a client's file that she needed

right away." Lawrence glanced at the car clock. It showed one o'clock in the morning. Felicia saw the look. "She's meeting with them tomorrow, but she wanted to review the file tonight."

"Baby?"

"Yeah?"

"Next time, let it go to voice mail."

Felicia rolled her eyes. Lawrence started up the car and pulled out of the parking lot. When they got to the interstate, Lawrence paused. I-75 North would take them to his place and I-75 South would take her home. "Which way?" he asked.

Felicia smiled, then said, "Seventy-five North. I want to finish what we started. Aisha has somebody at our place. Oops," she said, clamping her hand over her mouth.

Lawrence chuckled. "I knew you two weren't talking about business. Let's forget about it."

Twenty minutes later they turned into Lawrence's subdivision and pulled up in front of a modest three-bedroom house.

Felicia peered into the dark. She saw a silhouette of someone on Lawrence's porch. "Who's that on your front porch?" Felicia asked.

Lawrence squinted. "Oh shit! That's Lorna . . . my *wife*."

Chapter 5

Derrick pulled his U-Haul in front of 1920 Peachtree and braked. When his frat brother Tarik went on and on about his newly acquired piece of property, he thought he was exaggerating. But looking at it, he realized that Tarik didn't do it justice. Even to his untrained eye, he could tell that it was an architectural masterpiece. The three-level house had a red-tiled pointed roof that sloped onto brick-covered walls, a porch that wrapped around the first level, and he could see a hint of a balcony peeking out from behind the house.

Derrick and Tarik happily hopped out the truck and stretched their legs. The two-day drive had put a dent in their friendship. They had argued more than two stepchildren fighting over their inheritance. But as soon as they stepped out the truck their dispute melted away into the warm Georgia sun, like they usually did over the years. Ever since their first meeting during freshman year at Howard, when they were thrown together as roommates, they had had enough clashes to rival Paris Hilton and Nicole Richie. But unlike those two, Derrick and Tarik had always ended the beef and moved on.

"Sweet," Derrick said, suddenly happy with his decision. Darla and Chicago was now a memory. He eyed Atlanta's skyline. He was so close to downtown that it felt like all he had to do was reach out and touch it. "This yours?" Tarik nodded proudly. "You joking."

"Naw, man. I got fifteen more like it," Tarik said modestly.

Derrick shot him a look of astonishment, which quickly turned to admiration. He didn't know his friend was rolling like that. He had come up, way up. "You the man," he said, and dapped him. He warily eyed the truck. "Ready to start unloading."

"Cool. Let's unload, shower and then head over to Club Noir. That place is bananas! Celebrities hanging out with us common folk. And you know who follow celebrities? Fine women," he said, answering his own question.

"Man, we just drove for six hours and I'm funky as hell. The only celebrities I plan on seeing are the ones on TV, and even then it's going to be a short visit. I'm already tired. As soon as we unload, I'm going to set up my bed and hit the sheets."

"You're getting old. I remember back in the day, when you could play basketball all day, help somebody move, then go out and hang until we saw the sun the next day."

"That's true," Derrick said wistfully. "Those were the days. And you were single then. What about your fiancée? Won't she have something to say about your hanging at the club?"

"It's cool. I'm getting married, not going to jail."

"Well, good for you. I've dodged that life sentence."

"Yeah, right! Darla's already got the cuff and is ready to throw away the key." Tarik laughed.

"Naw, man, that fell apart."

"Word?"

"Yeah. I had to cut it loose, something was missing."

"She had a pussy?" Tarik asked.

Derrick nodded.

"She had a mouth?"

"Yeah," Derrick answered.

"And two hands?"

"Yeah, man," Derrick said impatiently.

"Well what the hell was missing? It looks like she had everything." Tarik and Derrick rolled with laughter.

"You're foul, man . . . just foul." Derrick jumped up on the bumper and pushed open the back door. It sounded like a muffled train going over the tracks as it retracted into the ceiling of the truck.

Tarik fished around in his pockets and pulled out a set of keys. "Here you go, man."

"I appreciate this, dawg."

"No problem. Ready to move in?"

"Of course. Let's get this show started. Let's unhook the car first." Tarik hopped up alongside Derrick. The company had offered to transport it for him, but he trusted them with his car about as much as he trusted himself in a roomful of strippers. In both situations, somebody was going to get screwed.

It took him less than ten minutes to get his car unhooked from the safety constraints and onto the street. He was about to pull it into the driveway next to the U-Haul truck when Tarik motioned to him.

"Park that thing on the street. We won't have enough room if you park it in the driveway." Derrick threw a doubtful glance toward the street. "It'll be safe," Tarik reassured him.

"It better be. This is my new baby," Derrick said, admiring his new purchase. As soon as he accepted the position he had run out and traded his BMW for the Benz he had always wanted, a midnight black convertible CLK500 Cabriolet. "If it so much as gets a ding on it, you're paying for any damages."

"Yeah, okay." Tarik chuckled softly as his friend parked his Mercedes on the street, practically pulling it up on the curb. "You're sure it's safe?" he asked, biting back a laugh as Derrick walked toward him.

"You think I should pull it up on the front lawn?" he asked, his voice tinged with worry.

"You're cool, man. You're cool." Derrick joined Tarik. "Don't forget your rent is due by the fifth of every month."

"I know that, brotha. We're straight."

"Just want to make sure. I don't want to have to evict your butt," Tarik joked. His boy was the most trustworthy person he knew. Next to his mother, there wasn't anyone else he trusted more in the world. They gripped his leather couch and slowly maneuvered it down the ramp. After much wiggling, pushing and praying they got it through the front door and set it down in the middle of the living room. Derrick did a 360-degree turn, then let out a low whistle. Tarik had e-mailed him pictures, but they didn't capture the character of the apartment. If he was impressed with the exterior, he was awed by the interior.

The two-bedroom upper-level apartment had polished hardwood floors that gleamed throughout and floor-to-ceiling windows that let in slices of sunshine. Built-in pine bookcases with a dark mahogany finish bookended the windows. And brass outlet covers glinted brightly. From the living room he saw that the kitchen was equipped with shining stainless steel appliances and granite countertops.

He couldn't wait to see the bedroom and the master bath. "Sweet. This place is laid."

"I told you I got you, boy. Don't ever forget it. This is one of my prime properties. In a couple of years this building is going to triple in value. I'll be able to sell it for a pretty profit."

"I ain't mad at you. My brotha has definitely come up. Let's finish unloading." As soon as they stepped outside a BMW came to a screeching halt in back of his Mercedes, missing it by a hair strand. "What the fuck!" Derrick shouted.

Tarik laughed. "See, you don't have to go to the models, they come to you." With eagle eyes, Derrick watched as a young lady stepped out the car.

"I don't care if she's as fine as Eva Pigford. Whoever that is needs to learn how to drive! Almost crashing into my car like she some damn fool. I just got that. It's not even a month old," he fumed. His eyes narrowed as the woman marched up the driveway. They grazed over her thick legs, handful of breasts and her chocolate skin.

She skidded to a stop in front of Tarik. "Whose big-ass truck is this? And why is it taking up the whole driveway? My movers are on their way and they won't be able to get in."

"Whoa, I didn't realize that I had to make reservations to move into *my* place," Derrick said.

"Yeah, you do," the lady snapped at Derrick. "Tarik, I made arrangements with you a week ago and you promised me that I wouldn't have any problems with moving in."

Tarik wrapped his arms around Aisha. "Calm down, we

just got here. We drove all the way from Chi-Town, we're tired and we're hungry. Show a brotha some sympathy."

Aisha glanced up at Tarik. "What were you doing in Chicago?"

"I flew up so that I could help my partner drive. Check it out Aisha, this is my boy Derrick. Derrick, this is Aisha." Aisha rolled her eyes and Derrick nodded curtly. "You might remember him from Howard. He graduated with us."

Aisha looked him up and down, then said, "I don't remember him. You really need to move," Aisha said, crossing her arms over her chest.

"We will," Tarik answered as he motioned to Derrick. "As soon as we unload."

"What!" Aisha sputtered. "*As soon as you unload?*" she asked between clenched teeth. "I didn't realize that the freakin' mayor of Atlanta was moving in. I suggest that you move that or—"

"Or what?" Derrick taunted. "You're gonna keep running your mouth. If so, I think I'd better invest in a good pair of earplugs."

"Screw you! You'd better move!" Aisha said childishly.

"Both of y'all shut up!" Tarik turned to Aisha. "Yes, I did say that it would be okay to move in today, but we got here a little faster than we expected." He glanced at her car. "I don't even see your furniture. You can either call your drivers and tell them to come in about three hours or they can come tomorrow. That's the best I can offer you."

Derrick and Tarik watched as the anger melted off Aisha's face. She grinned sheepishly. "I'm sorry, Tarik. A customer just called and told me that he isn't renewing his contract with me. I guess I was taking it out on you."

"We'll try to get out your way as soon as possible. Go on and call your driver. And take a look at your apartment. I put down some new tile in the kitchen. It's the bomb. I think you'll like it. I put the same tile in your sister's, just a different color."

"Oh, she'll love that. You know how much she loves a nice kitchen."

"I know. Where is she?" Tarik nonchalantly asked.

"At the Georgia World Congress Center. She got a catering job."

"Cool."

"I'm going to take a look at the apartment."

Derrick's eyes locked onto Aisha's behind as she sauntered up the stairs.

"Damn! She's living here?" Derrick groaned. "Which apartment belongs to her?"

"The one right below yours, and her sister, Felicia, will be living across the hall from her. I'm surprised that she isn't with her. They're closer than two welded metal balls."

"Don't tell me that all Southern women are like her."

"Naw, man. She's cool. Like she said, she's having a bad day."

"Well, she definitely wasn't the welcome wagon. Whassup with her?" Derrick asked, not being able to get the image of Aisha out his head.

"She's single. I'm not sure if she's seeing somebody right now. I would be surprised if she wasn't. Aisha's the type of lady who keeps a man."

"So she's one of *those*?"

Tarik's brow puckered. "One of what?"

"The kind of lady who *has* to have a man."

"Aisha *likes* to have a man, but not for the reason you think."

"Oh really. So what's her reason?"

Tarik eyed his friend. "Think about it. A dime piece like that. She owns her own business, has a nice ride, she doesn't need anybody to pay her bills. So there's only one reason."

"Oh!" Derrick said, finally comprehending. "She wants someone to fuck with?"

Tarik laughed. "Don't be so surprised. Not every woman is looking to get married. They want to have their cake and eat it too. Well in this case their *hot dog.*"

"Damn! It's like that?"

"To hear her sister tell it. She changes men just as fast as the day changes. And she enjoys it. She pretty much does what she wants."

"Sounds like a ho to me."

Tarik's spine stiffened. "What did you say?"

"I said she's a ho," Derrick repeated with a laugh.

"Watch what you're saying. I'm closer to Aisha than my own sister."

Derrick chuckled nervously. "Come on, man. I'm just calling it how I see it. If it sounds like a ho, talks like a ho and acts like a ho, then it's a ho," he said half-jokingly.

"Derrick," Tarik warned. "Watch your mouth."

"And if I don't?"

"Do you really want to find out?" Tarik quietly asked, sizing up his friend. Where Tarik was several inches shorter than Derrick, he had one advantage over his friend. And they both knew what it was: Tarik's black belt in karate.

"I was joking," Derrick said.

"You don't talk about my friends like that."

"My bad. We cool?" Derrick held his fist out to his friend.

"Yeah." They touched fists. Derrick nodded. "Not to keep

talking about her, but if I wasn't engaged, I wouldn't mind dating someone like her. There won't be any broken hearts, no miscommunications, just sex."

"But if she's just having sex, how many men is she just having sex with?"

Tarik sighed. "Don't get it twisted. Aisha is not a *ho*. She's a lady. I've known her and her sister since we were in kindergarten. Like I said before, I admire her. She's going for hers. As long as nobody gets hurt it's all good." He glanced up at the sky. It looked like the sun was getting ready to play hide-and-seek with the moon. "Let's get going. It'll be dark soon," Tarik said.

Derrick pulled himself out of his thoughts. *Just sex, no broken hearts* raced through his head. I think I know what I want for my housewarming gift, he thought.

Chapter 6

Aisha opened her apartment door and yelled, "Hey, girl, you coming over?"

Felicia pulled her door open. "I'll be right there, give me a minute."

"Bring over your red top, I want to wear it tonight."

"You already have it. I gave it to you last week."

"Are you sure? Let me check." She picked up her phone before taking the hop, skip and a jump it took to get into her bedroom. By the time she was there she had her sister on the phone. "Are you sure I have it?" she asked while thumbing through her closet.

"You have it," Felicia insisted. "Remember, you wore it with your off-white linen pants."

"I did, didn't I," Aisha answered. "I wore it when I went out with Tom, and I think I stuck that outfit right . . ."

Felicia heard the dull scraping of coat hangers moving across the metal bar while her sister rapidly rooted through her clothes. Suddenly she heard a laugh. "You found it?"

"I did," Aisha said happily. "See you in a sec." They hung up.

Suddenly Felicia yelled from her apartment. "Do you have the prospecting list?"

"I told Tiffany to give it to you."

There was silence, then: "I found it. It was stuck under some papers. I'll be right there!"

This was the mode of communication they had developed after living apart for over a month. They were either talking on the phone with each other or opening their front doors and yelling across the hall at each other like they were at a Falcons game.

Five minutes later, Felicia traipsed into her sister's apartment. She stood on the threshold and wondered for the thousandth time why her sister was an accountant and not an interior decorator because her apartment was laid. She had been in her apartment for only a month, but it looked like she had been living there for three years.

A pink cotton candy–colored sofa decorated with fuchsia and white throw pillows dominated the living room. Bamboo-accented end tables and a coffee table enveloped the couch. A citrus green room divider stood in front of the window. Behind it sat Tiffany's desk. Through the open door she could see the bedroom filled with brightly colored objects that made her think of a tropical island. Pictures of her and her sister were dotted throughout the room.

I really miss living with her, but at least now I can wake up refreshed and not like I spent the night being tortured by the sandman, Felicia mused. The undereye bags had deflated, but she still missed their closeness. Whenever either one of them didn't have a date, they would spend hours watching old Bill Cosby and Sidney Poitier movies and stuffing their faces with popcorn.

Aisha suddenly popped into the living room.

"This is so beautiful. You sure you didn't get it all from Macy's?" Felicia asked while still admiring her sister's apartment.

Aisha laughed. "I told you that it's Target with a little Wal-Mart and IKEA thrown in."

"I love it! You need to come over and hook your sister up," she said, thinking of her lone white sofa, single plant, bed and a chest of drawers that sat in her apartment like Salvation Army castoffs. The only room that had any life was her kitchen. Energy pulsed from the room. Pots and pans hung from the ceiling and on the wall, fresh herbs grew on her windowsill, and something was always simmering on the stove. Ever since her Aunt Hattie had taught her how to cook when she was no taller than her knee, she had taken to cooking as a princess does to shopping.

Aisha walked across the room to her armoire and began pulling out sheets of paper. She glanced over her shoulder at her sister. "I still can't believe the rent on this place. It's amazing. I don't know how Tarik can afford to give it to us at this price."

"I told you he'd take care of us," Felicia said smugly.

Felicia strolled to the kitchen to make them a snack. She stood at the threshold and shook her head in disbelief. Aisha's kitchen was so empty, she was almost positive that if she said something the echo would come back. "I bet she doesn't even know she has a kitchen," Felicia mumbled. "And what did you do with the shopping list I made for you?" she called to her sister.

"I stuck it on the refrigerator door." Felicia glanced at the door. Sure enough, there it was. Looking as untouched as the day she had given it to her. Felicia pulled open the refrigerator door and sighed. Her pickings were slim. There was moldy cheese, an eggplant, mushrooms and a red bell pepper.

"Interesting items. But I can make it work." She cleaned the vegetables, sliced them up and stuck them in the oven. "Let's see what she has in the cabinet. 'Old Mother Hubbard,'" Felicia sang. "Her cupboards are bare. Well, except for this," Felicia said as she pulled out a can of tomato soup. "I think we have lunch."

Twenty minutes later Felicia walked into the living room balancing a tray with two plates with grilled vegetable sandwiches, potato chips and bowls of soup.

"You found all this in my kitchen?" Aisha asked, amazed.

Felicia laughed. "I know . . . I'm surprised too. That kitchen is about as barren as a seventy-year-old lady's womb."

"Funny," Aisha said before biting into her sandwich. "Mmmm, this is good." She sat back in her chair and slowly chewed her food, then took a sip of her soup. "And you found this in *my kitchen*?"

Felicia laughed at her sister. "Yeah. I bet it's something that I had given you. You love to go shopping but you hate shopping for food. Figure that out."

"I don't get all excited about food like you do," Aisha said, shaking her head. "I remember now. Last week I went out with a chef, he offered to cook dinner for me. So he must've left some stuff over."

"You never noticed it was here?"

"Nuh-uh. I don't go in that kitchen. It's like it got something against me, like it can sense my fear."

"No, you're just too impatient to prepare the food like you're supposed to, then sit back and let it cook."

"I know . . . but I just don't have the time. Between FAACS, dating and trying to fix up this apartment I feel like I'm in one of those big gerbil wheels."

"Well, you've got to eat. Let me show you a couple simple dishes that you can make."

"Yeah, sure," Aisha responded, her voice vague. Felicia pinned her sister with a raised eyebrow. "For real, as soon as I find some time. We will spend a whole day in the kitchen. You can show me whatever you want." They were silent as they enjoyed their food.

"You know Lawrence called me again."

Aisha's eyes widened. "Again? What the hell is his problem? You told him to kiss your ass, didn't you?"

"I would've, but I think he would've taken it literally and think I was trying to get back with him. He still wants me," Felicia explained. "So he'd take any little thing that sounds like a commitment."

"That's pathetic. Besides, he's married."

"Separated," Felicia corrected her.

Aisha set down her sandwich. "Semantics. You're not thinking about going back to him, are you?"

Felicia shrugged. "I don't know. I was in love with him," she said quietly. "And we had so much fun together. Besides, I think he's close to asking me to marry him. He's been acting all weird. We were at Kroger last week and he picked up a bridal magazine and started reading it. Besides, I'm not like you," Felicia said. Her sister currently had four men in her rotation that she could call at a moment's notice. But she still kept her heart as secured as Fort Knox.

"You just be yourself. Don't settle for him. You want some-one who's going to be able to invest one hundred percent of himself in the relationship. Not anything less."

"I know, but . . ."

"But what, Felicia?" Aisha asked sternly.

"I'm seeing him tomorrow," she confessed.

"You're what?"

"Well," Felicia said, squirming in her seat. "He said that he wanted to talk."

"That's why they have phones."

"All we're going to do is meet for lunch, then talk. That's all. I promise."

"What time are y'all meeting?"

"Eleven thirty."

"I want to see you back here at one o'clock, not a minute later."

"Aisha!"

"One o'clock. Remember, I'm the slut in this family," she joked.

"Speaking of sluts, what happened to Miguel?" Felicia said, changing the subject. She hated it when Aisha appointed her-self her official caretaker.

Aisha rolled her eyes. "What do you mean, what happened to him? The same thing that happened to all of them. I got tired of him."

"You got tired of another one?" Felicia repeated.

"Yep. You know men are just like a boring book—you can throw it out if it doesn't catch your interest in the first few pages."

"One day you might meet a bestseller and won't even know it."

Aisha sniffed. "I doubt it, but if I do, I'll be sure to award him a Pulitzer," she joked.

"Where's Tiffany? Isn't she supposed to be working today?"

"Yeah, but she had to take her son to the doctor," Aisha answered. "Nothing serious," she said, reassuring her sister after seeing the concerned expression on her face. "Just his yearly physical."

"Ooh, guess who's moving to Atlanta?"

"Who, girl? I'm not in the mood to play."

"Mia."

"Mia from Howard?" Felicia nodded and Aisha's lips curved into a smile. "That's wonderful. It'll be just like old times. We had so much fun in school. Why is she moving here?"

"She got a new job. She was getting tired of Denver. Not enough chocolate for her."

"Well, there's more than enough chocolate here. We have a ton of different flavors, ranging from creamy dark to frothy white. It'll be just like old times."

Felicia's heart jumped an extra beat. "Yep, just like old times," she whispered, then louder, "I guess it's time to talk about FAACS. How are the numbers?"

Aisha shook her head. "We lost another contract," she admitted, while giving her sister a tight smile.

Felicia's heart fell to the floor. This was their second client in two months. "Who?"

"Max Beauty Systems."

"What? They came to *us*. They needed *us*."

"I know, but apparently they no longer need us. She has her brother doing the accounting."

"Yeah," Felicia snorted. "Probably accounting them right into the ground. I bet six months from now her system is going to be so fucked up that she's going to be so far into debt that they're going to need a supersize bulldozer to pull them out."

"She was paying us five hundred a month. Add it up. That's six thousand dollars a year we're losing. We need a big client."

"You have any prospects?"

Aisha shook her head. "The big companies think we're too small to handle their needs and the smaller companies don't want to pay for our services. Think, what can we do?" Aisha rubbed her forehead. Talking about it made her head hurt.

"Maybe we need to repackage our services."

Aisha mulled over her sister's comments, then: "What do you think we should do?"

"It seems like we're offering a little too much. Maybe we need to specialize. Like focus only on tax preparation?"

"I'm going to keep doing that. That's our bread and butter. But that's not enough business to keep us alive."

"What about if we hold free seminars on investment planning?"

"Hmmm, I like that," Aisha answered, her voice excited. "We can hold a monthly seminar with about—"

"Fifty people," Felicia finished for her.

"Yeah. Then we can explain our services—"

"And people can sign up."

"Yeah, good idea, girl. I don't know why I didn't think of this before."

"Because I'm smarter than you. That's why," Felicia joked.

"Yeah, right. When you were like two years old."

Felicia's phone rang. Aisha half listened to her sister's side of the conversation. A big smile was on Felicia's face when she clicked off the phone. "Wow!"

"What are you so excited about? Looking like you just won the lottery."

"That was a job offer to cater a wedding."

"Cool!" Aisha said. "How did she hear about you?"

"She tasted some of my food at a baby shower I did last month. You remember the one with the same sex-couple?"

Felicia nodded. "When's the wedding?"

"In a couple of months. She plans on having over a hundred guests. And she said she's flexible with the menu. So you know what that means. . . ." Dollar signs shined in Felicia's eyes.

"That's good," Aisha said dryly. "You know that the quarter ends about that same time?"

Aisha didn't have to elaborate. Felicia knew that the end of the quarter was their busiest time. "It'll be okay. This job shouldn't interfere with FAACS," Felicia assured her sister.

"And we'll be kicking off the new informational financial seminars about that time."

"It's fine. I have everything under control."

"Just make sure you do," Aisha said sharply, and Felicia's eyes widened at her sister's sudden mood change.

"Whoa! What's wrong with you? You know that I keep everything separate. One never interferes with the other."

"Maybe it's about time you made your choice. Do you want to become the next B.Smith or are you with me?" Felicia stared at her sister. "So are you with me or not?"

Chapter 7

Derrick sauntered over to his French doors, pulled them open and took a deep breath before settling into a chair to enjoy the warm Georgia breeze from his deck. "Man, it's good to be home."

He had taken to Atlanta's nightlife faster than a little boy to softball. In the three months since he had moved south, he had hit every hot club, eaten at the trendiest restaurants and dated some of the most beautiful women the city had to offer.

He plopped down into one of the patio chairs, his long legs splayed in front of him. Creases of worry wrinkled his forehead. He pulled out his cell phone, flipped it open, then began dialing. He was about to hit the talk button when words floated up to him. He immediately recognized Aisha's voice. He closed his phone and inched to the edge of his seat.

"Ooh, you're a big boy," Aisha moaned.

"You like it, baby?"

"I do. I do."

"You sure it's cool to do this outside? Won't your neighbors see us?"

"Naw, we're cool. That big tree is blocking us," Aisha said, and Derrick imagined her pointing to the tree.

"Your mouth feels good."

"You like what I'm doing?"

Derrick heard a grunt. Then: "Suck my dick. Make me think I have Hoover on me."

"Who the fuck is Hoover?"

"The vacuum, baby . . . the vacuum. Ooh, God it's better," the man moaned. "Suck it, Hoover." Slurping sounds drifted up to Derrick. "Do me, Hoover. Break my head," the man chanted incoherently, then: "Aw shit, Hoover!" The man screamed loudly as he released.

Derrick's mouth was dry as though he was the one panting and screaming. "Aw shit," he whispered to himself. He tiptoed into his apartment and headed straight to his bathroom.

In one swipe he stripped off his sweatpants and boxers and kicked them into a corner. His penis sprang out in front of him long and hard. He reached into his medicine cabinet for a small jar of Vaseline. He scooped up a handful.

Positioning himself in front of the toilet as though he was going to pee, he put his left hand on the wall behind the toilet to brace himself and his right hand grabbed his dick. He slowly began stroking himself. He threw his head back, closed his eyes and parted his full lips. His hips rocked back and forth in sync with his hand. An image of Aisha's lips on his dick danced before his closed lids. "Aw, Aisha," he moaned as his strokes got faster and longer. His grip tightened. "Be my Hoover," he groaned. "Suck me, baby, suck me." He flexed his butt and his gasps bounced off the bathroom wall. His legs were as wobbly as an electrical cord. He slumped against the bathroom wall. His dick pulsed in his hand, squirting every ounce of his essence out. "Shit!"

He pulled off the rest of his clothes then hopped in the shower. "It's a little late for a cold shower," he joked to himself as he lathered himself up. Then he stood under the showerhead to rinse himself off. He stepped out the shower and immediately dried himself off. "Now I need to do what I had planned on doing earlier." He threw on a pair of sweats and a T-shirt, grabbed a beer out the refrigerator. He was at the balcony door when he remembered the voices. I don't need to broadcast my conversations to the entire neighborhood, he mused. He backpedaled and dropped down on his couch.

He took a big gulp of his beer before he clicked on his cell phone and called his mother.

"Hi, Mom," he said, smiling as soon as he heard her voice.

"Hey, baby," his mother replied. Ruby was the family matriarch, who ruled everyone with her quiet strength and charm. "How're you doing?"

Derrick sipped on his beer while he updated his mother on his new job and life. "Where's Phil?" He asked about his father. Normally midway through their conversation, he'd interrupt his mother with some trivial thing that only she could do.

"Oh, he's out," Ruby answered vaguely, and Derrick knew what that meant. He was out with one of his mistresses.

"When are you going to leave him?" Derrick almost moaned. He and his mother had been having the same conversation for years.

Ruby laughed lightly. "For what, playing poker?"

"He's not playing poker. We both know that. He's out screwing around."

"Watch your mouth. That's your father."

"Mom. Come on. We've had this conversation over and over again."

"And it looks like we're going to keep having it."

"We will until you start listening to me."

"Where am I going to go? I'm a sixty-year-old woman."

"Women get out of marriages all the time."

"I'm at a point in my life where women my age are happily retired. Not running away from home. I'm too late for a midlife crisis."

"Mommy!" Derrick pleaded, gripping his beer bottle by the neck. He wanted to crack it over somebody's head. "You're not too old. Are you too old to sit back and watch your husband screw anything with humps?"

"Derrick, I told you once about talking like that. Do it one more time and I'm going to hang up on you," Ruby warned. "We both know that your father made some mistakes," she said, stumbling over her words. "But he, Reverend Joe and I worked it all out."

Derrick sighed. The holy Reverend Joe was just as bad as Phil. They both were frequent visitors to the popular Chicago booty clubs. "What did you all work out?" Derrick asked, more out of curiosity.

"Your father and I went to marital counseling with Reverend Joe. It was intense. I learned things about your father that really explained his behavior."

"I say a dog never stops shitting in the same place," Derrick mumbled, remembering the time his mother spent crying when Phil was gone for days without even a phone call.

Or when he was in high school and discovered that he had two half brothers and three half sisters, one of which was in the same grade as he.

"What did you say?" Ruby snapped.

"Nothing, Mom."

Ruby began updating him on family gossip. "Oh yeah," Ruby stated right before they were about to hang up. "That girl you used to date stopped by a couple of days ago."

He frowned. "Who, Darla? What did she want?" he asked. She never went over to his parents' house unless he was with her.

"Well, nothing much. She just wanted to say hi. She's so sweet. She baked me a pecan pie. I barely got a sliver of it. I couldn't pry it out of your father's hands. Not that I need it . . . I really need to lose—"

"So she stopped by to drop off a pie? That's it?" Derrick asked, his voice a little sharper than he intended.

"And to talk. I told her about your new job and your big apartment," Ruby answered, then: "Oh yeah, she asked me for your address."

"You didn't give it to her, did you?" he asked, thinking of the restaurant episode. "Mom, please tell me you didn't give it to her."

Chapter 8

"You're giving him five dollars?" Aisha yelled, her slurred voice jumping over the loud music.

"Oh yeah!" Mia laughed. "Hell, with that big package, I'd give him a twenty but I'm pacing myself."

Aisha, Felicia and Mia sat on the edge of a crowd of a hundred women ogling and groping male strippers. It was two o'clock in the morning and the three friends had already eaten dinner, seen a movie and visited two different clubs where they danced until their feet felt like they had been run over by a truck. In the two weeks that Mia had moved to Atlanta the three friends had been spending their weekends as though they were college freshmen.

Mia whistled loudly as the stripper danced off the stage. He was quickly replaced with another dancer. His muscular body glistened under the hot spotlights. Easing to the edge of the stage, he slowly gyrated his pelvis in Mia's face.

"Damn you're fine," Mia shouted, and stuck a five-dollar bill into his G-string. "May I bring you home with me?"

"It's a good thing you're a lawyer," Felicia yelled in her friend's ear. "Otherwise you'd be in the poorhouse after an evening of throwing five-dollar bills at half-naked men."

Two hours later Aisha, Felicia and Mia staggered into the apartment. "I'll see y'all later," Aisha slurred as she stumbled into her apartment. Felicia unlocked her door, she and Mia fell in.

Mia wrapped her arms around Felicia and pulled her close. "You smell like shit, baby," she whispered. Cigarette smoke clung to Felicia's clothes like a two-dollar bottle of perfume.

"You really know how to get a lady hot," Felicia said half-jokingly. After not seeing each other for years, she and Mia had comfortably picked up their college relationship.

"Thanks for the compliment," Mia said as her hands slid down and cupped Felicia's butt. She gently kneaded it while Felicia nuzzled her neck.

"I've missed you so much. I've been waiting for this all day. I don't know how I was able to keep my hands off you."

"I know how," Mia teased. Then: "Because you knew how much fun we were going to have behind closed doors."

"Is that why?" Felicia asked as she rained tender kisses on Mia's lips.

"Yeah." Mia unzipped Felicia's dress and gently pushed it over her shoulders, letting it puddle at her feet. Felicia kicked it away. "Stand back," Mia ordered, and Felicia instantly complied. "I never get tired of looking at you. You haven't changed much. You look almost like you did in college."

Felicia cocked her head at her lover. "Almost?" she asked, going along with Mia. She used to tease her all the time in college.

"Your titties have gotten bigger. Your body's a piece of art."

"I feel like art shopping," Felicia said while she slowly unbuttoned Mia's blouse, then pushed it over her shoulders, where it fell to the floor.

"Bedroom?" Mia asked, and Felicia nodded. Mia grabbed her hand as she led Felicia to the bed.

"Take off your clothes. I want to see you," Felicia instructed. She loved her friend's body. Her melon-size breasts, small waist and big butt made it hard for her to keep her hands to herself.

"Would you like me to dance for you?"

"Ummm, I'm all out of dollar bills," Felicia said with a laugh.

Mia winked. "I can think of other ways you can pay me."

"Are you wearing that G-string I like so much?"

"Maybe, maybe not," she teased.

Felicia reached over and turned on her CD player. "Dance for me," she softly requested. Tyrese's voice filled the room, Mia began swiveling her hips, then slowly unzipped her low-slung jeans. She shimmied the pants over her hips, past her thighs and calves, then kicked them off.

Felicia flushed at seeing her lover standing in front of her in nothing but a bra and G-string. "You're gorgeous, girl, just gorgeous! Come here." Felicia sat up and planted her feet on the floor. Mia sauntered over to the bed and stood between Felicia's legs. Felicia tugged off the bright red G-string.

"Kiss it, baby," Mia commanded. Felicia grinned up at her before lowering her head and nestling her face between Mia's legs. Mia moaned softly. "You do it so good." She cupped the back of Felicia's head, pressing it hard against her clit.

A wave of heat washed over Felicia as her tongue slid over Mia's button and the soft folds of her pussy. Felicia's hands made their way up to Mia's behind and tenderly caressed it. Suddenly Mia's grip tightened and her body tensed. Felicia increased the pressure on Mia's clit, pushing her over the edge.

Mia wobbled. Felicia steadied her, then pulled her onto the bed. "You okay?" she whispered to her lover.

"Whew, girl, you leave me weak in the knees," Mia said, her voice shaky.

Felicia snuggled against her friend. "I'm so glad to see you again."

Chapter 9

"Damn, girl, you put your foot in it today," Tarik said around a mouthful of potato salad.

"Thanks," Felicia replied happily as she looked around Tarik's backyard. It looked like everybody shared his consensus. Nearly all of his guests had a plateful of food. Ribs hung over plates, potato salad, fried and barbecued chicken, baked beans, macaroni salad, hamburgers with her special seasonings, and hot dogs were flying off the grill as though they had wings. Even Tarik's fiancée, Tara, had a plateful, and she rarely ate more than a container of cottage cheese a day. It helped a lot that the weather cooperated. The July sun splashed them all with warmth. "I appreciate the gig. There's strawberry shortcake, peach cobbler *and* banana pudding for dessert. "

Tarik let out a low groan. "All my favorites. You really should do catering full time."

"God, I wish I could! But I can't leave Aisha, she'd die. FAACS is her life. She lives and breathes FAACS."

"But you'd die if you stay."

Felicia laughed nervously as she began arranging the napkins on the table until they resembled a sunburst. "Don't be so melodramatic. I'll be okay."

"Yeah, right! You're the only person I know who's fiending for the Food Network. You probably go to sleep with it on."

"Hardly," she denied, rolling her eyes. But sometimes it *was* on when she fell asleep. She took a deep breath, then announced, "We might be losing FAACS. And I don't want Aisha to lose her company."

"Yeah, but you won't be getting all teary-eyed if and when she loses, it will you?" Tarik challenged.

"That's mean. I care about the company as much as Aisha does."

Tarik fixed her with a stare. She bowed her head.

"When are you going to tell her, Felicia? When are you going to tell her that you want to cater full time?"

Felicia shrugged. "Dunno. But check it out. I'm not going to tell her now, especially since she might lose the company. This would be like sticking a knife in her heart. I won't do it. I won't," she vehemently insisted. "We don't have to be identical twins to have a special bond. We were conceived at the same time. We lived side by side for eight months. We were born within minutes of each other."

"I know all that," Tarik protested. "You share the same DNA, but you're two separate people."

"We are and we aren't. Physically, yes. But sometimes it seems like we share the same mind. It's a spiritual thing. I can't explain it," Felicia said to Tarik's questioning look.

"No, I don't understand it. But I want you happy. So when are you going to break the news to her?"

Felicia sighed deeply. "As soon as she gets a big client, then I'll tell her," she decided.

"You'd better. If you don't I will," he threatened.

"Tarik! You'd better not."

Tarik rested his hand on her forearm and gazed into her eyes. "I'll do it because I care about you."

Felicia blinked at him, his hand hot on her arm. "You care about me?" she croaked.

"Of course. You're my friend, I care about what happens to my friends. You're too good a cook to be sitting in front of a computer all day. You know you're happiest when you're up to your elbows in pasta."

Of course he cares about you, he's your best friend. What the hell were you thinking? she scolded herself. "Ewww, ugly image. But you're right. I'm content and at peace while in the kitchen. You know me so well," Felicia said, flashing Tarik a dazzling smile.

John, a man who Felicia occasionally hired to assist her with catering jobs, carved his way through the crowd and skidded to a stop in front of her. "Hey, we think the meat is going bad. Can you come smell it?"

"That can't be right. I got it last night. But let me check it out. The last thing I need is to be responsible for an outbreak of food poisoning." Felicia hurried toward the house.

"You'd better tell her!" Tarik called after her. "Or I will," he mumbled.

"Or you will what?"

Tarik smiled to himself before turning to glance down into his fiancée's eyes. Her five-foot body was made taller by her three-inch wedgies. With her bronzed skin, full lips and shoulder-length hair, she looked like a miniature Naomi Campbell.

"I'll make love to you until you can't walk."

"Oh, like you did last night," Tara snapped.

"I was tired," Tarik said while nervously glancing around to make sure no one overheard her comment. "You know I spent all day helping Felicia set up." He pulled Tara close to him, then put his mouth close to her ear. "But I'm okay now. Let's take a trip up to my bedroom," he whispered.

Tara pushed him off. "It's too hot," she barked.

"My house is air-conditioned," Tarik said. "Come on," he pleaded gently while tugging at her hand.

"No!" Tara snatched her hand from his. "I don't want to. Besides, I didn't bring anything else to wear. You know I hate taking an outfit off then putting it back on ten minutes later."

Tarik ignored the ten-minute comment. "You have a whole closet full of clothes upstairs," he argued.

"Those are all *work* clothes. I don't have anything casual."

"Sure you do. You left the outfit that you wore to the cookout we went to last week."

"Yeah. But almost everybody here has already seen me in that. You know my rule about people seeing me wearing the same thing within a two-week period."

Tarik resisted the urge to roll his eyes. "Nobody's paying any attention to what you're wearing."

"You think so?" She scanned the crowd until she found her girlfriend, Tasha. She trotted over when Tara motioned to her. "What was I wearing last Saturday?"

Tasha thought for a moment, then said, "Your Marc Jacobs cargo pants and cropped top. Why?"

Tara tossed Tarik a look before sauntering away with Tasha at her side. Tarik shook his head. "And that's the woman I want to marry," he mumbled to himself.

◆ ◆ ◆

Derrick strolled into the party with a lady clinging to his arm as though he was one second away from running off without her. He had met her last week at the QuikTrip. He was filling up his Benz and she her Honda Accord. By the time his tank was filled, he had learned that her name was Gail, she was twenty-eight, had two children and was temping right now until something permanent came along. Normally Derrick would've overlooked her, but the way she looked in her shorts made him change his rules.

As soon as Derrick walked in Tarik was at his side. Derrick made quick introductions. "Why don't you get something to eat?" Derrick said, pointing her toward the grill.

Tarik watched her stroll off, then gave Derrick the pound. "So why you bring sand to the beach?" Tarik whispered in Derrick's ear.

"My bad, man," Derrick replied, glancing around at the crowd. There were beautiful unattached women everywhere. It was like a candy store. "If I would've known you put it down like this, I wouldn't have bothered."

"These are mostly Tara's friends," Tarik explained.

"Don't matter whose friends they are, they all look good. Let me do a little reconnaissance before Gail fills up her plate. I bet I can get a couple numbers before she comes back."

"Do your thang, dawg!" Tarik said as Derrick slipped into the crowd.

"It's so good to relax," Tiffany said, eyeing the crowd. "Thanks for inviting us." She inched forward in her chair to watch her five-year-old son, Tyrone, who was standing in front of a boy who looked like he was already a member of a junior varsity football team. She could tell by Tyrone's stance, his legs wide apart and his chin jutted out, that he was getting ready to fight. "Oh Lord," she murmured. For some reason Tyrone thought he could beat any and every thing, but he was no bigger than a sleeping frog. She was halfway off the chair when the young boy slung his arm over her son's shoulders. Tyrone grinned at him as though he was his new best friend. Tiffany gave a sigh of relief, then settled back into her chair. "There are some fine brothas up in here. I love the summertime." Men meandered by in tank tops showing their glistening muscles and shorts that showed off muscular calves.

"Me too," Aisha said as her eyes followed a tall mahogany brother strolling past. His white drawstring pants hugged his perfectly orbed behind. And his T-shirt clung to his chest as though he was sewn into it.

"I'll second that," Mia stated. Her eyes bounced back and forth to the half-dressed men *and* women. "There are some prime rib and beefcakes strolling around here."

Tiffany continued taking in the walking masterpieces until she saw a familiar face. A little ways off stood Derrick, holding a conversation with a lady whose mouth was slightly parted with awe. "Isn't that your neighbor?" Tiffany asked, pointing.

"Derrick? Derrick's here?" Aisha asked as her hand automatically went to her hair. Even though her hair was slicked back and she had added a ponytail extension that swung down her back, she still nervously smoothed it down.

"Ooh, somebody's got a crush," Tiffany teased.

"No I don't!"

"Well what's up with all this?" she asked, and looked in a pretend mirror and mimicked Aisha's movements.

"It feels windy," Aisha replied, her tone defensive.

"Yeah, right. It's just the wind from you whipping your head around to find Derrick."

"He is fine, isn't he?" Aisha finally admitted.

"Yes he is. I wouldn't mind it if he and I were the last two contestants on *Survivor*."

"You're nasty, girl, just nasty," Aisha laughed, shaking her head. "I wonder if that's the lady he was with last night," she said, straining to see the woman who had her arms locked around Derrick's waist. "They were tonguing each other down at the front door."

"You were spying on him?"

"No!" Aisha huffed. "I heard something and I looked out my window and saw those two lips locked together like they were glued to each other." The lady in Derrick's arms pulled away just enough for Aisha to see her face. "Yep, that's her. They practically broke the headboard through the wall."

"Sounds like a serious fuck session."

"It was *multiple* fuck sessions. I didn't get to sleep until four o'clock in the morning."

"Why? Wishing it was you and not her?" Tiffany asked.

Derrick had seen Aisha as soon as he and Gail walked into the backyard. But with Gail hanging on to him like he was the last man alive and with Tiffany by Aisha's side, he couldn't get a break. Luck was with him when Gail had to go the bathroom to refresh her makeup and Tiffany had walked away dragging a little boy.

Derrick stood in the shadows and eyed Aisha as she ate an ice cream cone. The music and conversations melted away as Derrick watched Aisha's tongue swipe across the mound. His mouth went dry when her lips cupped the scoop. "Shit, Hoover," he mumbled as he imagined her lips on his penis, and it suddenly began to grow with a quickness that took him by surprise. Fortunately for him the pants he had on camouflaged his situation. But to be on the safe side he forced himself to think of Dennis Rodman in a wedding gown. He instantly deflated.

Derrick sauntered over to Aisha and plopped down in the empty chair next to her.

"Hey!"

"Like chicken, huh?" Aisha asked, nodding at his plate. It was filled with barbequed *and* fried chicken. Derrick grinned and Aisha's mouth went dry and her crotch got wet. *Nobody should be that fine.* "Um, where's your date?"

"She went to the bathroom. She should be right back." They people watched for a little while, then: "I heard your sister catered all this. She really should do it professionally."

"Nah," Aisha answered with a wave of her hand. "This is just something she does to earn a couple bucks. She isn't serious about it."

Derrick swallowed some chicken. "She should be, she definitely got some skills. Her cooking is off the chain. She can really make some dough. No pun intended." Derrick laughed at his joke.

"She's making enough dough with me," Aisha snapped.

"That's all good. But I don't think she should sleep on this."

"Felicia knows what she's doing. We're a good team, she

won't do anything to mess us up." Aisha angrily bristled in her chair like an aggravated peacock. "Since when did you turn into a career counselor? Next time I need some career advice I'll be sure to ask you because you obviously have all the answers."

"Hardly. But I can recognize skills when I see them."

"That's What Friends Are For" blared. "Oh, that's her now," Aisha said, reaching for her phone.

"Hey, girl." She listened, then: "Yeah, I tasted the wings and they were delicious." She shook her head as though her sister could see her. "No, they weren't too salty, they were good." She was silent as Felicia talked. "Sure, I'll talk to you later."

"Did she leave already?"

"Nope, she's in the house."

"Oh," Derrick answered. Suddenly his mouth turned up into a smile. "I bet you have some skills."

"Damn right! I'm a CPA, I have a BA in accounting, my MBA in finance and I'm president of my own company. Damn right I have some skills."

"I wasn't thinking about those kind of skills," Derrick murmured. Aisha held her breath as his eyes roamed over her body then stopped at her mouth. "I would love to take you out, then find out what you can do with those lips."

Aisha gasped. "You're asking me out, while you're on a date? That's so disrespectful!"

"She's not my girl," Derrick answered. "We just met."

"Girl or not, you don't do stuff like that."

"I'm sorry, my timing is off. It's just that I rarely see you at the apartment. But I would really like to take you out."

Aisha frowned. "Aw hell naw! We'll go out when President Bush is elected for a third term."

"That won't happen," Derrick protested.

Aisha winked. Just then his girlfriend strolled up.

She was what Aisha called a T.A.W., typical Atlanta woman. She had the shoulder-length hair with the blond highlights, Prada'd and Gucci'd down, and the hand shaped in a permanent claw for clutching her men.

She glanced at Aisha, tossed her a fake smile, instantly dismissing her, then turned to Derrick. "Hey, baby, come on. I want you to meet a friend of mine. I didn't know she was going to be here," she said, then reached for his hand.

"Talk to you later," he said as he let himself be led away by Gail.

Aisha watched them go. She shook her head. "What a player. And he's not even smart about it. How dare he ask me out while he's with another woman? You'd better learn how to play the game," Aisha said. She would bet her favorite G-string that Derrick never stayed with a woman long enough for him to even bother to remember her last name.

Moments later Tiffany returned.

"Damn, girl. I might have to take a plunge in the pool," Aisha said while fanning herself with her hand.

"That fine-ass Derrick got you hot?" Tiffany asked.

"Yeah, do you think I should do something about it?" she asked.

Chapter 10

Derrick backed into his driveway and pulled his golf clubs out the car. The mid-September weather provided the perfect opportunity for him to get out and hit some balls with his boss. At seven o'clock that morning the green was already highly trafficked. If everything keeps flowing in the right direction, then I might be partner this time next year, he thought, whistling to himself as he made his way up to his front door. It was four months since his move to Atlanta, and his life had been going smoother than the Temptations' dance moves. Chicago seemed like a lifetime ago.

Suddenly he heard his name being called and he panicked. "Oh shit! I don't think I have a date tonight." He did a mental check of his calendar and it took him only a second to remember that this evening was all his. He had planned on cracking a six-pack while watching the game. Oh well, she's here now, he thought as he pasted what he hoped was a sincere smile on his face and then turned to the voice. As soon as he saw who it was, the smile fell from his face, faster than a cheating man's boxer briefs.

"Darla? Darla?" he repeated, surprised. "What are you doing here?"

Darla slammed her car door shut and took her time walking up the driveway. She stopped right in front of him. "I see you got your Benz," she said, eyeing the car while ignoring his question. "It's nice. Is it everything you thought it would be?"

Something in her tone made Derrick take a step back. This wasn't the same sweet and classy lady he had left in Chicago. "What are you doing here?" Derrick repeated.

"I came to see you. I need to talk to you."

"You need to talk to me? You could've called."

Darla shrugged. "I could've, but I didn't, now I'm here. Let's go inside."

Derrick opened his mouth to object, but something in her eyes told him that it wouldn't be a wise thing to do. "Let's go." They were silent as he led her into his apartment.

"Nice place," Darla said, looking around. "I want something to drink."

"Do I look like your servant?"

Darla smiled. "The more you argue with me, the longer it'll take for you to find out why I came. So if I were you, I'd get jumping."

What the fuck! Who is this lady? Derrick thought.

Darla saw his reaction and she winked at him, causing Derrick to almost trip over his feet on his twenty-step trek to his kitchen. By the time he returned with bottled water and a glass filled with ice cubes Darla had made herself comfortable on his couch.

Darla eyed the glass, then slid it in Derrick's direction. "You know I don't like cubes. I prefer crushed."

"Why don't you just be happy with the ice cubes?"

Darla shook her head. "Nope. I want crushed."

Derrick snatched up the glass, stomped to the kitchen and promptly replaced the cubes with crushed ice. "Happy now?" He slammed the glass down. "What do you want?"

"You're looking good," Darla said. He slipped off his jacket, exposing a Sean John polo that clung to his chest and biceps.

"Whassup, Darla? Thanks for the compliments, but I know you didn't come all the way from Chicago to make small talk."

Darla shook her head. "No I didn't. I felt that my news would be better delivered in person."

"What?" Derrick said impatiently.

"Remember your last weekend in Chicago?"

Derrick shrugged. "Kinda, I hung out with my boys, that's all I remember."

"You don't remember calling me?"

"Nope."

"You don't remember calling me and inviting me over to your place at three o'clock in the morning?"

"Nope."

"You don't remember us making love?"

"Aw hell no! None of that happened. You're making that stuff up."

Darla shook her head, incredulous. "Either you're one hell of a liar or you truly don't remember. Well, let me help you. You called me, crying and saying how much you missed me and that you wanted to see me before you left for Atlanta. So me and my stupid ass believed you and went over to your place. We made love. Then I never heard from you again.

It's a good thing your mom likes me so much. She really influenced my decision to tell you. Because I wasn't going to," Darla confessed.

"What? Rewind. I feel like I stepped into the middle of a conversation. What weren't you going to tell me?" Derrick asked impatiently.

"My parents told me that you have a right to know. And I guess they're right."

"What should I know?" Derrick asked cautiously, and his stomach slowly twisted.

"I'm three months pregnant," Darla announced.

"Wow, Darla, congratulations. Why are you telling me?" Suddenly his eyes grew bigger than his coffee table and his blood dropped down to his toes. "No!" He shook his head and backed away. "No!" he repeated.

"Yes!" Darla smirked. "It's your baby, Derrick. You're going to be a daddy."

Chapter 11

Felicia trudged up the steps to Tarik's door. The oversize insulated bag she was carrying slowed her progress so much so that she felt like she was walking in quicksand. The two-second trip up to his front door felt like twenty minutes. As soon as she reached the door she gratefully placed the bag on the ground, knowing that Tarik would carry it into the house for her.

She rang the doorbell, then rubbed her shoulder. "Boy, that bag was heavy. I don't know why—" Tarik opened the door and Felicia's mouth dropped. She couldn't tear her eyes away from his bare chest. It wasn't that she hadn't seen his chest before, she had—at the beach, while he worked in the yard and a couple of years ago when he helped her paint her bedroom. But that was before he started working out. Now he looked like he could be a Calvin Klein model plastered on a billboard. His chest rippled with muscles that weren't there a year ago.

Sweat trickled down his muscled pecs, down his well-defined biceps and into the elastic waistband of his shorts. Felicia gulped deeply. Damn!

"You don't know what?"

"Huh?"

"When I opened the door, you were saying 'I don't know why' and then you stopped."

"Oh!" Felicia shook her head to clear it. "I was saying that I don't know why I'm carrying this big bag of food," she answered before nudging it with her toe.

Tarik grinned, before leaning down and picking up the bag as effortlessly as though it weighed less than a newborn baby. "Good, you brought the food. Can't wait to taste it. I've been saving my appetite all day. Come on in." He held the door open. She squeezed past him.

"Is Tara home?" she asked loudly, then braced herself for the answer.

Tarik shook his head. "She's out," he answered, and Felicia exhaled slowly. "I'm sorry for this," he said while motioning to his bare chest. "But I just finished working out." He grabbed a towel and swiped it over his chest and arms. Felicia inhaled sharply; Tarik glanced at her.

"I thought I was going to sneeze," she lied.

"Don't be sneezing around my food," he drawled. "What did you bring me?"

Tarik was her official tester. Whenever she made a new dish he was the first to try it. "Tortilla turkey wraps, mixed green salad with dried cranberries, walnuts, diced chicken and grape tomatoes, and confetti rice pilaf. And for dessert, manhandler cookies. I have oatmeal raisin, triple chocolate chip, macadamia nut and triple fudge."

"Let's have at it." He carried the bag to the kitchen, where they both unpacked it and filled their plates.

"Aren't you going to put on a shirt?" Felicia asked. It didn't take long for her to notice that every time Tarik brought his fork to his mouth his biceps bulged.

"I'm cool," Tarik answered. He took a bite of the turkey wrap. "This is good."

"And healthy," Felicia quipped while averting her eyes from his muscled torso.

The hand that was halfway to his mouth stopped midway. He stared at her as though seeing her for the first time. "What's wrong?" Felicia asked, laughing. Tarik looked like he had just found out he had just sold one of his properties for a seven-figure amount. "You looked a little stunned."

Tarik stuffed a forkful of confetti rice in his mouth, then quickly swallowed, barely chewing it. "It's your food. It's off the chain. You got me in a daze."

Felicia laughed. "You're sweet. I'm glad you enjoy it. It's hard to make healthy and delicious meals. Are you almost ready for some cookies?"

"Sure."

Felicia stepped up and walked over to the counter. "Which kind?" she called over her shoulder.

"One of each," Tarik answered. "Pile them on."

Felicia shook her head while stacking cookies on a plate. "Here you go," she said, placing the food in front of them. "Would you like some of my homemade strawberry lemonade or milk?"

"Both!" Felicia turned around to get the drinks, but stopped at the sound of Tarik's voice. "Let me get them. The least I can do is help out. Sit down and give those size tens a rest," Tarik teased.

"Size ten!" Felicia huffed. "I'm a six and a half. I don't have clown feet. Unlike you," she said, glancing at Tarik's bare feet. "What size do you wear?"

"Thirteen!" Tarik answered, then went to the counter for the drinks.

"You have mountain-climbing feet."

"Nuh-uh, your sister," Tarik teased, and Felicia burst out laughing.

"Your brother," Felicia shot back.

The chirping of Tarik's cell phone cut through their laughter. He trotted over to the kitchen counter and glanced at the display. "It's my baby," he announced.

"Tell her I said hello." Felicia smiled. And resisted the urge to gag. She hated his fiancée; she was as phony as the hair she sometimes wore. She tilted her head and studied Tarik while he chatted with his wife-to-be.

His shorts were hanging low on his hips. A speck of something caught Felicia's eye. She leaned forward and sucked in a breath of air. Tarik shot her a look of alarm. She smiled weakly, signaling that she was okay. *When did he get that sexy mole? Why haven't I noticed it before?*

Tarik clicked off his phone. "I need to make a run over to Tara's girlfriend's house. Both of them are giving a presentation to the mayor tomorrow, and she wants to use me as her guinea pig. Wanna come? I'm sure they'll be glad to have an extra person to critique them."

"Hmmm, no thanks," Felicia said, pulling herself out her chair. "I guess we can hang out another day." She gathered up her things and walked to the door. "Talk to you later?"

"Give me those." He grabbed her items out her hand and Felicia followed him to her car. He stuck everything in the trunk. "Talk to you later." With a furrowed brow Tarik watched her drive away. "There's something different about Felicia. And it's making me hot. This is so wrong," Tarik said. "So wrong."

Chapter 12

Aisha buried her face in her arms and sighed deeply. Fortunately her bedroom door was closed. On the other side of the door were two people with whom she dreaded talking. "They'll be okay," she muttered. "They're big girls. They can deal with it. I'm moving heaven and earth to make sure everything turns out okay. Well, I'd better get jumping." She got up off the chair, winked at herself in the mirror, then strolled out into the living room. "Okay, ladies, I have some good news and some bad news," Aisha announced to her sister and Tiffany.

"Are you going to fire me?" Tiffany asked fearfully.

Aisha turned startled eyes on her assistant. "Why would you ask that?"

"Because you had me move the Taylor Manufacturing file to the client cancellation drawer. That's the second account we lost this month."

Aisha laughed nervously. "You're way ahead of me. That was my bad news. And your job is fine . . . for now," she tacked on quietly. Tiffany's jaw dropped and Aisha hurriedly explained. "I'm sorry, Tiffany, but if we keep losing customers the way we are then we will have to let you go," she said sadly before glancing at Felicia, who gave a small nod of understanding.

Tiffany clenched her teeth and crossed her arms over her chest. She loved Aisha and Felicia but she hated working for them. She always felt like an outsider. With a mere look or a movement of the head, they had silent conversations that only they understood.

"What's the good news, girl?" Felicia asked. "I think we need some."

Aisha smiled at her sister. "Well, all our hard work has paid off. KBS is giving me an opportunity to present to their top executives the services we can provide them."

"Woo-hoo!" Tiffany shouted. "This is it, girl. We're going to be rolling in money. And I won't lose my job!"

Felicia hugged her sister. "I know. Now we don't have to worry about any other companies leaving us, 'cause KBS will be throwing money at us."

"Hold up, y'all. We haven't gotten the job yet. And I still have to create my presentation. They haven't told me when they want me to come so we got to be ready."

"So this account will either make us or break us?" Felicia asked, looking into her sister's eyes, and immediately felt ashamed of herself when she had the urge to sigh with relief. After much contemplation and bullying from Tarik, she decided to resign from FAACS. But now wasn't the time to tell her sister about her decision. I'll do it when it feels right, Felicia decided before settling back in her chair to listen to Aisha.

Aisha nodded. "We need this account, girl. If FAACS is going to survive we need this account like the Lakers need Shaq. I'm going to need all of your help. I'm going to warn you, there might be some overtime. But just remember, we're doing this to secure our future, so sometimes sacrifices have to be made."

"I'm here for you, girl. If I have to, I'll bring Tyrone and he'll sleep over while we work," Tiffany solemnly offered.

Aisha laughed. "Thanks. But I hope it doesn't come to that."

"And you know that I'm here for you," Felicia said. "Just tell us what to do."

"Ooh, now you'll get a chance to meet that fine-ass Lance Forbes. Forget the job, I want *him*," Tiffany joked.

"Hush! The only thing I know is that we'd blow up if we get this KBS gig. Did you see their revenues listed in the latest issue of *Black Enterprise*? That company is growing so fast. It'll be heaven to have them as one of our clients," Aisha said. "And I can't believe that with all their money they haven't updated their accounting system. I hadn't seen anything move that slow since Uncle Rob had his hemorrhoids operated on."

"Speaking of fine-ass men," Tiffany cut in. "Did y'all see your neighbor today? I saw him on the way in. Brother knows he can rock an Armani."

"Was he by himself?" Aisha asked.

"Yeah, as far as I saw. Why?"

"Because he must think this is a motel, the way he keeps bringing women in here and they act like they struck gold. To make it worse, I can hear his friends showing their gratitude."

"What? Outside his door?" Tiffany asked.

Aisha shook her head. "His *bedroom* is right over mine."

"Maybe you should tell him to keep it down," Felicia offered.

"Yeah right! I'll tell him that his playtime is keeping me up at night."

"Join the club. Now you have a little taste of what I had to go through. Karma is a bitch. What goes around comes around," Felicia said.

"This has nothing to do with karma. It's just a case of a horny neighbor, nothing more, nothing less."

"Okay, keep believing that," Felicia murmured.

Aisha rolled her eyes at her sister. "*Anyway,* it does make me wonder," Aisha said, grinning wickedly.

"What?" Tiffany asked.

"I wonder if Derrick is as good as he sounds?"

"Maybe you should try him out."

"Maybe . . . maybe I should. But y'all know he had the nerve to ask me out while he was on a date. So I'm not looking to get caught up with somebody I can't trust." Aisha's voice turned serious and she fixed her gaze on Tiffany, then Felicia. "Y'all listen carefully." She paused to make sure she had their attention, then: "We need to get this account, it's *imperative* that we do so. Getting it will allow us to soar or keep us above ground. And I want to soar. Don't y'all?"

Chapter 13

Felicia tugged at the blankets. Trying to get them from her bed-mate was like trying to pull a tissue from under a boulder. "Oh crap!" she uttered when the towel protecting the pillowcase shifted under her. Halting her wrestling with the blankets long enough for her to readjust the towel, she resumed her fight.

"Stop hogging all the blankets," she grumbled while nudging him in his back.

Lawrence turned around to face her. "You cold?" Felicia nodded. "Well I can make you hot."

"You've already made me hot more times than I can count." Felicia grinned before pecking Lawrence on the lips. When they had met for lunch, never in her wildest dreams did she imagine that they would end up in bed. "Now I just want to relax." Felicia pulled the blankets over her and Lawrence wrapped an arm around her waist and pulled her closer. She nestled against him tightly, his body heat warming her. His penis pressed against her back. She sighed happily before drifting to sleep.

"Let's Go Crazy" blared and Felicia jumped as though a gun had gone off. "What's wrong, baby?" Lawrence mumbled, sounding like he had a mouthful of M&M's. He had slipped into a coma-like sleep.

"Just the phone," Felicia said, trying to slow her heart. "I'll be right back." She slipped off the bed, plucked up her cell phone and padded into the bathroom. "Hello," she whispered into the phone.

"Felicia?"

"Yeah, what's up?"

"Why are you talking so low?"

"Um, because—"

"Where are you?" Aisha asked.

"Um, I had a catering job."

"This late?" Aisha asked as she glanced at her clock. It read eleven o'clock.

"I'm, um, done, but I, um, um, have to clean up now."

"Oh, well, I was just checking up on you. I stopped by your apartment and you weren't there."

"I, um, should be home in about, um, an hour or so," she answered vaguely.

"Do you want me to wait up for you?"

"No, um, don't wait."

"Okay, I'll see you tomorrow then."

"Bye."

Felicia slumped against the bathroom wall. "I hate lying," she muttered. "There's too much stuff to keep straight."

Felicia tiptoed back into the bedroom praying that Lawrence had gone back to sleep. At the bed her glance automatically went to her sock-encased feet. Lawrence hated for her to walk on the rug then get into bed—he hated the germs.

His rule was that she could wear socks to bed only if they were freshly laundered and if she put them on while in bed.

"Maybe he won't notice," she whispered. She noiselessly pulled back the blankets, eased one half of her body in, then, when nothing happened, she slid in the other half. Whew! She pulled the cover over her, then closed her eyes.

Suddenly Lawrence's voice boomed throughout the bedroom. "You're not wearing those dirty socks, are you?"

"They aren't dirty. I just walked to the bathroom on *your* rug," Felicia replied defiantly.

"Don't you think you should take them off? You know how I feel about germs in my bed."

"You bring germs into your bed every day. Nobody's one hundred percent germ-free," Felicia protested. "They're flying all over. Look, there's one on your face right now."

"No there isn't," Lawrence answered, but he couldn't resist running a hand over his face. Felicia grinned. "So you're not going to take them off?" Felicia shook her head. Lawrence pulled back the covers and Felicia held her breath as his eyes roved down her body, starting at the top of her head and moving down to the tops of her toes. His perusal was strictly nonsexual. It was more as if he was studying a bug. "What about I spray your feet with Lysol?"

Felicia opened her mouth to protest. He was never this bad. Not resting her head on his shoulder, having him watch her wash her hands or even boiling his cutlery were all bizarre habits that she had learned to tolerate, but this? "Lawrence?"

"Please?" he begged, looking like someone on his knees begging his executioner for his life. His eyes were wide with fear, his bottom lip trembled, and his nostrils flared.

"Umm, sure," Felicia uneasily agreed, and he flicked on the light.

What? Felicia mouthed as he reached into his nightstand drawer and pulled out a can of Lysol and foot covers. He slid the covers over his bare feet before standing up. Then, wearing a mask of determination, he pulled back the covers and sprayed his side of the bed, then motioned for Felicia to roll over. Shocked into a daze, she did as he instructed and watched as he sprayed her side of the bed and her feet.

"That's enough," Felicia protested when she felt her socks getting saturated.

He set the can of Lysol on the floor, pulled off his foot covers, tossed them in the wastebasket, clicked off the lights, then slid into bed as though nothing bizarre had transpired. "What did your sister want?"

Felicia had closed her eyes and now they whipped open. *Shit! Shit! Shit! I just want him to take his Lysol-smelling ass to sleep.* "What?"

"What did your sister want?"

"Oh, she was just checking up on me."

"She didn't know that you were over here . . . with me?"

Felicia's eyes adjusted to the dark, and she could make out Lawrence's profile. He was lying on his back with his hands behind his head. "Um, no, she didn't."

"Where did you tell her you were?"

"A catering job."

"So you haven't told her about us?"

"No."

"Why not?"

"I don't want the arguments, the lectures."

"About what?"

Felicia smacked her teeth. "You're still married, Lawrence."

"Separated."

"Semantics. In the eyes of the law you're still married."

"In the eyes of the law? I think there are more eyes involved in this than necessary."

"In mine too," Felicia admitted.

"I want to get a divorce," Lawrence said, and Felicia heard the frustration in his voice. "It's just that we have property to split, pensions and 401(k)s. It's a lot of shit that needs to be divided."

"So when? When are you gonna get your divorce?" Felicia whined, and immediately hated it. She never wanted to be one of those whiny women begging their lovers to leave their wives. "I feel in limbo. Almost like I'm in purgatory," she said softly.

Lawrence reached over and clicked on the light. Felicia groaned and covered her eyes with her hand. "I'm not holding you against your will, Felicia. You're always free to go."

"I know," Felicia moaned. "But it's so easy to pretend that you are just separated and not really married. You know, when I think of a man being separated I also imagine that the wife is on a vacation, and one day, out of the blue, she'd return ready to resume her position as wife."

"It's not like that!" Lawrence protested.

"What do you call rolling up to your house and finding her sitting on your porch?"

"Bad timing," Lawrence answered. "She and I are really going to get a divorce. Believe that! But I want to know whether you want to hang with me until everything's settled."

"I don't know," Felicia answered meekly.

"And if so, would you tell your sister? I don't plan on tip-toeing around like some punk because you're afraid to talk to your sister about us."

"I hate hiding too," Felicia said, conveniently forgetting that she and Mia spent the night before licking each other like lollipops. "But I don't feel like dealing with Aisha right now. I need some time to sort this whole thing out." And to decide whether I want to stay with this germ nut, she thought.

Lawrence eyed her. "How much time do you need, Felicia? Tell me that: How much time do you need?"

As soon as Felicia opened her mouth, "Let's Go Crazy" blasted from her cell phone.

Chapter 14

Aisha sat at the bar of the Sun Dial restaurant. At seventy-three stories up, on top of the Westin Peachtree Plaza Hotel in downtown Atlanta, it was a perennial favorite because of its breathtaking views of the city and delicious cuisine. But today the view wasn't on her mind. She nervously crossed one leg over the other, then uncrossed them, then quickly repeated the movement. "I have to get this contract," she muttered to herself. Her heart pounded against her chest. An image of her closing down FAACS and standing in the unemployment line waiting to sign up for weekly unemployment checks flashed before her eyes. "I can't lose FAACS. And I won't," she vowed before turning her attention back to her work. Today was her meeting with Lance Forbes of KBS. "That's What Friends Are For" played softly, slicing into her thoughts, and she clicked her cell phone on. "Hey girl!"

"Have you met with him yet?" Felicia asked, and Aisha rolled her eyes.

"You know the meeting isn't until twelve o'clock. And you

know Mr. Forbes won't show up before then. You know how he rolls. I wish that I had an opportunity to meet with his executive board like we planned."

"Why? This puts you face to face with the decision maker. Hundreds of people would love to be in your shoes right now."

"I know. But the more people to influence *him* the better."

"Doesn't matter. I heard that Lance Forbes makes his own decisions. It doesn't matter if a million people liked you. If he's not feeling you, then . . ."

"You're right. I'm nervous and not thinking right."

"You got this, girl! Call me after the meeting, okay?"

"I will," Aisha promised.

"Right *after*. Even before you get to your car."

"I told you I'll call."

"Okay, I'll talk to you later. Don't forget to call me!" Felicia shouted before her sister clicked off the phone.

"God, I hope craziness doesn't run in the family," she muttered before turning her attention back to her presentation. In one hand she held a bottle of Evian and in the other she held a blinding pink highlighter. She still had a few minutes left before Lance Forbes arrived, so she began to meticulously review her presentation for the hundredth time. Over the past week she had become so familiar with the document that she was quoting it in her sleep. After reciting a few key points, she set down her highlighter long enough to run a hand over her already perfect hair.

She nervously glanced at her watch. It was two minutes to twelve. Lance Forbes had a reputation for punctuality. He never arrived a minute early or a minute later than the appointed time. He always came precisely on the dot. Aisha absentmindedly took a sip of water. "Well, two more minutes before my life will change—either I'll be a rich lady or a bag lady."

"What about bag ladies?"

Aisha swirled around and looked up into a pair of honey-colored eyes. *Lance Forbes.* He broke his rule by showing up one minute early. His five-foot-eleven muscled frame was covered by a jet black Armani suit. She glanced down at his feet. She knew enough about men's shoes to know that the pair he wore wasn't from Wal-Mart. From her limited knowledge she deduced they were Prada. He wasn't very tall but he gave off a power that almost left her breathless.

"Atlanta—downtown Atlanta is filled with bag ladies. I-I mean bag people," she stuttered, then wanted to cover her face with a cocktail napkin. She quickly composed herself. "But that's not important," she said. "Why don't we get our table, it should be ready." They strolled over to the maître d', who instructed them to follow him.

Lance motioned for her to lead and his eyes leisurely followed her progress, running up her well-muscled legs, tight behind and swinging hair.

Aisha sat in her chair, and even before she could settle in the sommelier sauntered over with the wine list, which was about the size of a paperback book. "Oh, nothing for me," Aisha protested. "I don't drink while I'm working," she said lightly before closing the minibook. The sommelier then rounded the table and hovered over Lance while he studied the list.

Lance glanced up from the minibook. "Who's going to report you?" he asked, his voice teasing.

Aisha shook her head. "Nobody. But I'm working and it's a rule that I have." *Especially when I'm giving a presentation that will hopefully save the company.*

Lance raised an eyebrow. "Never?" he asked, almost taunting her. Aisha shook her head. "What about a glass?"

"I don't think so."

"Come on now. I thought the client was always right."

Aisha studied him, not knowing if he was testing her or really wanted her to drink with him because he didn't want to drink alone. "Okay, half a glass."

"Good. I would hate to be the only one drinking."

He studied the wine list and Aisha regarded him. His skin was as smooth as whipped chocolate. He had thick glossy eyebrows and a wide sensuous mouth. *Damn he's gorgeous!* "I'm sorry, what were you saying?" Aisha asked, pulling her eyes away from Lance's mouth and inching them up to his eyes.

"I said, I think we'll have the Bollinger 1997 Grande Année Brut Champagne."

"Champagne? I can't have champagne in the middle of the day," Aisha protested.

"Why not?"

"It seems so . . ." She cocked her head searching for the right word. "Decadent," she decided.

"It's good to break the rules once in a while. Trust me, I know," he said confidently. He motioned to the sommelier, who had taken a few steps back, but was hovering close by like a hummingbird. Moments later the sommelier returned with the champagne and glasses.

"Are we celebrating something special?" the sommelier asked.

"I am," Lance said, looking into Aisha's eyes.

"And what is that, sir?"

"I'm having lunch with a beautiful lady."

"Aha! That is something to celebrate."

Aisha felt her face tingling and was grateful for her lush coloring—otherwise he would see her blushing like a naïve twelve-year-old. Feeling self-conscious, she averted her eyes.

"You're embarrassed," Lance observed.

"A little," Aisha admitted.

"You're a very beautiful lady. I'm sure you get attention from men all the time. How many men are you seeing now?"

Aisha laughed nervously. "Umm, I'm not seeing anybody," she answered, then cleared her throat. "Maybe we should order lunch."

"Maybe we should," Lance replied smoothly.

It wasn't until after they'd eaten and Lance talked her into a second glass of wine that they got down to business.

"So if you let FAACS handle KBS's accounting system conversion, we'll not only get you up and running faster than anyone else, but the new system will be more efficient. You'll be getting the Mercedes of systems, it will do everything you've ever wanted and then some. Just by installing this system, I can guarantee that you'll see a ten percent increase in productivity from your workers."

"Those are ambitious promises," Lance answered.

"We can do it!" Aisha insisted. "We have a proven track record—"

Lance held up his hand. "I know all about your track record. I do my research," he said in response to Aisha's questioning look. "What do you like to do when you're not working?"

"I'm sorry?" Aisha asked, confused by the sudden change

in conversation. This man changed subjects more than Monique changes her outfits at the BET award show.

"You're a young lady who owns her own business. I know that you have to do something to relax. You can't stay that beautiful by working all the time."

"Oh. I don't have much time for fun. Do I—I mean— do—we—" *Slow it down, girl.* She took a calming breath, then: "Does FAACS have the job?"

"May I pamper you?" Lance asked, ignoring her question.

Aisha placed her hands on the table, palms down, and leaned toward Lance. "If pampering involves giving me your business, then yes, you may pamper me."

"I've never had any of my propositions for fun interpreted that way before," he answered slowly. "It's different," he muttered.

"Well, FAACS is a unique firm. We can—"

Lance held up his hand, signaling her to stop. "I know what you can do for KBS, but what can I do for Aisha?"

"Just give me the job. That'll be sufficient."

"Is it?" Lance asked. He cocked his head and his eyes slowly roamed over her face, passed her neck, moved over her shoulders and stopped at her breasts. Aisha's nipples immediately hardened. Lance chuckled. "I think you need something more," he decided.

"Mr. Forbes, I don't mix business and pleasure. My grandmother told me, 'Never stroke the trunk of the man who owns the tree,'" she said primly.

"Your grandmother is a very smart lady. But for me business is business and pleasure is pleasure. They're two different things. As far as I'm concerned one has nothing to do with the other," he said, his voice smooth.

"I just don't think it would be a good idea," Aisha argued. "I've seen the careers of many phenomenal—I mean totally bad—sistahs who in the boardroom put the fear of God in people with just a look and were ruined because of one slipup in judgment. I don't want that to be me."

"That won't be you," Lance said soothingly. "You're already two steps ahead of the game—you're a visionary and you're too smart for something like that to happen to you. You're focused on what you want. And I admire that."

Aisha beamed at him, flattered by his compliments. "Thanks. But do we have the job?"

"Let me take you out. I know a spot that has dinner and jazz," Lance said. "All we'll do is hang out. Then if you decide that you don't want to do it again, I'll honor that request."

"Do we have the job?" Aisha repeated. She was beginning to feel like a parrot.

"What about if I give you my decision this weekend?"

"Umm . . ."

"I'll pick you up Saturday . . . at noon."

"Why can't you tell me now?" Aisha pressed.

"Because I think my answer would be best served with dinner," he answered with a smile.

"But if you tell me your decision now, I might concede to a congratulatory dinner."

"But what's better than anticipation? The rush of not knowing?" Lance saw a flicker of defeat cross Aisha's face. "So I'll pick you up at noon?"

Aisha sighed. Lance was more persistent than two bald women fighting over a clearance-priced wig. "Twelve in the afternoon? I thought you meant dinner, not lunch."

"I did. It'll take a minute to get to where we're going."

"I'm not going to have to pack, am I?" Aisha nervously asked. She had read about him in one of the tabloids. He was well known for his extravagant gifts.

"Not unless you want to," he drawled.

Aisha eyed him over the rim of her glass. "Pack for dinner? Seriously. Where are we going?"

Parlez-vous français? (Do you speak French?)

Aisha had taken French 101 in high school and she racked her brain for the translation and a response. *"Un petit peu. Pourquoi?"* (A little. Why?)

"Because I want to take a beautiful lady where they speak this beautiful language."

"You're taking me to France?" Aisha asked excitedly, her apprehension melting away faster than snow on a sun-filled day in Rochester, New York, after a snowstorm.

Lance shook his head. "Not quite, but just as quaint."

"Where? Where?"

"Montreal."

"Montreal? Like in Canada?"

"Yep!"

"Oh wow! I've never been there. I've been to Toronto but never Montreal. I almost went to Vancouver, but something happened and I couldn't make it. I wanted to—"

Lance chuckled softly. "So does that mean you'll come with me? You want to hang out with me in Montreal?"

Chapter 15

Derrick picked up his cell phone before trotting to his balcony for his weekly phone call with his mother. Pressing his cell phone against his forehead, he debated whether he should tell his mother about her new grandbaby. Sometimes she made him more nervous than some of the senior partners at the firm. Her tongue could slice him up with such precision that she'd cut him down to a five-year-old boy. He peered over the edge to make sure no one was within hearing distance. Seeing that the coast was clear, he pressed in his mother's number, going as slowly as possible. His fingers felt as though they were made of lead. The phone rang. He held his breath and wished for it to go into voice mail. But his mother picked up.

"Hey, baby!"

"Hey, Momma."

"What's going on?"

For the next thirty minutes he amused her with stories about his coworkers, the cases he was working on, Atlanta and his neighbors.

"That was funny," his mother said between laughs. "You have such a gift for storytelling. You should be a writer or something."

"Thanks." His mother was always encouraging him. Even in kindergarten, when he would bring home his finger paintings and she told him that he could go on to be the next Picasso. Back then he didn't know Picasso from G.I. Joe, but the way she said his name he knew that Picasso was somebody important. "But I don't think I have the patience to sit in front of a computer trying to come up with characters whose lives are more exciting than mine."

"Have you heard from Darla?" she suddenly asked, and Derrick nearly dropped his cell phone with surprise.

"Yep. She stopped by," he replied casually.

"Stopped by! She stopped by Atlanta? That's odd. Why did she fly all the way to Atlanta to see you? Why couldn't she have called?" his mother mused, and Derrick could see her tapping her forefinger against her chin, a habit she developed whenever she was trying to figure out a mystery.

Derrick took a deep breath; he had visualized this moment. He had even practiced saying the words in front of a mirror. But somehow, placed in the limelight, he got stage fright. His hands began sweating so much that he almost dropped his cell phone. He swiped them across his sweatpants. "She's pregnant," Derrick pushed out, and braced himself for the onslaught of curse words. His mother was a church lady, but she was known to forget God whenever she got pissed.

"Say what?"

Derrick repeated himself.

He was so surprised at her next question that he was left momentarily speechless. "Is it yours?"

"Umm, yeah . . . I guess. She said it was. I asked her the same thing," he answered. "I don't think Darla would lie about something like that."

"You never know. Some women see a man accomplishing things and she tries to jump on his ship." His muscles began to uncurl and loosen up. This isn't going too badly, he thought with relief. "Maybe you should get one of those DNA tests," his mother suggested.

"Darla isn't like that. . . . I mean she is . . . kinda," he answered, his words coming out tangled just like they were in his head. "What I meant was, this wasn't intentional, but she turned into the type of person who would destroy a brother's ship then throw him a life jacket."

"What do you mean it wasn't intentional? It takes two people to make a baby. How did this happen?"

"Mom!" Derrick almost squeaked, feeling like a teenager.

"I know where babies come from and I've long given up the illusion that you're a virgin. Especially after I found your stash of *Playboy* magazines when you were thirteen. Now tell me what happened."

Derrick took a deep breath and gave his mother the G-rated version of the situation. Telling her the bits and pieces that he remembered. Most of that night was still foggy to him.

"So you were drunk but she wasn't?" she verified.

"Yes ma'am."

"Since she hadn't been drinking she should've pushed you off. A smart lady would've done that."

"That's true," Derrick quickly agreed.

"I'm not excusing your behavior. Drinking and driving," she said with a snort. "I don't ever want to hear about your doing that again. Do you hear me!"

"Yes ma'am," Derrick answered meekly, hanging his head as though his mother was standing in front of him shaking her finger.

"But I'd keep an eye on Miss Darla. She got you and she got you good. Any woman who'd take advantage of a drunk man would do anything to get what she wants."

Derrick held his breath while his client looked over his newly drafted will. Robert Doyle, a seventy-two-year-old multimillionaire who had made his money in franchising his soul food restaurant, had picked Derrick's law firm to handle his estate after he died. He hated his former lawyers, who thought just because he was over seventy years old he was as gullible as a newborn baby.

One of his wrinkled pecan-colored fingers jabbed at the paper. "What does this mean?" he asked.

"Just that you're naming us executor of your will."

"That means in the event of my untimely death y'all get to distribute my assets."

Derrick smiled. "That's right, Mr. Doyle. But we will only distribute them the way *you* tell us to." Suddenly his smile turned into a frown as his cell phone began vibrating. He didn't have to look at it to know that it was Darla. She had been blowing up his cell and home phones for the past two weeks. Seconds later the phone stilled and Derrick refocused his attention on Mr. Doyle, who was pointing his wrinkled finger at him.

"Did you draft this?" he asked Derrick.

"I did," Derrick answered proudly.

Mr. Doyle snorted. "At three hundred bucks an hour I

think my five-year-old great-granddaughter could've done a better job. Hell, I bet I could've gotten her to do it for a lollipop," he chortled.

Derrick smiled weakly. Working with Mr. Doyle was like working with a puckered teenager. He was arrogant, knew it all and was moody. The past three months were miserable. When he wasn't meeting with Derrick, he was on the phone with him half a dozen times a day making changes to his estate. But Derrick grinned and tolerated the man. He was billing crazy hours. Every phone call and visit was duly noted.

Derrick was daydreaming about what he wanted to do with the money. A scuba-diving trip to Mexico would be perfect. He'd call up one of his girls and have her pack nothing but a bikini and toothbrush. Who would it be? he mused. All of a sudden Aisha's face popped up. The loud banging of the conference room door being slammed open pulled him away from the sparkling blue water and Aisha. Suddenly he was back in the conference room, with its oversize wood table, dark blue carpeting and old man Doyle.

"Derrick! There you are!" Darla squealed as she raced into the room and stopped at Derrick's side.

"Darla?" For the second time in less than three weeks Darla had surprised him. "What are you doing here?"

"I need to talk to you."

"You can call me," Derrick hissed close to her ear. "Not come running down to my job like some ghetto chick. You have more class than this."

"You calling me ghetto!" Darla yelled.

Aw shit! Derrick's face tightened with horror. What happened to the lady he left in Chicago? And why was her evil twin trying to fuck up his gig? "I'm not calling you ghetto. Bad choice of words," he apologized. "Let's go to my office."

Darla swooped around him and settled into a cushioned conference chair. "I'm not going anywhere. As soon as I get into your office you're going to leave and come right back here." She nodded at Mr. Doyle.

"I'm Robert Doyle," he said, holding out his hand and introducing himself.

Darla looked at him, then down at his hand as if it were a piece of dog shit. Then turned her attention back to Derrick. "I want to talk now," she demanded.

"Now isn't a good time. Can't you see that I'm in the middle of something?" Derrick ran a hand over his face. "I'll call you later tonight. I will, I promise. Just leave," he begged.

"You know where I just came from?" Darla asked, her voice deadly calm.

Derrick rolled his eyes. "Where?"

"The doctor."

Derrick's eyes went wide. "Is everything okay?"

"Now you would've known the answer to that question if you were with me. But yes. I'm okay."

"Darla, why are you here? Why?"

"To talk to you, young man," Mr. Doyle supplied.

Derrick turned his gaze on his client and resisted the urge to yell. "What do you want to talk about, Darla?"

"Our baby," she announced, and Derrick winced and Mr. Doyle's sharp glance took in the scene, suddenly understanding the situation. He shook his head. Young people. Nowadays they spit out babies like they were manufacturing toys.

"Let's go into my office." This time Derrick pulled Darla

from the chair and grabbed her elbow so that she couldn't escape. "Excuse me, Mr. Doyle. Make notes on anything you don't understand. I'll be right back to answer your questions." As soon as they got on the threshold of the conference room leading out into the hallway, Derrick turned and locked his gaze with Darla. "If you so much as make a sound before we get to my office I'm going to have security up here so fast that people are going to think you're trying to rob me. Are you going to chill until we get to my office?"

Darla nodded, then was stiffly escorted by Derrick to his office. As soon as his door was closed she whirled on him. "What the fuck is your problem! How come you can't call me like you're supposed to? I'm not walking around carrying a fucking toaster, Derrick—this is your baby in here," she yelled while pointing at her stomach.

"You don't give me a chance! As soon as you leave one message, two minutes later there's another one," he grumbled.

"That's not true," Darla denied. "I only want to make sure that you're involved with the pregnancy."

"I am, I mean I will be. Don't press me, Darla. I'm just too busy for this."

Darla's eyes narrowed. "Too busy for your child? Yeah, I can see that you're too busy. Too busy buying new cars and this," she said, eyeing a brochure for a new house that was sitting on his desk. "So while I'm living in a one-bedroom apartment you're having a new house built?"

"I didn't tell you to quit your job, pack everything up and move here," Derrick snapped.

"No you didn't, but considering the circumstances I thought it would be a good idea. Here, this is for you." Darla slipped her hand into her purse and pulled out a three-page document and handed it to Derrick.

"What's this?"

"My pre- and postnatal contract," Darla announced.

"What the fuck!"

"Yep! You're not the only one who knows about contracts."

"What the hell is this?" Derrick asked, flipping through the document. Words like *baby, doctor, visit, labor, delivery* and *custody* flew by him.

"This is a little something that I had a friend draw up for me."

"I can tell by the gibberish that a *real* lawyer didn't create it."

"*Whatever.* Basically what it's saying is that you have to accompany me to all my prenatal doctor visits, you will be with me during delivery. Labor is optional. We still need to hammer out the custody arrangements. After the baby's born, I'm not sure if I'm staying here or moving back to Chicago. But there's a stipulation that covers—"

"This is bullshit!" Derrick shouted.

"Bullshit or not. You'd still better sign it." Darla leaned over and snatched a pen off his desk. She held it out to him.

"What's this for?" he asked, looking at the pen as though it was a hand grenade.

"I want your John Hancock. I want you to sign it right now. I want the promise that you're always going to be in your child's life. Go ahead and sign it!" she ordered.

Chapter 16

Tarik and Felicia walked hip to hip through the mall, chatting and laughing. They were shimmering with happiness and it was more contagious than the flu during December. Occasionally Felicia's hand would touch Tarik's shoulder as she tried to emphasize a point or he would find himself touching her hair or arm.

"Let's do Neiman Marcus," Felicia suggested. "I heard that the men's department just got a new shipment of clothes."

"Cool. Lead the way."

Neiman Marcus was empty, the store had only been open an hour and the salespeople were stumbling around like zombies and watching them through half-closed eyes.

"Hmmm, I don't know," Tarik said as he studied a thick cable-knit turtleneck sweater. "Do you think this makes me look too—"

Felicia shook her head. "Not at all. I think it's hot. I like that color on you," she answered, admiring how the off-white looked against his skin.

"I like it too. Maybe I'll get it in this color," he said, picking up a watermelon-colored sweater. Felicia shook her head.

"I don't like that." At those words, Tarik immediately dropped the turtleneck.

"I'll be right back. Let me take this off." He strolled toward the fitting rooms. He enjoyed going shopping with Felicia. It was like hanging out with his best friend sans the testosterone. Tara hated to go to the mall with him. The only way to get her to accompany him was to bribe her. Their deal was, if she didn't pout he'd buy her something before they left. It had gotten so stressful that he had begun leaving his fiancée home and bringing Felicia.

Moments later he returned to her side to find her holding out a pair of Juicy Couture Travis 1974 jeans with a multicolored stripped Hugo Boss button-down draped over it. "What about this?"

"Cool, it might work for the weekend. Hold on to it."

"I think the colors in the shirt pick up the brown in your eyes," Felicia teased, then playfully fluttered her eyelashes.

"You sure know how to compliment a brother."

"That's 'cause I love you like a big brother."

"Then can you give me some sisterly advice?"

"Whassup? What's wrong?" Felicia asked, instantly concerned. "Let's Go Crazy" exploded from her purse. She shot Tarik an apologetic look. "I'll be quick." She kept her promise—the call was less than two minutes. "What's going on?"

"Would you ever cheat on your boyfriend?"

Mia popped into her head. *It isn't like she's my girlfriend.* "No, never have, and I pray that I never will. Why?" Her eyes suddenly widened. "Are you saying that Tara is cheating on you?"

"Drop it down a notch. I don't need half of NM knowing my business," Tarik hissed.

Felicia tugged at his arm. "Come on. Let's walk through the mall." She left the items on a table. "Maybe we'll come back and get them later." Once they were in the mall Felicia turned to her friend. "Why do you think Tara's cheating?"

"I don't think it, I *know* it."

"How do you know for sure? I know that Tara can be a little self-centered sometimes, but I don't think that she'll cheat on you. She really does love you. I just can't see it," Felicia said.

"Well, she is," he insisted.

"How do you know?"

"I hired a private investigator to follow her," Tarik admitted.

"You did what? Why would you do something like that? That is so sneaky. Why couldn't you just ask her?"

Tarik looked at her as though she had asked him to stop in the middle of the mall and lay an egg. "Oh yeah, right. I'm supposed to ask my fiancée if she's smashing some other dude and expect her to tell me the truth? That's bull."

"It's better than sneaking around spying on her."

"Whose side are you taking?" Tarik asked, glaring at her.

"Naturally I got your back. You're my boy and everything. But I'm looking at it from a female's point of view. I wouldn't want anybody spying on me. I'm sorry," she said softly once she realized how she sounded. She gently touched his hand. "Tell me why you hired the private investigator."

"I sensed something was going on. She would say that she was going out and later when I would ask her about it she told me that she never told me that. And whenever I had asked her how she spent her day she got very defensive or vague. She was acting sneaky, like she was trying to hide something from me. And not only that, she was beginning to act mean."

"More so than usual," Felicia muttered.

"What?" Tarik asked, straining to hear her.

"Nothing. What did you find out?" Felicia glanced down and noticed his hands balled into fists. The urge to reach out and uncurl them overcame her but she squished it. *He needs to get some things off his chest, not be appeased,* she decided.

"She's seeing a judge," he said quietly.

"No! A judge?"

"Yep."

"The kind of judge who listens to trials and hands out prison sentences? That type of judge?"

"Yep."

"Oh. Maybe they're just good friends," Felicia offered.

"That's some bullshit. You should've seen the way they were tonguing each other down. I don't greet any of my females friends like that."

"I'm so sorry, Tarik. So what are you going to do?"

"I'm going to have to cut her loose."

"Maybe you should take some time to think about it. You two are living together, and in less than four months you two are going to be married in one of the most lavish weddings that either family has seen. Dang, y'all got over three hundred people on the guest list."

"Take some time to think about it?" he repeated, his voice incredulous. "I've thought about it. She can have the house and I'll take a loss on the wedding. I just want her gone."

"Aren't you being a little rash?"

Tarik shook his head. "I've known for about three weeks."

"Oh."

"And this isn't the first time," Tarik admitted.

"Oh, Tarik, no!"

Tarik nodded. "Yeah, about a year ago she met a professional football player at a club. She was flying back and forth to Miami so much to see him that she had collected enough frequent flyer miles for us to take a trip," he said, his tone full of contempt and laced with sadness. "So you see, I'm not acting irrationally."

"No, you're not," Felicia agreed. "So what excuse did she give you for not being at home?"

"It was all business related. All she told me was that she was scoping out locations for parties."

"And you didn't do anything then?"

"I was about to . . . but it ended. I'm sure he broke up with her, because she wouldn't have done it. Then everything was okay until the judge—that's when her job got busy and she couldn't spend as much time with me as she used to."

Why the fuck did you take her back? was on the tip of Felicia's tongue, but she swallowed it. "I'm really-really sorry. You know that I'm always here for you. I'm just sorry that you have to go through this."

"I'll be okay," Tarik said, offering her a weak smile, but his eyes belied his attempt to be strong, their usual sparkle dulled by pain.

"Give me a hug," Felicia said suddenly.

"Here?" Tarik asked, furrowing his brow. "Right in the middle of the mall?"

Felicia shrugged. "Sure, why not? Come here," she said, then opened her arms, and Tarik stepped in. She pulled him to her and gave him a soul-fortifying bear hug. "Do you feel a little better?" she whispered, and she felt Tarik's nod. "You ready for something to eat? You want the food court or a restaurant?" she asked while stepping out his arms and studying his face. The pain was still there but at least the smile he offered was sincere.

"Food court is cool."

"Okay. I'm not sure what I want. Let me check out a couple places and I'll meet you."

Twenty minutes later they were seated, Felicia with two slices of pepperoni pizza with an inch-thick layer of cheese hanging off her plate and Tarik with chicken swimming alongside green peppers and onions in a spicy red sauce slapped over rice. "Yuk! I don't know how you eat that stuff."

Tarik shrugged. "It'll do. Of course it's not your cooking."

"Thank you. You know that I'll cook for you anytime you want. Just let me know when."

"Will do," Tarik promised before stuffing his mouth full of chicken.

"So . . ." Felicia began. "When are you going to break up with her?"

"As soon as she gets back in town. She's in the Caribbean on a business trip."

"Damn, she's bold. I hope you're taking the ring back," Felicia said, thinking of Tara's 3-karat platinum ring. Every time she glanced at it, she got the urge to slip on a pair of sunglasses.

"Damn right. And if she decides to act crazy, I'll show her the pictures."

"I still can't believe you hired somebody to follow her *and* take pictures," Felicia said. She'd never expect this behavior from Tarik—it was something straight out a reality TV show.

"I needed proof. My gut said something was wrong, but I needed some concrete evidence." Suddenly a pregnant lady waddled by and Tarik smiled wistfully, his voice softened. "There was a time when all I could think of was getting Tara like that. But now . . ." He shook his head.

Felicia reached over and patted her friend's hand. "I'm sorry that it ended like this. You're such a sweet guy and Tara is stupid not to realize what a great catch she had. I want to tell you something but I don't want you to get mad."

Tarik shook his head. "You can't do anything to make me mad. Especially not with everything I have going on. Whassup?"

"Well, I never really—" Felicia hedged, then she took a deep breath. "I never liked Tara."

Tarik set his fork down, surprised. "You didn't like Tara?" Felicia shook her head. "All this time she and I dated, you never *liked* her?"

"Nope," Felicia said, and took a bite of her pizza.

"Why didn't you tell me?"

Felicia snorted. "And would you have listened?"

"I-um-um, maybe," Tarik stuttered.

"Exactly my point. Man, you were so deep into Tara that Jacques Cousteau wouldn't have been able to pull you out."

"Fuck I was stupid!"

"Don't be mad at yourself. You're human, you can't help how you feel," she said thinking of Lawrence. Even with all his idiosyncrasies and marital problems she still loved him.

"The next time you see me falling for somebody like Tara, shoot me please."

"With a shotgun or pistol?" Felicia teased. They were silent as they ate their food. It was beginning to get cold. Felicia glanced across the food court and spotted the pregnant lady. She had gotten her food and was carrying it to her seat. A wistful expression crossed Felicia's face. Tarik caught it and followed her gaze.

"You want one?"

"No-yeah-maybe, yeah," she finally admitted.

"Damn, that was like getting you to admit you like watching *The Brady Bunch* reruns. It's not a bad thing. We all want families . . . even me."

"I'm sorry she did this to you."

"I'll be okay. I just need to take a trip to Las—"

Suddenly a loud shriek sliced through the din, leaving behind silence. "What happened?" Felicia craned her neck, and when she saw where the sound came from her heart jumped into her throat. The pregnant lady lay sprawled out on the floor looking like a beached whale. "Tarik, do you think we should do something?" Felicia asked, but turned to find Tarik heading in the direction of the lady.

He pushed his way into the newly formed crowd and stood at the perimeter. Everybody looked on like scared rabbits. The lady was Hispanic, with a stomach the size of an exercise ball, and from what he learned about pregnancy from his sister, he guessed that she was about eight months pregnant. Her eyes were squeezed shut and her hands clenched at her sides, while she uttered low moans mixed with words in her native tongue.

Tarik knelt beside the lady. *"¿Está bien?"* (Are you okay?)

Her eyes flew open, then stretched to the size of her stomach. Tarik wasn't sure if it was because she was surprised he was black or that he knew how to speak Spanish. He was suddenly grateful for growing up in the diverse neighborhood that he had. Puerto Ricans, blacks, whites and Italians all lived together peacefully.

No, señor. Yo no puedo andar. (No, sir. I can't walk.)

Tarik glanced down and noticed that her ankle had swollen to the size of a cantaloupe.

"Did somebody call an ambulance!" he shouted to the crowd.

"I did," a female voice answered from the group.

"Thanks!" Tarik told the caller. *"Usted será bien. Una ambulancia está en su camino."* (You'll be okay. An ambulance is on its way.) The lady nodded, then bit down on her lip. *"¿Viene el bebé?"* (Is the baby coming?)

"No, señor."

"Bueno. ¿Cómo se llama usted?" (Good. What's your name?)

"Adonia."

"Ah, esto significa a una señora hermosa." (Ah, that means a beautiful lady.)

Adonia nodded, then gave a smile, which quickly turned into a grimace.

Felicia stood among the crowd watching Tarik sitting on the food court floor in his Dolce & Gabbana pants, cradling the lady's head in his lap. She was transfixed as he murmured softly to her while stroking her hair.

Felicia cocked her head and studied her friend. *I wonder what it would be like if Tarik touched me like that.* The thought jumped into her head so unexpectedly that it felt as though a bolt of electricity had shot through her, and she gasped.

"Are you all right?" a lady standing next to her asked, her face scrunched with worry.

"I'm fine," Felicia mumbled. In a daze she retraced her steps through the crowd and plopped down in a chair. Prince blared through her phone and she automatically reached for it. Then her hand dropped to her side. "I can't talk to Aisha now." *Why would I want Tarik to hold me and to stroke me? Me and Tarik? Why?*

As soon as her heartbeat returned to normal and she felt sane, she made her way back to the crowd, then eased to the edge. Minutes later the paramedics arrived, tearing through the crowd like bullets.

Tarik held Adonia's hand while the paramedics wheeled her through the mall and into the ambulance.

Adonia grasped his hand. *"Gracias. Que Dios le bendiga."* (Thank you. God bless you.)

Tarik squeezed her hand softly before strolling back to Felicia.

"You were awesome!" she gushed as they made their way out of the food court. By an unspoken agreement they both decided they were no longer hungry.

Tarik shrugged. "I was being a concerned citizen."

"Being a concerned citizen is picking up litter. Being a concerned citizen is knowing what you want when you get to the cash register at McDonald's. Being a concerned citizen is telling someone they dropped a dollar bill. But you were amazing! You almost had me thinking you were a candy striper," she joked.

"Whatever."

"You did a good thing," Felicia said softly. "Where did you learn to do that?"

"I didn't do anything."

"You did," Felicia insisted. "While most of the people were looking as though this was an episode of *CSI,* you jumped in and helped."

"I didn't even think about it. I just went for it, I guess my instincts took over. I'm glad I was able to. Hey, where you going?" he asked. Felicia had suddenly veered right.

"I thought you wanted to go back to Neiman Marcus," Felicia explained.

"I'll go back later. I'm in the mood for some sneakers. And it's down this way," he said, and grabbed her hand. Felicia felt a shock of energy go through her. She trembled, then snatched her hand away. "What—what's wrong?" Tarik asked, confused by her behavior.

"Nothing, I just, um, put some lotion on my hands and I didn't want to get any on you."

Tarik arched an eyebrow at her. "Do I need to call an ambulance for you?"

Felicia laughed. "I'm fine. Let's finish shopping." She peeked at him out of the corner of her eye. *Me and Tarik?*

Chapter 17

Aisha, Felicia, Mia and Tiffany were crowded in a booth at Aisha's favorite Thai restaurant.

Plates filled with duck, lamb and shrimp covered the table. In the middle of it all was a nearly empty bottle of wine. "I want to make a toast," Aisha announced. They all held up their glasses. "To my girls. Thanks so much for all the overtime and putting up with me while I rewrote the presentations so many times that I dreamt about it. And thank you, Tiffany, for your hookup at Kinko's. Otherwise a sistah would be broke paying for color copies and binding. To the continued success of FAACS!"

"To continued success," Felicia, Mia and Tiffany repeated. They clinked their glasses. Mia reached under the table and stroked Felicia's thighs, causing Felicia to sigh into her glass of wine.

Aisha took a sip of her wine, then suddenly spied the nearly empty wine bottle in the middle of the table. "Hold up. Let me get another bottle. We have a lot of celebrating to do." She motioned for the waiter. Once he sauntered over to their table she placed her order.

"To the lady who got the million-dollar coochie," Mia quipped.

"Yeah, to the lady who's keeping us from living on the street," Tiffany added.

"Y'all shut up and stop being so damn dramatic. I got the job because my presentation was off the chain. Besides, I didn't go to bed with Lance until *after* he told me we had the contract."

"What would've happened if you had turned him down, especially after he had taken you to Montreal?"

Aisha shook her head. "That's not Lance. He knew all along that he was going to give me the contract. He loves mind games, especially chess. We're all pawns in his world. Fortunately for me, I know this; however, he doesn't know that I'm the queen. And as y'all know, the queen is the most powerful piece on the board." Aisha took a sip of her wine and relaxed in her seat.

"You're awesome, girl." Tiffany beamed at her. "What was it like having a man charter a jet for you? That is so sexy!"

"Sexy," Mia mouthed to Felicia.

"It was cool," Aisha answered nonchalantly, oblivious to the seduction going down. When she first got on the plane she was impressed by its opulence, from its plush leather seats to its well-stocked bar, the plasma TV and full-size bed. But a part of her couldn't help but mentally renovate it. The red carpet would have been replaced with something lighter and the bathroom would've been gutted and redone. Then: "There's nothing in the world like it," she said, excited. "It's one of the best experiences in the world. And he even flew a little. Not long, just about five minutes. He's working on getting his pilot's license. But I was duly impressed."

"So are you officially a member of the mile-high club?" Tiffany asked. Felicia and Aisha exchanged glances and smiled at each other. "I guess you are," Tiffany said, answering her own question, and sipped her drink.

"We're set, ladies. His check cleared today," Aisha said while picturing the six-figure amount. "We won't have any money problems for a long time."

"So now I can get that raise?" Tiffany slipped in.

"We'll talk about it later," Aisha said. But knew that she would give it to her. She deserved it. She had always been a conscientious worker, but during the past couple weeks she really stepped up to the plate and proved to be invaluable.

Felicia's head throbbed while she watched the exchange between her sister and Tiffany. The promise she had made to Tarik rang in her ears and she grimaced. Now isn't the right time to tell her, she decided. Aisha looked happier than a fly on Brad Pitt and Angelina Jolie's wall. I'll tell her as soon as she gets a grip on the new account, Felicia decided. She grasped Mia's hand and squeezed it.

"So how was he? Did his dick size match his wallet size?" Tiffany asked, and the twins stole a look.

"Oh yeah!" Aisha crowed.

"So when are you going to see him again?"

Aisha shrugged. "Whenever. The good thing is that from a business standpoint I won't be seeing him that much. I'll be working with his CFO. I think he mentioned something about calling me. I don't remember."

Tiffany's eyes widened. "You don't remember? A man that rich and fine is flying you all over and icing you up and you're acting like he's Johnny the Clown?"

"These earrings are nice," Aisha said while stroking her

1-karat diamond earrings. "Yes, he's rich and all, but that's not enough."

Felicia knew that her sister cared about Lance about as much as she cared about her favorite pair of shoes. She was looking for her soul mate. A man who could not only make her come by the wink of an eye, but someone whose very presence radiated peace to her very soul. Felicia nervously cleared her throat, then: "Do you think best friends could ever be lovers?"

"Maybe, girl," Tiffany said. "I mean, anything is possible. My cousin Lil D used to hang out with her friend Crunko. From the time they were in kindergarten till they were seniors in high school, they were best friends. Nothing happened until Lil D came home during a break from college. It could've been seeing him in his mechanic's uniform, but ever since then they been together. They talking about getting married next year. So yeah, I guess it's possible."

All the while Tiffany was talking Aisha was studying her sister's face. She looked about as nervous as a virgin on her honeymoon night. "Why would you ask that?"

"I just wondered," Felicia answered. "It seems like the ideal situation. They know each other inside and out. They know each other's faults and they're cool about it. You know, there are no surprises. None of that Dr. Jekyll and Mr. Hyde shit. You know how you meet someone and all you get is their date face, which quickly cracks after three months. With your best friend you already know everything. It just seems like a perfect situation."

"For whom?" Aisha asked quietly.

"For two best friends," Felicia whispered.

"You and Tarik?" Aisha asked.

"What?" Tiffany asked, surprised.

"Yeah," Felicia admitted, and she felt Mia suddenly stiffen, then shift away. Felicia looked at her, surprised. *It's not like we're a love connection,* her look said. Mia met her gaze before snatching up her glass of wine. She took a deep gulp.

"I don't believe it," Aisha said, and sat back in her seat stunned. At one time she had entertained the thought that her sister and Tarik were more than friends, but Felicia always vehemently denied the allegations.

"Me either. Tarik was always my friend, my big brother. I never looked at him *that* way. I'm blown away by these new feelings for him. Now whenever I see him I don't know what to say or how to act. We used to hug all the time, but now I can't even do that. I get so hot just by his touch. So I make excuses for him not to touch me. I think he's getting mad."

"So what happened? Tell us everything. Let me refill my glass," Tiffany said as she grabbed the bottle of wine and poured herself another drink. "Anybody else want some?" Tiffany asked while dangling the bottle at Aisha and Felicia.

"Sure, why not?" Aisha, Felicia and Mia said at the same time.

Once her glass was filled, Felicia told them about the incident with the pregnant lady. "And something inside me melted when I saw him sitting on the floor taking care of that pregnant lady. I saw a side of him that I had never seen. I knew he was nice. But tender and caring . . . it was such a turn-on."

"But doesn't he have a fiancée?" Mia asked.

Felicia shook her head. "He left her. That crazy bitch cheated on him. And not just one time, she was out of control." She told them about the private detective Tarik had hired to follow Tara.

"Wow!" Tiffany said. "This is just like that TV show *Cheaters*. Man, I would've loved to see that tight-ass, Tara, busted."

"I'm glad that he finally got rid of her. I always thought there was something foul going on with her. He's a good man. If I was ready to settle down, I'd scoop him up," Aisha said.

Felicia laughed. "You'd have that poor guy dead in a week."

"I would love to have him," Tiffany chimed in. "He's a BMM."

"BMM?" Felicia asked. "What's that? I've never heard that phrase before."

"Brother making money," Tiffany quipped.

They all laughed.

"So now that he's free, sis, are you going to tell him how you feel?"

Felicia gave Mia a sidelong glance, then averted her eyes. She thought about Lawrence and her stomach knotted up worse than a bad braid job, then she pictured Tarik and the blood rushed to her face. "I am. I don't know when or how. I need your help. Tell me what to do?" she pleaded with her sister. "You have experience with dumping men faster than week-old Chinese food, but do you know how to keep a man?"

"Of course I do," Aisha huffed.

"Without using your coochie," Felicia amended, causing Tiffany to giggle.

"Funny." Aisha laughed, then focused on her sister. "How can Felicia get Tarik?" she wondered out loud. Suddenly a grin spread over her face.

"Did you come up with something?" Felicia asked, excited.

"Maybe. Maybe not," Aisha teased.

"Stop playing around. Tell me. I know you have something."

Aisha sighed deeply. "I guess I'll tell you. Okay, young ladies, gather around." She motioned for Felicia and Tiffany to lean in. As soon as their foreheads were almost touching, Aisha whispered, "Listen closely, this is what you got to do."

Mia shot up in her seat. "Hold up! Let me use the bathroom before you give out your advice." She turned to Felicia. "Come on. I want to borrow your lipstick." Felicia followed her friend to the bathroom.

Once inside, Mia rounded on her friend. "What the hell is going on here?"

Felicia blinked. "What are you talking about?"

"You're in love with Tarik?" she spat.

"Yeah," Felicia answered, bewildered. "What's wrong with that?"

"What about us?"

Felicia frowned. "Us?"

"Yes, us. You and me. The lady who's been serving up orgasms to you."

"We were lovers . . . just lovers. That's the way it's always been. You always knew about Lawrence, now Tarik. I *never* hid anything from you. I never thought I did," she said quietly.

Mia grabbed Felicia's hands and gazed into her eyes. "I want us to be a couple. I love you."

Chapter 18

Aisha glanced out the car window at the passing scenery, then occasionally sneaked a peek at Lance, who was driving his car with the concentration of a diamond cutter.

After hanging out a couple of months, Aisha and he had simmered down to seeing each other once every few weeks. With the exception of working on his account, she found he rarely crossed her radar. Now he had tempted her with an invitation to what he promised to be a "celebrity-drenched event."

Aisha noted that his BMW cost twice as much as her car and had three times the features. The top was down on his car and the air flowed sensuously over her skin. She had never been in this part of Georgia before. An hour outside of downtown Atlanta, all the houses were breathtaking works of art that reminded her of mini European castles. Her eyes were strained as she studied the homes as though she could peer inside to see the secret of their owners' success.

"Damn! This is how I want to roll," she said longingly.

"You will if you keep going at the rate you're going."

Startled, Aisha turned to Lance. She didn't realize she had spoken out loud. "Thanks. That's quite a compliment coming from you, *Mr. Black Businessman of Atlanta.* You're running a multimillion-dollar company, starting a clothing line and a record company. I'm impressed. How do you do it?" In the time they had spent together she had seen him conduct business meetings while driving, strolling through the airport and once having sex.

"Baby, haven't you learned anything yet by watching me?" Aisha shook her head. "Always remember three things. Stay focused. Always have a goal in mind. And never, ever take no for an answer," he said ticking the items off.

"That's too easy," Aisha scoffed.

"It worked on you, didn't it?" Lance asked with a smirk.

"You caught me during a weak moment," Aisha teased, then: "Now that I think about it, that's how I got your business."

"How so?" Lance asked.

"I was focused, my objective was to get your business and I didn't take no for an answer," she finished proudly.

"Two out of three isn't bad," Lance muttered.

"What? I did all three."

"*I* let you have all three. I gave you the business," Lance added, answering her unspoken question.

"You didn't give me anything. I worked for it," Aisha huffed as she squared her shoulders and faced Lance.

Lance chuckled. "You're right, baby. I didn't give you anything. Keep working hard. You'll be CEO of your own company one day," he said.

Aisha's heart worked double time. "Why you condescending ba—" His laughter cut her off and she glared at him through narrowed eyes. Suddenly she remembered what she had told Felicia and Tiffany—he liked to play mind games. *Screw him, I'm not getting sucked into his game,* she decided.

After closing her eyes and taking a deep breath she leaned back in her seat, looking as relaxed as a well-fed goldfish in an aquarium at a day care. "Do you miss not having a Mrs.?" Aisha asked, her voice innocent. Lance cut his eyes at her. Aisha laughed. "Hey, I'm just asking, I'm not looking to add those three letters to my name. At least not anytime soon."

"I enjoy my freedom too much. I don't like having my time regulated by anybody."

"We're too much alike," Aisha said with a laugh. "Where's this party anyway? It seems like we're almost to South Carolina."

"Another fifteen minutes."

She glanced down at her outfit. Her little black dress looked sophisticated in her apartment, but the farther they drove and the bigger the houses got, the more underdressed she began to feel. "What's the dress like?"

"Chill. You're fine. I wouldn't be with you if you weren't," he replied arrogantly. Aisha opened her mouth to protest, but he continued, "Yolanda and Ken are good people. Trust me, nobody's gonna be paying any attention to what you're wearing."

"I like what you're wearing," she said, taking in his outfit. "Easy access." *So he wants to play games. I hold the record for being the biggest cock teaser,* Aisha thought, gloating to herself.

He cut his eyes at her. "For what?"

"For this," Aisha answered as she unbuckled her seat belt, slid over to Lance and slipped her hand into his pants. Even before she had her hand wrapped around his penis he was as hard as one of the diamond earrings he had given her.

"You gonna do that *now?*" Aisha nodded. "Right *here?*"

"Yep," she replied with a grin before bending over and losing her face in his lap.

"Shit!" Lance groaned when Aisha's mouth found its mark. "Do your thing, girl. Do your thing."

Aisha ran her tongue over Lance's dick, occasionally stopping at the tip, where she sucked it a little harder. She took a deep breath before inhaling his dick, pulling it whole into her mouth, his hairs tickling her nose.

The car swerved and she bumped her head against the steering wheel. "Hey, be careful. I don't want a concussion," she said while rubbing her head.

"You might get one. If you keep doing what you're doing I'm gonna jam my dick so far up in you that I'm going to poke a hole right through your head."

"Yeah, just don't mess up my hair," Aisha warned. She had spent three hours at LaTonya's Wax and Curl getting it hooked up. Resuming her position, Aisha cradled his balls while blowing wisps of warm air on his dick. He tentatively thrust his hips toward her lips. She teasingly pulled back. While tenderly stroking his balls, she covered his tip with her mouth creating a suction that caused his hips to work overtime.

Lance's moans filled the car, and just when she felt him tense she lifted her head.

"Why did you stop?" Lance asked, his voice strangled with frustration and anger.

Aisha pulled a tissue out of her purse and daintily dabbed at her mouth. "I just realized that we could have an accident. And I don't want that to happen," she said.

"Damn an accident, finish what you were doing," Lance ordered.

"Naw, baby," Aisha drawled. "What would happen to KBS if you get hurt? I'm only thinking of you."

"Whatever," Lance grunted. "Cover the wheel while I readjust my pants."

Aisha muffled a laugh before grabbing the steering wheel.

"What's the occasion for the party?" Aisha asked while peering at her reflection in the car's lighted mirror. She pulled out her lipstick and reapplied it. Lance had calmed down once he realized she wasn't going to finish the job.

"None. Just chilling. Yolanda and Ken are both lawyers, so they like to have little get-togethers just to relax. And babe, they have this awesome hot tub that seats a dozen people. It's off the chain!"

"You should've told me, I didn't bring my swimsuit!"

"I don't think that's going to be a problem." Lance smirked.

"What? What do you mean by that?"

"Here we are," Lance announced as he stopped at a gate. He pressed the intercom, announced himself and moments later the gates slid open. Aisha caught her breath. "It's the bomb, isn't it?"

Aisha nodded. A half dozen spotlights beamed on the three-story house splashing it with light, making Aisha feel like she was attending a Hollywood premiere. It took them five minutes to drive up the tree-lined driveway to get to the house, only to be stopped by dozens of cars already filling the racetrack-size driveway.

"No valet?" Aisha asked as Lance pulled behind a Bentley.

"Naw, like I said, they're good people. They don't get all caught up."

"This isn't caught up?" Aisha asked, nodding toward the house.

"Well, they do work hard. A brother gotta have something to show for his money. I can't wait for you to see the inside. It's laid."

Aisha smiled. "I can't wait to see it." Lance rang the doorbell. She said, "I hate showing up empty-handed. We should've brought something . . . at least a bottle of wine."

"We're good. I brought Ken back a little something from Cuba the last time I was here."

Lance punched the doorbell and almost immediately the door swung open. Standing on the other side was what Aisha could call a butler, but he was dressed for WWE wrestling. At six foot seven and three hundred pounds, the man wore a formfitting shirt and leggings that molded his muscles and his crotch, leaving little to the imagination.

"Hey, Dawg!" Lance said before dapping him down.

Aisha nodded politely, then eased into the house. Her eyes were as wide as one of Dawg's pecs.

"I told you it was the shit!"

She and Felicia had taken an art appreciation class at Howard so she recognized several of the paintings in the foyer as original pieces of art: Annie Lee, Charles Bibbs and Lester Kern.

They entered a huge room. Aisha suspected that it normally

served as a living room since several couches were pushed up against the wall. Huge crystal chandeliers dangled from the twenty-foot ceiling. Thick ornate wallpaper covered the walls.

Aisha critically studied the room. *I would get rid of that wallpaper and use a darker color. They need something to make this room feel more intimate. And I wouldn't have pushed the sofas against the walls. What happens if people wanted to sit down and talk? It won't happen the way they have it set up.* In less than one minute she had mentally redecorated the room, rearranging furniture and painting walls until she created her own paradise.

Mingling in the middle of it all was an attractive crowd of people who looked like they had all just finished a photo shoot. This is better than a Jack and Jill, Aisha happily thought. Lance must've felt her vibe because he grabbed her hand and pulled her into the crowd.

She found herself in a sea of Sean John, Prada and Dolce & Gabbana, and she navigated it all as though she was a regular. Occasionally she paused long enough to soak up the smells. Expensive perfume and cologne caressed her like a lover. Soft laughter and murmurs could be heard.

"I'll be right back. I see somebody I need to talk to," Lance said before hurrying off, leaving her standing alone in the middle of the floor.

Aisha shrugged, then sauntered over to the makeshift bar for a drink. She settled against the bar with drink in hand, then peered through the crowd for the promised celebrities. She wasn't disappointed. Standing across from her was an Academy Award–winning actor. I didn't know he was in town. He's not that tall, she observed. A little bit away she saw a famous rapper guzzling champagne like he couldn't afford a whole vineyard.

Shaking her head, she finished her drink before cutting her way through the crowd, occasionally stopping on the fringes of small clusters of people to eavesdrop on their conversations. There was the stirring discussion on why black people named their babies after cars. And the heated debate that caused her to pause a little longer: When will Americans accept a black president?

"Whew! It's hot in here," Aisha said, while fanning herself. By then she had spoken with several people who were interested in having her give them a presentation on FAACS. Her bag was brimming with business cards. She sauntered over to Lance and kissed him lightly on his earlobe.

"Let's take this outside," Lance said, already pulling her away from the crowd. They slipped through a set of French doors and discovered that there were just as many people outside as there were inside.

There were dozens of white wrought-iron tables sprinkled throughout the yard with little votive candles placed in the middle, twinkling like stars. Swinging from the trees like lighted jewels were Chinese lanterns. "Beautiful," Aisha breathed. The whole yard made her think of a fairy wonderland. She turned to the chairs to sit down, but Lance tugged her. "Hey, I'm beginning to feel like one of your pets the way you keep pulling at me."

"That can be arranged," Lance said. "I want to show you the hot tub," he said. And before she could respond, he pulled her across the yard, weaving in and out of clusters of people who dotted the manicured lawn. Lance came to a stop in front of a row of sky-kissing pine trees. Felicia squinted as she peered into the dark, she didn't see any signs of a hot tub.

"Hey, where are the spas?"

While still tugging at her, Lance stepped through a small gap that, while practically invisible, was big enough to let adults through. *He's been here before* breezed in and out Aisha's head so fast that she didn't grasp it. On the other side of the trees, surrounded by a ten-foot-high privacy fence, were two spas. Several six-foot-tall torches were jammed into the ground, lighting up the area, giving it a cozy feeling. Aisha noticed that one tub was already filled with ten people but the other had only five people. One of the men stood up and stretched. Water trickled down his sun-toasted body. He climbed out of the tub and sauntered across the yard as though he was fully clothed.

"He's naked!" Aisha hissed in Lance's ear.

"That's the best way," Lance joked. "Come on," he said, tugging at her. This time Aisha snatched her arm away.

"I'm not getting undressed in front of all those people," she protested.

"I told you, nobody's paying any attention to you. These are grown folks who've seen and done everything."

"Well, I'm a grown folk who's done and seen everything I want to, so I'm not going to do it." She turned around and started walking toward the trees.

"Come on, Aisha. It's cool. It would be like going topless in Brazil."

"I've never been and don't plan on doing any sunbathing anywhere," Aisha called over her shoulder.

"It's not that deep, Aisha," Lance said between clenched lips. "All we're going to do is get undressed and sit in some water. Really, how bad is that? I can't believe that you're so old-fashioned. You don't strike me as the type. Or maybe you're scared? I forget you Southern ladies don't get a chance to experience much. My bad. It's cool. Let's go."

Aisha stopped, then crossed her arms over her chest. Suddenly she felt overdressed, like she was wearing a fur coat while everyone else was wearing shorts. "I'm not scared," she announced with a glare. "And for the record, I'm not old-fashioned. I'll do it," she decided. "Where do I get undressed?"

Lance grabbed her hand and pulled her to two small white wooden buildings that reminded Aisha of oversize doll houses. They were two stories high, with four windows in front, one with pink shutters, the other with blue and a door that look like a graham cracker. "Which one is for the ladies?"

Lance smirked. "Take your pick."

Aisha marched over to the one with the pink shutters and entered a large rectangular room with six lockers built into the wall, where keys were dangling from the locks. "God, high school gym all over again," she grumbled.

"I know," a voice murmured.

Startled, Aisha whipped around and found herself eye-to-eye with a breathtakingly beautiful naked woman. If Aisha had to guess, she would say the lady was half African-American and half Asian. Her thick luxurious shoulder-length hair looked like the swatch of hair Aisha had sitting in her closet and her skin was the color of a lightly toasted marshmallow. Aisha averted her eyes. It wasn't that she was unused to seeing a naked lady, she saw them all the time at the gym. But there were certain rules and etiquette to follow. And standing around talking to another lady who was naked was the number one no-no.

"Hey, I thought I was by myself," she said self-consciously before inching over to one of the benches with her back turned toward the lady.

"I'm Koi," she said.

Aisha peered at her over her shoulder. "Aisha," she replied when Koi didn't move an inch. Aisha pulled down the straps of her dress. She glanced again to find Koi in the same spot. Rolling her eyes at the locker, she let her dress fall away.

"This must be your first time here?"

Damn, why isn't she leaving? "Yeah it is."

Koi chuckled. "I can tell. You're about as nervous as the only brotha at an NHL game. You shouldn't be, you have a nice body . . . from what I can see," Koi teased.

"Thanks."

"You'll have a good time in the spa. It's really relaxing."

"I guess," Aisha murmured while folding up her clothes and placing them in the locker. She kicked off her shoes and felt Koi's eyes on her as she bent over to pick them up and place them in her locker.

"You came just in time. Things are gonna start jumping off soon."

"Really?" Aisha asked, eyeing the key, not knowing where to put it since she was as naked as the day she was born.

"Stick it on the board."

"What?"

"Your key, stick it on the board," Koi answered as she pointed to a corkboard. Sure enough, there were keys neatly lined up.

"Thanks." Aisha stepped over to the board, grabbed a tack and stuck her key alongside the rest of them. "Will it be safe here?"

Koi waved her hand. "Please. Have you seen the people at the party?" she asked with a snort. "Put together, they have more money than a small country. They are not casing the locker room. Believe me." She was silent, then: "Who did you come with?"

"Lance," Aisha said, then heard Koi giggle. "What's so funny?" she asked, placing her hands on her hips.

"I love me some Lance."

Aisha arched an eyebrow. "So you know Lance?" she asked, not at all surprised. This wasn't the first time she had run into one of his former bed partners.

"Yeah," Koi drawled. "He's cool. Lance and I always have a good time whenever we're together. He always brings me fun toys to play with," she said while her eyes roamed over Aisha's body.

"He's with me tonight so I don't think you two will do any playing," Aisha snapped.

"We'll see," Koi winked before sauntering out the room.

Aisha tentatively stood at the door. She peered into the darkness looking for Lance. Fortunately she didn't have to go far, she smelled him before she saw him. Using the glowing red tip as a beacon, she navigated through the dark to him. "What's that?" she hissed as soon as she got to his side. She was so upset with Lance for smoking the weed that she didn't notice how the warm air caressed her body like a million tiny fingertips.

"Just something to relax me, baby," he answered before taking a deep puff.

"I thought the spa was supposed to relax us."

He held the joint out to her. "Here, try this. It'll calm you."

"Oh hell naw. I'm not doing that shit. I'm here, I'm naked,

but I'll be damned if I smoke that shit. Get it away from me!" she said as she pushed his arm away.

Lance shrugged. "More for me."

They strolled over to the tubs. One was still filled, but the second had emptied out with the exception of one person, Koi.

"Hey, Lance," she called. "Come on in." Lance didn't waste any time getting into the hot tub. He moved faster than a lobster with its claws touching boiling water.

Aisha followed him, and by the time she got in, Koi was sitting so close to Lance that she might as well have been sitting on his lap. "Where've you been? It's been a minute."

"Busy, girl. You know I got KBS, and I got so much shit happening that I can't come out and play that much."

Koi rolled her eyes. "You know what they say about all work and no play?"

"Yeah. It gives Lance a limp dick."

"You don't have one now," Koi said. She clasped Lance's penis and began stroking it. "You're nice and big now."

Aisha watched in shock as Lance reclined and opened his legs. His eyes drooped closed, and his lips curved up into a smile. "Lance?" Aisha barked. "What the fuck is going on?"

Lance opened his legs wider, giving Koi even better access. He opened his eyes long enough to wink at her and say, "Just relaxing, baby."

"I'm leaving." Aisha stood up.

"How're you gonna get home?"

"I'll have somebody take me."

"Like hell they will. They know me. Half of the people here are my clients and the other half are dying to be my clients. They won't do anything to fuck up their business. So sit down," he snapped.

"Then I'll call the police," Aisha argued, already halfway out the hot tub.

"Do you even know where you are?"

Aisha looked toward the house. All she could see through the trees was the lights. She didn't know where she was. She hadn't paid attention to the street signs or the house number. Defeated, she sank back into the tub. Suddenly Lance started moaning, and slurping sounds could be heard. It reminded Aisha of a thirsty dog lapping up its water. Aisha's stomach rolled when she looked over her shoulder and saw Koi's mouth on Lance's penis. *Aw, God, this is a nightmare.* She turned her back while Koi gave Lance a blow job. Two minutes later Lance grunted and Koi squealed with delight.

"So are you sharing tonight?" she asked Lance, then she looked slyly at Aisha.

Aisha pressed herself against the hot tub wall as if trying to make herself disappear. Her mouth was open with shock, and the blood rushed through her as though she was sitting in a pot of boiling water.

Lance laughed at the expression on her face. "Give it a try, baby. I think you'll like it. Besides, I know you're still hot, especially after what happened in the car. Let Koi take care of you. She's good, I haven't had any complaints."

Koi winked and ran her tongue over her lips before motioning to Aisha. "I've already got a good look at her and I like," Koi said, as if her approval was all that was needed to make Aisha her lover. "C'mere, I want to taste you."

Chapter 19

"So what are you in the mood to eat tonight?" Aisha asked Lance.

"You, baby, all covered in caviar," he drawled before running his tongue over his lips.

"Um, wasn't that lunch?" Aisha teased.

"Sometimes things taste better the second time around," Lance shot back at her.

"Well—"

Suddenly one of his phones rang. Aisha had learned early on that he kept three different phones, two for work and one for personal business. With one hand on the steering wheel, he snapped open what she had dubbed his "fun" phone.

Aisha frowned but was silent as Lance talked to Koi. Her head snapped up when he told her that he'd be seeing her later that night. He clicked off his phone and placed it next to him in a little compartment. He continued driving as though he had just announced that it was pitch dark outside.

Aisha sucked her teeth, then: "So you're seeing Koi tonight?"

Lance's eye twitched at the irritation in Aisha's voice. "You know that she and I occasionally hook up."

"Did you forget our rule?" she asked quietly.

"What rule?"

"That we keep our shit separate. I don't want to know what you got going on and you don't need to know what I'm in. After that Koi shit, I thought we agreed that when we're spending time together, it's just us, no one else."

"I didn't forget. I had to speak to her."

"That's disrespecting me."

Lance pulled his gaze away from the road long enough to shoot her a look of confusion. "How am I disrespecting you? You're not my wife and you certainly aren't my lady. So how am I disrespecting you? Please enlighten me."

"You're talking to other women in my presence," Aisha hissed. "Like I said, I don't care what you do when we're not together, but I will not tolerate your talking to other women when we're together. My phone rings off—"

"Hold up! You said you will not *tolerate* me talking to other women. Who the fuck do you think you are? My mother?"

"I'm not trying to be your mother. All I'm saying is that I respect you when I'm with you. My phone is ringing off the hook whenever we're together, but you don't see me picking it up all the time."

"Unless it's your sister," Lance grumbled as he pulled his car in front of a Brazilian steak restaurant.

"I have to talk to my sister," Aisha snapped. The valet opened the car door and Aisha stepped out.

"You two talk more than two teenage girls on crack," Lance shot.

"Whatever," Aisha said before following him into the restaurant.

Upset with Lance's attitude, Aisha barely touched her dinner.

Aisha surreptitiously studied Lance while he savored the last bit of beef. Then: "So how often do you and Koi hook up?"

Lance sighed. "I thought we were done talking about this."

"I'm just curious. Tell me."

"We see each other whenever. It's not that serious. You and I got our thing and Koi and I got our thing. Besides, I just added another flava to the mix. I need to rev up my shit." He sniffed, then nodded at her still full plate. "I thought you were hungry?"

"And I thought it was just going to be you and me. I understand what our relationship is about. But I don't like being a part of your crew."

"So now you're asking for exclusivity. A couple hours ago you told me you didn't care what I did when I wasn't with you. So why're you flip-flopping?"

"I'm not *flip-flopping* and I never wanted exclusivity with you."

"What did you want?"

"The contract," Aisha answered in a strong voice. "You knew that. You were just a bonus."

Lance smiled, pleased with Aisha's frankness. He respected a person who spoke their mind. Lance didn't comment as he laid his platinum card on the table for payment.

"I'm not giving up Koi. She's fun and cheap. It doesn't take much to please her. You, on the other hand . . ." he said, letting his sentence drift off. "Help me to understand. If it was just sex between us, why do you care who else is in my bed?"

Aisha arched an eyebrow at him. "You just said it, who else is in your bed. That's exactly what I was thinking about during dinner. I don't like coming after some other woman. Especially someone like Koi. I want you to stop seeing her."

Lance reached under the table. His hand snaked up her leg and slid between her legs. Aisha yelped, and slapped his hand away. "What are you doing?" she hissed.

"Checking to see if you got balls, because you must think you're my daddy, talking to me like that. Nobody tells me who to sleep with. And speaking of bed partners, Koi really likes you, she keeps asking about you. Her tongue should be insured by Lloyd's of London, she's that good. She'd probably make you scream louder than I do."

"Whatever. I don't understand why you socialize with someone like her. She's nothing but a ho."

Lance laughed loudly. "Well if she's your definition of a ho, what are you?"

Aisha furrowed her brow. "What do you mean?"

"I mean that the both of you take and take and never give anything. And both of you spread your legs faster than a crack ho."

"I'm not like that. I own my own business."

"So does Koi."

"Really? What is she, Atlanta's version of Heidi Fleiss?"

Lance nodded while his lips fractioned up into a smile and Aisha's eyes grew big. "Don't knock it. She's getting paid. She easily cleared six figures last year . . . tax free. You should think about soliciting her for a client."

"Hell, she's a high-class ho. It's her coochie that should be insured, not her tongue. But she's the ho, not me."

"You're both either flat on your backs or knees to get what you want."

"I told you. Sex with you was a bonus. Nothing more. Just stop seeing her."

"Stop seeing her?" Lance repeated the demand as though the concept was foreign to him. "That's not going to happen anytime soon. She and I have an arrangement that suits us."

"What about me? Don't you care about what I want?"

His remark didn't come until they were both in his car and driving on Atlanta's rain-slicked roads. Aisha glanced straight ahead. The rain was pelting the car so hard that it sounded like bits of hail were showering them.

"What about you?" Lance asked, coldly eyeing the lady who had shared his bed for the past couple of months. He admired her skills in bed as well as her business sense. She was a young Madam C. J. Walker. But he wasn't looking for that combination right now. He wanted freaks—fun, easy-access freaks. And Koi fit the bill. And nobody was going to tell him otherwise. He was thirty-two years old, too young to settle down with one woman. "You can either stay on the team and play by the rules or get cut," Lance said calmly.

"I guess you'd better cut me," Aisha snapped. I don't need to see you, just keep me on your payroll, Aisha thought smugly.

"Fine," Lance answered. "You won't see me anymore and as of two seconds ago, your project ended."

"No . . . that's not right, Lance," Aisha said, panicked, her voice tightening with stress and her body coiled as though ready to jump on him. She needed this account. There were people who were relying on her. She forced herself to relax. Leaning forward, she fixed Lance with a pointed stare.

"What's not right is some businesswoman coming out to play and not knowing the rules of the game," Lance said arrogantly.

"You're messing with my money, Lance." Aisha decided on a different tactic. "We work well together and you enjoyed my work. I think we can keep it strictly professional," she said.

"Is that so? You really think that?" he asked, taking his eyes off the rain-soaked road long enough to glance at her. Aisha nodded. "Well you're a lot more stupid than I gave you credit for. You've fucked up. You're trying to tell me what to do," Lance said. He suddenly turned the wheel sharply and braked at the curb so abruptly that Aisha had to reach out to brace herself on the dashboard. "Get out!" he ordered.

"Don't put me out here!" Aisha begged. "It's raining."

"Get your ass outta my fucking car. Don't make me call the police, because I will," he threatened. He grabbed one of his cell phones. "I'm gonna say it one last time, get-the-fuck-out-of-my-damn-car."

Aisha stared at him, her mouth open wide. He met her gaze unflinchingly as he reached across her and opened the door. "Please!" Aisha implored.

"Get out!" he barked, then shoved her out. Aisha stumbled and before she could right herself, he pulled the door shut and sped off into the night.

Aisha's face was wet, a mixture of tears and rain, as she trudged down the street. "I don't know how I'm going to tell Felicia about this! Damn, Aisha, you fucked up!"

Chapter 20

Derrick tossed his gym bag into his car, stepped inside and rested his head on the steering wheel. Even an hour-long sweat-popping, muscle-grueling workout did nothing to rid him of his stress.

No situation was more Advil-popping than being in the middle of siblings fighting over their mother's will. Four hours of his day had been spent playing negotiator, mediator and peacemaker to such a family. The whole thing wrung every ounce of emotion out of him.

"What a fucked-up day!" he groaned. "If days were boxing gloves, then I got my butt beat bad. I definitely earned my money today."

Not only did he have to act as referee, but the firm lost a big case, his secretary quit, and Darla showed up at the office once more, acting like a baby mama on meth.

Derrick pulled himself up and frowned. "Crappy weather." He stuck in a Boney James CD, hoping that it would mellow him out.

He carefully navigated his car through the rain. The last thing he needed today was an accident. "Wouldn't that be the fucking cherry on top," Derrick chuckled mirthlessly.

He drove along, and with each mile his muscles relaxed and he was able to enjoy the music. It wasn't until he was halfway home that he saw a lady marching down the street. Umbrella-less and coatless she looked as though she had showered fully clothed. Rain rolled off her in rivulets. "There's something about her that's so familiar," Derrick mumbled to himself as he slowly cruised on.

Derrick stopped at the stoplight and peered into his rearview mirror. "There's something about her. That walk." Derrick had a niggling feeling in the back of his head that he knew her. Even sopping wet and bowed over, she still barreled down the street as though she owned it. Derrick couldn't take his eyes off her. He was staring at her so hard that he missed the green light and was sharply reminded to move when the car behind him honked. He pulled off slowly, resting his foot on the gas with just enough pressure to inch forward. The driver of the car behind him honked angrily, then swung around him and sped off.

Suddenly it hit him. "Oh shit, that's Aisha!" He looked in the rearview mirror for a break in traffic, then at the first opportunity swerved toward the curb and pulled to a stop.

"Hey, Aisha!"

Aisha turned toward the car. Instead of a BMW at the curb there was a Benz. She was so surprised to see the driver that she was frozen with shock, standing so still that she looked paralyzed.

"This isn't the best time to exercise," Derrick joked.

With an embarrassed shake of her head, Aisha turned on

her heels and resumed walking. Derrick kept his foot on the brake as he crept alongside her. Her feet were sloshing inside her sandals. Suddenly one of the four-inch heels broke, cracked into a dozen little pieces like a twenty-five cent piece of Chick-O-Stick candy. "I'm not going to cry. I'm not going to cry," Aisha repeated to herself. She squared her shoulders, put one foot in front of the other and limped on.

Derrick shook his head. "Stubborn! Fine as hell, but stubborn as fuck!" He slowed his car to a crawl. The broken heel had reduced her speed, making her inch along like a wounded animal. "Would you just get in!" he called from his car. "You're going to be a prune by the time you get home. I'm sure all the dirty rainwater is wreaking havoc on your skin *and* hair." Aisha immediately stopped and her hand instinctually went to her hair, which was slicked to her head like a shrunken skullcap. "Come on."

Aisha looked at the open car door, then peered inside at Derrick, staring at him like a mouse at a block of cheese, trying to decide if there was a trap involved. Then she shrugged, limped over and slid into his car. Not a sound was made as Aisha pulled off her saturated sandals, then with the aplomb of a queen she reached under her dress and pulled off her sopping panty hose. She held them in her hand like a heap of dog mess as if deciding to wring them out, then she tossed them into a corner.

The car was dark, but Derrick could see Aisha's dress clinging to her like a ninety-year-old lady's skin. The dress was wrinkled, but not so much that it hid the fact she was cold. Her nipples stood out like headlights.

Derrick turned on the heat and Aisha flung him a grateful smile before adjusting the vents so that one blew on her face and the other on her feet. She ran a hand over her head and a wave of water ran down her back.

Derrick bit back an expletive as the water dripped off her and onto his leather seats. Instead he asked, "You wanna talk about it?"

Aisha shook her head, then changed her mind. He did pick me up, she decided. "Well, girl meets boy, boy screws girl, end of story," she said succinctly.

"The end? I doubt that. You were gonna walk home?"

"I'm not in the mood to talk about it," she snapped. Then her voice softened. "Listen, as you can see, it's been one of those days."

"Join the club," Derrick mumbled.

"Thanks for picking me up. I really do appreciate it."

Neither said anything on the drive home. Aisha wracked her brain for revenue-generating ideas and possible ways to lure Lance back. And Derrick's eyes kept wandering to Aisha's profile. With her makeup washed away by the rain, she was naturally beautiful.

Aisha saw his glances out of the corner of her eye. She let him get an eyeful before turning to him. "What?" Aisha snapped.

"What?" Derrick asked and quickly shifted his gaze to the road.

"You're staring at me."

"No I'm not," he denied.

"Yeah, right. Just don't do it again," she demanded before shifting away from him and focusing her attention outside. She stayed in that position until they got home.

Derrick pulled the car into the driveway and neither moved. They both watched the rain hitting the windshield, then being whisked away by the wipers. "Why don't you come into my place," Derrick said. "It looks like you still need to talk."

Aisha looked at him and for the first time saw his clothing. His T-shirt pulled across his chest, showing her firm pecs the size of oranges. His sweatpants were loose but not so loose that she couldn't make out his toned thighs and the bulge where his legs met. A shot of desire hit her clit. "Sure," she mumbled, and followed him inside. But she paused at her door.

"Come on," Derrick coaxed, seeing her hesitation. "You still want to talk, don't you?"

"I guess," Aisha admitted, then followed Derrick up to his apartment.

"Take off your clothes," Derrick demanded as soon as the door was closed.

Aisha shrank against the door and clutched her purse to her chest. "What?"

"Come on now, get your mind out of the gutter. You're all wet," Derrick explained with a grin. "I want to give you something warm to wear so that you don't catch cold."

"Oh," Aisha said, a little disappointed.

Derrick sauntered off to his bedroom, a smile playing on his lips. He didn't miss Aisha's look of disappointment. He rummaged through his dresser drawer until he found a T-shirt he thought would fit.

"Here you go. The bathroom is right down the hall. Why don't you take a shower?"

"That sounds delicious." She sighed with relief as she headed toward the bathroom.

Derrick went into the kitchen. "Hey, do you want something to eat?"

"No!" Aisha called back, then: "On second thought, maybe some soup or something."

"Consider it done," Derrick answered, and quickly got busy. By the time Aisha emerged from the bathroom, the dining room table was almost set and Derrick was standing over the stove stirring a pot filled with bubbling food.

"Wow! I wasn't expecting this!" Aisha said. And Derrick almost dropped the pan he was holding. He thought the T-shirt he had given her would be a perfect fit, but he neglected to consider her height. While the T-shirt was hanging off her, covering her knees, it still gave him a phenomenal view of her calves, and on top of that her nipples stood out like two captains in the navy, saluting him. "I left my wet clothes in the bathroom. I'll be sure to grab everything before I leave. I don't want you to get into trouble with any of your girlfriends," she said half-jokingly.

"No problem," Derrick mumbled, trying to tear his eyes away from her breasts. "Have a seat."

Aisha sat at the table and watched as Derrick finished putting out the place settings and glasses. "I wasn't expecting anything so nice. You're pretty talented," Aisha teased. Although the dinnerware was heavy-duty ceramic, the light pastel pattern was bright and cheery. She felt better. The shower did wonders for her, somewhat alleviating the pain of losing the KBS account. Lance and the lost account were something she'd deal with tomorrow.

Derrick didn't tell her that an ex-girlfriend had shown him how to set a perfect table. Instead he said, "Thanks. Here you go." He placed a basket of sourdough rolls on the table and Aisha's eyes widened with astonishment. They had come from the freezer and the chowder that he was going to give her was, ten minutes ago, just a hard brick in the freezer.

"Was I in the shower that long?"

"Yeah, I thought maybe you drowned," Derrick teased.

"If I did, then I'm in heaven." Aisha hungrily eyed the clam chowder Derrick ladled into her bowl. The walk must've worked up my appetite, she decided.

Derrick's mouth fractioned up into a smile. Five minutes ago, the steaming chowder was as hard as a popsicle. "I do what I do."

Derrick went into the kitchen and pulled two frozen lobster tails out of the freezer. They were supposed to be for his date tomorrow, but something told him that Aisha would appreciate them more. He quickly seasoned them before sticking them in the broiler. Derrick made his way back to the dining room and sat down. He reached for Aisha's hand.

Her eyebrows shot up into her hair. "You want to hold my hand?"

"I want to bless the meal," Derrick quipped.

"Oh."

For the second time that evening Derrick heard disappointment in her voice. He quickly thanked God for the meal.

"This is good," Aisha moaned while sipping the soup.

"Do you want me to leave the room?"

"Huh?" Aisha looked up at him, her face in a frown. Her face relaxed when she realized he was joking. She giggled and Derrick felt a jolt of electricity go through him and he got as hard as a frozen block of clam chowder. She looked cute.

"You were putting a hurting on the chowder. Want some more?"

Aisha nodded and she glued her eyes to Derrick's bottom as he walked to the kitchen. Nice ass. I wonder if it tastes as good as it looks, she mused. I bet he does, just like a tasty nugget of luscious creamy dark chocolate.

Inside the kitchen Derrick rested against the counter, giving himself time to soften. "That's not going to happen," he muttered. Just the thought of her legs and the way her hair fell over her face when she bent over to eat made him hard.

"What are you doing, catching the lobster?" Aisha yelled.

"Yeah, I have to, they all heard you were in the house and ran away," he laughed as he walked through the door carrying a platter of lobster tails.

"More wine?" Derrick asked.

"Please," Aisha answered, holding her glass out for more. She smiled at him as he poured the liquid into her glass.

Her body flushed. She wasn't sure if the heat was from the chowder or Derrick.

Derrick watched in amazement as Aisha's knife and fork moved with lightning speed. "Ummm, the lobsters are dead, you don't have to worry about them trying to get away," Derrick teased.

Aisha looked up from her plate. "I didn't realize how hungry I was," she explained while slowing her pace.

"Don't slow down just because of me. Keep inhaling. Hopefully you'll clean the plate so that I won't have to."

"Eww!" "That's What Friends Are For" popped through the air, causing Aisha to hop out of her seat. "Where's my purse? I need to take that call."

Derrick pointed to his sofa. Her purse rested against the cushions. Aisha hurried to it and clicked her phone open. "Hey, girl." She paused, then glanced at Derrick before answering. "I'm at a friend's." She shook her head. "No, not Lance. I'll tell you about it tomorrow. I will . . . I promise."

"Lance?" Derrick asked as soon as she returned to the table.

Aisha shook her head. "Felicia."

Derrick wanted to ask her why she didn't tell her sister that she was in the building with him. Why is she lying to her sister? he wondered. Instead he asked, "So whassup with you and bruh man?"

Suddenly the anger that Aisha thought she had under control threatened to erupt. "He ruined my business. Because of him I might have to close."

Derrick didn't know the ins and outs of what happened, but the most important thing that he learned in Business 101 was to never put your eggs in one basket. He told her so.

"I know," Aisha snapped. "I have degrees in finance *and* accounting. I should've known better, but I never knew that a man couldn't separate business from pleasure."

"I'm sorry I asked. I thought after bruh man made you fend for yourself in the pouring rain you'd be ready to get some things off your chest."

"I do . . . just not now. Just thinking about it will piss me off again. And I'm having too good of a time. I don't want to spoil it." She stuck her wineglass out. "Top her off."

"That's beer."

"And?" Aisha asked arching her eyebrow. "I want a good buzz tonight. Besides, it's not like I have to drive."

Derrick obliged her and filled her wineglass. "I hope you're not a slutty drunk."

"Sometimes." She flirted while imagining his bare chest. "Let's talk about something else," she said, pulling herself away from her fantasy.

"Agreed." Derrick shifted the conversation to attending historically black colleges and both wondered why neither one of them remembered the other from their Howard days.

"I'm sure our paths must've crossed," said Aisha. "Especially since you and Tarik hung together."

"Maybe, but I would've remembered meeting you," Derrick drawled.

"Yeah, right! You seem like the type of man who goes through women like they're boxes of chocolate. So if you did meet me back then, all I would've been to you was a piece of double-dipped dark chocolate with caramel in the middle."

Derrick nervously cleared his throat. She was right. During his college days he had women throwing their panties at him like they were groupies and he took full advantage of it. "That's not true," Derrick cajoled. "If I ever got a taste of you, I would become a lifelong chocolate lover," he whispered at her with a wink.

Aisha studied him over her wineglass. His midnight black eyes were shrouded by thick lashes and his full lips were turned up into a smile. *I think I'd better get us back to a safer subject,* Aisha thought. She asked him about his childhood and they launched into a discussion of their favorite memories.

"You went fishing?" Derrick asked, incredulous. No way could he see the manicured and pedicured glossy lady sitting in front of him baiting a hook. "Me too!"

"Yeah, I went fishing." Aisha grinned. "And I loved it. My dad and I used to go fishing at least once a month. He'd pull out his little rowboat and we would spend all day on the lake."

"I did the fishing thing with my uncle. It was cool. I bet you stopped when you became a teenager."

"Well, I stopped when my dad passed away," she said sadly, and Derrick gave her hand a quick squeeze. She quickly brightened. "But a year or so before he passed, I caught more trout than he did," she boasted.

"So did you use live bait or fake?"

"Live, of course," Aisha sniffed as though the question was an insult.

"Bobbers or floaters?"

"Neither. Those are for amateurs. There's nothing like getting a tug on your pole letting you know that you've snagged a fish."

Oh, I would love to have you tug on *my* pole, Derrick mused. "Maybe we can go up to Lake Allatoona . . . you know, to fish," Derrick said, impressed.

Aisha nodded. "Maybe," she agreed with a giggle, and Derrick found it cute.

They had moved to the sofa and two empty bottles of wine lay between them. By then Derrick had pulled off his shirt and Aisha's T-shirt was inching up way past her thighs. Aisha's skin shimmered and before she knew what happened, Derrick suddenly reached down and pulled her feet into his lap.

"What are you doing?" Aisha chuckled.

"Just giving you a foot massage. I think every lady should have one at least once in their life."

"I agree," Aisha murmured as Derrick's hands sensuously moved over her sore feet. It was hard to believe that a couple of hours ago, they were soggier than a newborn's diaper. "Ah, that feels good," Aisha sighed, while reclining on the couch and spreading her legs.

Derrick's hands slowly inched their way up her right leg and gently massaged her calf, then he moved to the left and did the same. Aisha gurgled happily and closed her eyes in happiness. He tenderly kneaded her thighs. Seconds later his hand crept to where her legs met.

Derrick slipped his finger into Aisha and her eyes flew open. She stared at him, her eyes two big question marks. As he inserted it in and pulled it out, Aisha's eyes fluttered closed and she began moving with him. Her hips flowed smoothly while his hand attempted to take her to an o.

"Awwww, D, keep doing that," Aisha moaned.

"I'm here to do whatever you want," Derrick said, watching her. He couldn't tear his eyes away. She looked so sexy, so uninhibited. Her legs were spread wide and inviting, her head was thrown back and she made soft purring sounds.

"Don't stop!"

"Baby, you can't pay me to stop," Derrick said with a grin as his hand glided over her stomach up to her breasts. Bending down, he gently pulled one of her nipples into his mouth and suckled. Aisha gasped then ran her hand over Derrick's head. Moans of ecstasy escaped her lips as he feasted on her breasts. Heat seared her body where Derrick's silky caresses washed gently over her.

Suddenly his movements stopped and Aisha's eyes flew open. "I asked you not to stop," she said as her lips turned into a pout.

"Sorry babe, but I wanted to change position," he answered, and his eyes glinted with desire as he knelt before her.

"I don't care, just keep doing what you were—" Aisha let out a strangled cry as Derrick reinserted his finger and gently tongued her clit. "Oh my God!" Aisha screamed as Derrick finger-fucked her. Her hips bucked as Derrick tenderly nibbled on her button.

Derrick pulled his mouth away. "You taste good baby," he drawled.

Aisha's body throbbed. "Please don't stop," she begged, then inhaled sharply when Derrick's thumb ran over her clit. Her legs snapped together, capturing his finger. "Don't stop," she chanted. "Please don't stop." Derrick continued his maddeningly slow and precise movements until her hips jerked and she gave a strangled cry. He stayed with her until her orgasm came.

"Umm, how about if I stick something a little bit bigger inside you?"

"Just a *little* bit bigger?" Aisha teased.

"Aw hell naw," Derrick said. "You see for yourself," he drawled. He stood up, slid his fingers under the elastic waistband of his sweatpants and in one swoop pulled off his sweatpants, shorts and boxers. His dick popped out at her. She glanced, then did a double take, her lips turned up into a smile. "See, brotha wasn't lying," Derrick bragged.

"No he wasn't," Aisha answered in awe.

"I hate to tease you but I got to take a shower. I don't like being dirty while doing the dirty and I'm sure you don't either."

"Go clean up for me."

Aisha reclined against the couch and watched Derrick saunter to the bathroom. She wished she knew how to whistle. Instead she clapped softly. "Looking good, baby."

"Well, you saw me coming toward you, I thought I'd give you a treat by letting you see me from behind," Derrick teased.

"I like," Aisha said. "I like very much." Derrick winked, then stepped into the bathroom. Moments later Aisha could hear the water. She looked down at her naked body. Is this the smartest thing to do? she asked herself. Should I do my neighbor? she mused, thinking of the women constantly traipsing in and out of his apartment. Well, it'll be a one-time thing, she decided as she settled against the couch. As soon as she did so, the bathroom door opened and Derrick strolled into the room. She saw his penis before she saw him. It stood at attention like a general in the marines. She couldn't wait to taste that. "C'mere." She crooked her finger, motioning Derrick to her. He stood in front of her. Aisha licked her lips before dropping down to her knees.

Derrick dropped his hand on her head. She looked up, questions in her eyes.

"We don't have to do this. I don't ever want anyone to say that I took advantage of a vulnerable lady."

Aisha grinned. "I'm a grown lady and this is what I want to do. I've been thinking about this since I first saw you."

"Oh yeah?" Derrick asked, grinning. He didn't know Aisha was feeling him like that.

"Yeah!" Derrick groaned when her lush lips covered his tip. She moved him in and out her mouth. Minutes later her movements quickened, then he tightened.

"Now do that while you're inside me," Aisha demanded.

"Will do," Derrick answered. He grabbed Aisha's hand and pulled her up so that they faced each other. Her lips parted in anticipation, and Derrick kissed her gently, moving his lips over hers so softly that they felt like ribbons of air.

He sat up and tugged Aisha along with him. Without saying a word he reclined on the sofa and pulled Aisha on top. She straddled him, wrapping her legs around his waist. Her lips found their way back to his. Derrick's hands roamed over her back, caressing and stroking it until her skin burned. Suddenly he lifted her and eased her onto his cock.

"Shouldn't we use a—" Aisha was getting ready to ask, but her words were sucked back in as soon as Derrick's dick found its way inside her. Derrick grabbed her behind and slowly began moving her up and down. Aisha swerved her hips, trying to feel every inch of him. "Condom." The word came out in one short puff.

Derrick pulled Aisha closer to him and nuzzled her neck, leading her to sigh and fall asleep. He scooped her up and carried her into the bedroom, where he gently placed her on the bed and slipped in beside her.

The sun had broken through the sky when Aisha slid out of bed and padded to the bathroom to take a quick shower. She threw on a T-shirt and made her way to the kitchen. "Let's see what your cooking-challenged behind can make," she said while scrutinizing the kitchen. Soon water was boiling and bread was in the toaster.

Derrick sleepily stumbled into the kitchen. He let out a loud groan when he saw what Aisha planned on feeding him. "That's hardly enough to keep me alive. Get out the kitchen, girl. Go sit down and let a man do his thing."

Aisha stuck her tongue out.

"Hey, you know the house rules—don't be flicking if you don't plan on licking."

"Well, depending on how good your breakfast is, there might be some licking," Aisha shot back before flouncing off to the living room.

It was dark when they got in last night and she didn't pay

much attention to his décor. Now she did; she looked around. She nodded her head impressed. His apartment was strictly male but very contemporary.

Spotting a photo album on the table, she glanced over her shoulder toward the kitchen. Derrick was bent over peering into the oven. "Nice ass," she mumbled before picking up the album. She settled on the couch, tucked her feet underneath her and began thumbing through the book. There were several pictures of Derrick and a very attractive lady, and in many pictures they were gazing into each other's eyes as though they were sending each other secret messages of love.

"Who's this woman you're all hugged up with in all these pictures!" she yelled to him. "What is your problem, girl, you just slept with him, not married him," she hissed to herself.

"Shit!" Derrick cursed, he had forgotten to put that away. Normally if he had a female coming over, he'd pack it away. "I really should burn it," he mumbled. He didn't have to go into the living room to see that she was pointing to Darla. The whole album was dedicated to them.

"Oh, someone I used to date," Derrick answered nonchalantly.

Aisha thumbed through the pages. There was picture after picture of Derrick and Darla at various events. "It looks like you two did more than date, it looks like it was serious," Aisha observed.

"Well, yeah," Derrick mumbled. "Are you ready—"

"When did you two break up?"

He was learning that Aisha was worse than a private investigator on steroids. "We broke up right before I moved to Atlanta."

"Did you break up *right before* or *because* of your move to Atlanta?"

"Why does it matter?"

Aisha shrugged. "Don't know . . . it just does."

"We, I mean *I* broke up with her right before I moved here. She's a wonderful lady, but I couldn't see myself married to her. And now that she's pregnant—"

"What!" Aisha shrieked, and the photo album fell to the floor forgotten.

"Oh shit!" Derrick dropped his head in his hands. By the time he looked up Aisha was standing over him, waiting for a response.

"What's going on? You left a pregnant woman? You're going to have a child?" she asked, rapidly firing the questions at him.

"I didn't know she was pregnant when I left. She just showed up here."

"Where is she now?"

"I don't know."

"You don't know?" Aisha asked, incredulous. Here's a man who she thought was different from other men, but he turned out to be worse than them all, a dirty low-down brother, one who catered to her every need, but was a snake in disguise. "You don't know where the mother of your child is?" Derrick shook his head. "Well, you know what? You'll have a lot of time to find her. Because I'm leaving!" Aisha stalked to the bathroom and snatched her clothes off the shower rack.

"Aisha, wait!" In response Aisha shot past him faster than a bullet. She opened the door and stomped down the stairs. "Aisha, let's talk about this!" Derrick called. But Aisha ignored him. Derrick slammed the door shut. "You and your big mouth. How the hell are you going to get her back?"

Chapter 21

Felicia pulled her car to a stop in front of Lawrence's house. She didn't have to worry about him being at home since it was the middle of the day. An empty suitcase was in one hand as she slipped her key in the lock and stepped inside. The house was as quiet as a funeral home.

Her plan was all set. She would pick up her belongings, then call Lawrence to meet with him later to tell him that she no longer wanted to see him. A sense of peace settled over her at the thought of finally being with Tarik. Aisha and Tiffany decided that she should woman up and tell Tarik how she felt about him.

Soft humming filled the house as she roamed into the bedroom and began filling her suitcase with her items. "Aw hell, why not play some real music." She went into the living room and stuck in Mary J. Blige's latest CD. Soon Mary's gritty voice filled the room and Felicia began swaying to the music. An hour and a half later and well into Jamie Foxx's new CD, she was halfway packed. What normally would have taken her half an hour was extended considerably every time one of her favorite songs came on and she stopped to dance and sing along. She had her music jamming more than Karaoke Night at the Apollo.

Lawrence's grandfather clock chimed two. She had originally hated the clock but now was grateful for it. Her stomach started growling and she realized that she hadn't eaten anything all day, not even breakfast. Dancing, she made her way into the kitchen and fixed herself a sandwich and a glass of wine. I'm really going to miss Lawrence, she mused. We had a good time, despite his unusual habits and his *wife*. I loved him.

Felicia shook her head. Why did it have to be this way? Why does love have to be so complicated? She let the question hang while she shifted her thoughts to Tarik. Anticipation made her face glow. Her feelings for her best friend had totally blindsided her. It amazed her that what she had spent close to a decade searching for had always been within her grasp.

The grandfather clock chimed three and Felicia finished her snack and hurried back into the bedroom. A few of her things still cluttered the room and she wanted to get them packed up. She had a catering job and she had to be there at six o'clock.

Her Kem CD was playing so loud that she didn't hear the front door open and slam shut. "What are you doing?"

She whirled around to find Lawrence standing at the door. His appearance surprised her so much that she dropped the blouse she was folding. "I'm, um, leaving."

His face sagged like a soggy napkin. "You weren't going to tell me to my face?" He looked so hurt that Felicia immediately realized that she had made a mistake. Sneaking wasn't the best way to do this.

"I was, when you got home," she answered softly before glancing down at her blouse. She wanted to pick it up but something told her that now wasn't the right time. But it *was* one of her favorite blouses.

"Why are you doing this?" Lawrence asked.

"I can't keep doing this. Us," she explained at his confused expression.

"Come on now," he said while reaching for her. Felicia pulled out of his reach. He moved as if he wanted to reach out again, but he dropped his hand to his side. "I know what this is about," Lawrence suddenly said. Felicia opened her mouth to protest but he continued talking. "You're tripping about my wife. Well, you don't have to worry about it anymore. I'm getting a divorce. See, that's why I'm home early. I got the paperwork to get the process started." He grinned as he proudly held up a handful of paper.

Sweat began popping out over her body. This isn't what she expected. "Oh!" Felicia answered. She eagerly reached for her blouse and snatched it up. *I have to get out of here.*

"And the good thing is that since we've been living apart we can do a no-fault divorce. It'll only take thirty days for it to become official. Then we can talk about taking us to the next level."

"Next level?"

"Yeah, baby. See, you think I haven't been thinking about us. I was thinking we could get engaged. We could be married this time next year."

Felicia rapidly began shaking her head. "No, no, no, that can't happen."

"Calm down, baby. It doesn't have to be next year. I know how you ladies like to have time to plan your weddings."

"No. It's not that," Felicia sighed, then glanced at her suitcase. Lying on top of the folded pile of clothes was a necklace Tarik had given her a couple of years ago for her birthday. "I just think we both would be better off if we saw different people," she blurted out.

"What are you talking about? I'm getting a divorce. *I want to marry you.*"

"I know you do and that's what I wanted too. But now . . ."

"But now what?" Lawrence almost barked.

"That's not what I want anymore," Felicia confessed quietly.

Lawrence snapped his fingers. "Just like that you changed your mind? Did you feel that way last night while we were making love? Or when I was eating your pussy the other day? Or did the thought pop up when I cooked dinner for you last week?"

Felicia's spine stiffened at the tone of Lawrence's voice. "I didn't plan on my feelings to change. It just happened," she offered lamely.

"Shit doesn't just happen," Lawrence countered. He studied her, and they locked gazes, and Felicia quickly broke the connection. Anger quickly replaced hurt in Lawrence. "Who is he?"

"Who's who?"

"Who's the dude who got you wanting to leave me?"

A hollow sound reverberated through the room and Felicia realized it was her laugh. "Nobody. There's nobody," she vehemently denied.

"That's bullshit! There is somebody. You can't even look me in the eye."

"Sure I can." Felicia boldly met his gaze.

Lawrence grabbed her chin, locking her into position. "So who is he?"

Felicia's eyes widened as half a dozen lies ran around in her head. "There's no—" Lawrence's grip on her chin loosened. "It's Tarik, I caught feelings for Tarik."

Lawrence's hand dropped. "Your boy Tarik? Your best friend Tarik? The one you told me over and over again that you were nothing but friends?" Felicia nodded and Lawrence chuckled nastily. "So all this time you were shopping, having dinner and going to movies you were trying to get with him?"

"No. It wasn't like that. And remember, he had a fiancée, Tara."

"How was it, Felicia? Help a brother understand how it went down."

"We did hang out," she haltingly started. "But as friends. Nothing more. Honest. I wasn't sitting around biding my time until he was a free agent. It wasn't like that. I was into us, at one hundred percent. I really was," she answered in response to his snort. "But like I said, my feelings changed."

"Did you two sleep together?" At the thought of feeling Tarik's arms around her Felicia's lips curved up into an elephant-size smile. "What the fuck?" Lawrence hissed at seeing the expression on her face.

"We didn't sleep together," Felicia said quickly, clearing up any misunderstanding. "We haven't done anything. He doesn't even know how I feel about him."

"So you're leaving me on a dream?" Felicia nodded. "Ain't this some shit? Here I am trying to wife her up and she's leaving me for a fucking dream?"

"It's the dreams that get us excited about facing another day," she mumbled.

"What did you say?" Felicia was saved by the sound of Prince. "Aren't you going to answer it?"

"I'll talk to her later."

"You'll talk to her later. Why not now, Felicia? Hell, you've picked up the phone while we were making love. Why not now?" he taunted. "Maybe I'll answer for you. I bet you never did tell her about us. Where's your phone?" he asked, looking around the room.

"Lawrence, chill. This is important. I want to talk to you," she said.

"Where is it?" He prowled around the room trying to find the source of the noise. In his search he snatched up clothes, shoved cologne bottles to the floor and was about to upturn the mattress when she screamed.

"Lawrence!" Fortunately the phone was in her purse, which was underneath the top of the suitcase.

"Get your shit and leave."

"You don't have to be an asshole about it," Felicia snapped, suddenly tired. She walked over to the closet and quietly debated whether she wanted to take her clothes off the hangers or just stick everything into her suitcase.

"An asshole?" Lawrence snorted. "How the fuck do you think I should feel? You come in here telling me that you're in love with someone else. Maybe you'd prefer it if I had helped you fold up your clothes and pack your bags."

"I'm not saying that you had to do all that."

"Yeah, well I don't plan on doing any of that punk-ass shit."

Felicia sighed and began pulling her clothes off the hangers. Fortunately she had taken most of her things a couple of months ago when they had broken up the first time. Her hands were filled with clothes when she turned around and faced Lawrence. "That's good because I didn't ask you to do any of that *punk-ass shit*!"

Before she knew what happened, Lawrence's hand came out of nowhere like a phantom and smacked her hard across her face. So hard that her head whipped around like the character in *The Exorcist*. The clothes flew out of Felicia's hands. Her mouth dropped open, too stunned to utter a sound. Their eyes met. Lawrence's filled with shock and Felicia's with hurt and pain. Lawrence reacted first. He stepped to her and pulled her into his arms. Felicia stood stiffly against him.

"I'm sorry. I'm sorry, baby. I didn't mean to hit you," he crooned while stroking her face. A red splotch was spreading across her skin as though someone had gone crazy with blush. In a daze Felicia reached up and touched her cheek. It was burning.

Felicia looked at the man she once cared for. The man she thought she knew. "Why did you do that?" He had never ever hit her before.

Lawrence shook his head. "I don't know. I'm sorry, baby."

"Why did you do that?" Felicia repeated.

"I don't want you to leave," Lawrence admitted.

"Hitting me isn't going to keep me here," she said angrily.

"I didn't know what else to do."

Felicia sighed and reached down and picked up her clothes. She smashed them into her suitcase, hangers and all, not caring if they got wrinkled. Lawrence watched her as she closed the suitcase and zipped it close. He was on her heels as she trudged through the house pulling it behind her as though she was going on a trip. She stopped at the front door.

"Don't you walk out that door!"

Felicia slowly turned to face him, then locked gazes with him. She cocked her head, then said, "Oh hell. I'm not walking, I'm running. What are you going to do now?"

Chapter 22

Felicia and Tiffany sat mannequin still on Aisha's couch. It was Saturday, their day off, a rarity. Ever since they had gotten the KBS account a day off had become about as nonexistent as an honest man. This was Felicia's first time seeing her sister since early yesterday, before Aisha went out to dinner with Lance, and she looked horrible. Her normally lush chocolate skin was gray, her hair stood up in spikes around her head, and even her sweatpants were ragged, a no-no for Aisha. Usually even in sweatpants she made shabby look chic.

Aisha nervously tapped her pen against her yellow pad. All morning, after she had finished cursing Derrick out, was spent thinking of ways to tell her sister and Tiffany that she had blown the KBS account. She saw the worry and fear in Felicia's and Tiffany's eyes.

"Thanks for stopping by. I-um-don't-know-how-to-tell-y'all-this," she stuttered and Felicia watched in amazement. Aisha was *always* on point. "But we—I mean I—lost the KBS account."

A collective sharp gasp went up. "What happened?" Felicia asked quietly.

"Well, to be honest, Lance got pissed at me because I told him that he should give up his little ho *and then* he wanted me to participate in a ménage à trois."

"So he got mad at you. So what? Get over it. Don't be a punk ass and cancel the contract!"

"People in Lance's position do not *get over it*. They get even. So he ended the contract and I have to return all the money he had given us, less the services we provided."

"How did this happen?" Tiffany wailed. She had already spent the bonus on late bills, and the raise was already calculated into her budget. Now she might lose her job.

Felicia patted Tiffany's leg. "Can he do this?" she asked quietly.

"Yep. He put so many stipulations in his contract that if I had farted, he would've rescinded."

"Why did you sign it?"

Aisha looked at her sister through narrowed eyes. "Why? It was a six-figure deal. This deal was going to put us on the map. I'm sorry that I let y'all down. I never should've slept with him," she said, shaking her head.

"Can't you call him?" Tiffany croaked, sniffling. Mascara made a river down her face to her chin.

Aisha patiently blew out a puff of air. "Lance doesn't give second chances."

"Please!" Tiffany begged.

"No. I'm not calling. We'll deal with this," she said forcibly. "And we will be okay, honest," she promised with a glance to Tiffany. "It's just a bump in the road."

More like a mountain, Felicia thought. "Maybe you should

think about closing FAACS. You could always go back to Corporate America."

"Hell no! We're not closing. This kind of stuff happens to small businesses all the time. We're okay for the next five months or so. After that . . ." She shrugged her arms. "But I do have some good news," she announced.

"What?" Tiffany grumbled.

"There's a grant that I can apply for. It's for minority women business owners. When we get it, it will save us. We'll be set for at least five years," she said, smiling.

"Oh," Tiffany said as she sunk lower into the couch. She knew that grants weren't guaranteed. She decided then that she had better update her resume and interviewing skills.

Felicia snorted. "A grant? We can't put all our hopes in something as uncertain as a grant."

"We have a chance of getting it," Aisha said when Felicia arched an eyebrow at her. She continued, "This particular foundation is giving away twelve grants, and we meet all the criteria. I think I e-mailed the information to you and Tiffany a couple of weeks ago."

Tiffany glanced up at her boss. Aisha noticed that her face was as twisted and tight as a woman in labor. "You sure you e-mailed it to me?"

"I did, but I'll do it again if you want," Aisha offered.

"No, let me check my e-mail." Tiffany shot off the couch and hurried to her computer, where after a few keystrokes the document was in front of her. She printed it off.

"Why don't you resend it to Felicia."

"All set," Tiffany said as she returned to her spot on the sofa.

"Thanks," Felicia murmured.

"The good thing is that it's already completed. I did it as

soon as I received it. But when we got KBS's business I completely forgot about it. Never again," she said, more to herself than to Felicia and Tiffany. She vehemently shook her head. "Never again will I put all my eggs in one basket. That was the stupidest thing I have ever done." She turned to her sister. "The application must be mailed out Monday, otherwise we're gonna be disqualified."

"Why don't we just mail it out today?"

"Because I want you to review it."

"You're the owner of the company," Felicia retorted. "Why am I looking at it?"

"Because you're co-owner, smart-ass. And I have all the data in. I just want you to proofread it. You're good at that kind of stuff. And don't worry about the numbers, they're all correct. Just read all the verbiage, make sure it sounds like I have some sense. Are you going to have time to look at it tonight?" Aisha asked her sister.

"I will. I have a couple catering jobs to do tomorrow and Monday, but they're small. I'll be sure to read it tonight."

"Come on, ladies, let's get excited. This grant will keep us in the black. We'll have money again. Let me see some excitement."

"Yay!" Felicia and Tiffany halfheartedly chorused.

"Need any help tomorrow?" Tiffany offered. She enjoyed working with Felicia on her catering jobs. Besides, now with everything happening with FAACS she could use the extra money.

Felicia considered her question. "Sure, I'm making about twenty-five cookie bouquets. I would *love* the help." She would enjoy the company. Working with Tiffany would make the time go by faster.

Felicia turned to her sister. "Are you still going to your conference?"

Aisha nodded. "I am. I've already paid for it. It'll be good to network with other business owners."

"What time do I have to get you to the airport?"

"Don't worry about it. I'm taking a cab. My flight is at six in the morning. I wouldn't drag the devil out that early to do an airport run."

"Thanks, girl," Felicia answered, relieved. She hated going to Hartsfield-Jackson International Airport. And she especially hated driving there before noon, navigating her way through all the traffic usually left her feeling like she had just run a 5K marathon.

"It's too bad that you can't make the conference."

"I know . . . I hate to miss the Black Women in Finance conference," Felicia said, infusing just enough regret in her voice to make herself sound genuine.

"Maybe next year. But I can't wait. It's going to be in Las Vegas this year. And y'all know the saying: 'What happens in Vegas stays in Vegas.' "

The ladies burst out laughing. "Just don't lose the business," Felicia teased.

"I almost did that once. I won't do it again," Aisha answered solemnly. "Don't you forget to mail out that grant application. That's the only thing that's keeping us from folding. Understand?" she asked, while leveling a gaze at her sister.

"Understood."

Chapter 23

For the tenth time that afternoon Derrick attempted to review Darla's legal document, her child support agreement. What he normally considered light reading was as complex as Chinese characters. He had as much interest in it as a toddler in a new Lexus. Suddenly a picture from the night before popped into his head. He wearily rubbed his eyes, but that didn't erase the image. Aisha was superglued on his brain, a naked, writhing, screaming Aisha.

"I can't concentrate on this right now," he said before shoving the document to the side. "All I can think about is Aisha. Shit! She got me feeling like I'm thirteen years old."

Pushing away from the table, he marched over to the refrigerator for a beer. He plopped down on his couch, popped open the beer and took a big gulp.

"Maybe I should go talk to her," he decided, but two sitcoms and two beers later he hadn't moved an inch. "Any day now," he joked. Just then his cell phone rang. He glanced at the display, then let out a groan. "What does she want?" he asked himself before clicking on his phone.

"Have you had a chance to sign the documents yet?" Darla asked.

"I'm looking at them now."

"Well, how long is it going to take you? I want to get this done as soon as possible."

Derrick stifled a sigh. "Just relax, you're only six months pregnant, what's the rush?"

"I want to make sure that you take responsibility for your child!" Darla shrieked.

"My child will be well taken care of. You knew that when you decided to get pregnant."

"When I decided to get pregnant?" Darla yelled. "*You* got me pregnant. It takes two people to make a baby, and I didn't do this on my own. Now you may fault me for keeping it, because I don't believe in abortion. But don't you ever, ever think that I intentionally got pregnant."

"Calm down," Derrick said.

"I just want to make one thing clear," she said, then paused. "Are you listening to me?"

"I am," Derrick answered.

"This is your baby and you damn well better plan on taking care of it. That document is just the beginning—keep playing with me and you'll be sorry," she hissed before clicking off her phone.

Derrick stared at his phone. "Why does my life seem like a rerun of *The Jerry Springer Show*?" he wondered out loud.

Chapter 24

Papers surrounded Felicia like a shawl. They had started off as a neat stack on her lap, but the later it got, the more they spread. As soon as she nodded off to sleep, they scattered like a bunch of cockroaches. Felicia's phone chirp startled her out of her sleep.

"Who's calling me at eleven o'clock at night? And on a Sunday?" she muttered drowsily.

"Felicia, I need your help," a panicked voice on the other end said. Felicia immediately recognized it as Diana Burberry, a lady she occasionally catered for.

"What's wrong, Diana?"

"Everything!" she wailed. "I'm sorry for calling you so late. But I have an event tomorrow—a luncheon—a corporate luncheon—but the caterer I had scheduled can't make it tomorrow. She and half her staff came down with food poisoning. Can you believe it? So they're useless right now. Anyway, I'm hosting a luncheon for fifty of Atlanta's top businesswomen. The mayor has already RSVP'd and they're expecting something innovative and different."

"Okay," Felicia mumbled while knuckling her eyes. She glanced down at the grant papers surrounding her, then returned her attention to Diana.

"I know this is very short notice. But I need you. I should've called you first, but the caterer is the niece of one of the vice presidents here. And you know how that goes. Can you help me out, Felicia?"

Yeah, nepotism still going strong. "Umm, I don't know . . ." She stalled while mentally reviewing tomorrow's schedule. Thanks to Tiffany, the cookie bouquets were done—all she had to do was deliver those to Georgia Pacific along with the brownies and the miniature cakes.

"I'll triple your normal rate. I really need somebody. And I want you. You're professional, dependable, your food is delicious and—"

Triple? Felicia's lips curved into a huge smile. "I think I can do it. What did you have in mind for the menu?" Felicia heard Diana's sigh of relief.

"It doesn't have to be anything special. At this point it can be hot dogs and pork and beans."

Felicia laughed. "Would you like your hot dogs grilled or boiled?" Felicia asked, and was met with dead silence. "I'm only joking."

"I thought so," Diana answered, laughing self-consciously. "But it's late and my nerves are burnt. I know that you'll come up with something unique and delicious. I'll fax you the contract."

"I'm so glad you're able to help me. I'm so crazy that I'm going to pull my hair out. Help me move this table," Felicia asked Tiffany. Both of them were dressed in sweatpants and T-shirts. As soon as she had hung up with Diana, Felicia had thumbed through her portfolio of past events to find a lunch that was easy to do yet innovative and different. As soon as she decided on her menu, she had run out to the twenty-four-hour Wal-Mart to pick up some missing ingredients.

Then she spent an hour throwing items into her food processor to slice, dice and chop her food into pretty little pieces. She was up at five o'clock in the morning to pack everything up, drop the items off to her first two jobs, take a quick nap, then hurry over to Diana's office. A quick call confirmed that Tiffany was going to meet her there.

Felicia surveyed the rooms, then quickly rearranged the tables. She draped a black tablecloth over the wood-topped table, then trimmed it with royal-blue-colored fabric. Reaching down into a large carton, she pulled out boxes of different sizes, then placed them on the table before covering them with shimmery fabric.

Suddenly Diana flew into the room, a blur of red, white and blue. Her red fingertips flew as she gesticulated wildly while throwing comments at Felicia.

"Everything looks nice so far. I knew you'd come through for me."

"Thanks."

"What's all these little things?" Diana asked as Felicia pulled out platters and bowls of colorful dishes.

"They're tapas," Felicia offered.

"Tapas? I've never heard of that." Diana eyed the small delicacies as though they were mini-pigs in a blanket.

Felicia stifled a sigh. No matter how innovative Diana requested, if it wasn't the same old catered lunch food—

chicken, tuna or ham sandwiches—she got worried. "Tapas are a Spanish specialty. They're really appetizers. But I have so many that I've decided to use them as a meal."

Diana scrunched her face up at the item Tiffany had pulled from the cart. "What's that? It looks like a blob of mayonnaise."

Tiffany looked at Felicia for a response. "It's Ensaladilla Rusa, Spanish potato salad. It's delicious. Give me some crackers and I can make a whole meal out of this by itself. You should try it."

Diana skeptically eyed the white bundt-shaped dish. "I don't know if this is substantive enough for lunch. Katie, the caterer who was scheduled, was going to have boxed lunches with sandwiches, potato chips, pasta salad and homemade cookies."

Felicia and Tiffany glanced at each other, and Tiffany lifted a questioning eyebrow. Felicia launched into caterer mode. "Actually, Diana, the tapas bar is even better. Not only is there a lot more variety, but it's something different. Not too many caterers offer this."

"But will it be enough food?" Diana asked, zeroing in on the mini appetizers.

"More than enough," Felicia reassured her. "I've made enough so that there's twelve pieces per person." She still saw the doubt on Diana's face. Felicia grabbed a plate and quickly snatched a selection of tapas from the buffet. "Here, try these." She handed the plate to Diana.

Diana took a bite from one, the other half quickly followed. After the first one she was tossing the tapas into her mouth as though they were peanuts. She burped loudly. "You're right, they are filling. I'm sorry. I'm just so stressed," she said before giving Felicia an apologetic smile.

"That's okay." Felicia filled her plate with additional tapas. "Take some for the road."

Diana gave her a grateful smile before traipsing down the corridor, balancing a plateful of tapas.

"Wow! Go on," said Tiffany. "Girl, I'm impressed. You really know how to deal with difficult people. I would've told her to eat the food and shut up."

"It's all part of the job. Let's finish setting up," Felicia said, unfazed by the incident. She had dealt with all types of people, some worse than Diana. "And the most important thing is that Diana already paid me, and she's happy . . . for now," Felicia whispered to Tiffany. Suddenly her phone rang. Felicia glanced at the screen and saw Mia's number. Ever since she had confessed her feelings, Felicia had been avoiding her like a redhead avoids the sun.

She grimaced before clicking on the phone. "Hey, girl."

"Where've you been? I've been blasting your phone all week."

"I know," Felicia answered while she fussed with cutlery. "I'm sorry, but I've been busy. Whassup?"

"I wanted to finish our conversation. You never did give me an answer."

Felicia peeked over her shoulder. Tiffany was on the opposite side of the room rummaging through boxes. "I didn't mean to hurt you," she whispered. "I thought our thing was light—you know, no strings. It's always been like that . . . *always*. What changed?"

"You're right. I guess it must be my new surroundings. I'm confusing loneliness with love," Mia chuckled.

"You're okay then?"

"I will be, trust me."

Felicia heard Tiffany walk up behind her. "I gotta go." She heard Mia call her name. "Yes?"

"Call me when you want to hook up again. You do know how to make a lady hot."

Felicia grinned. "I will." She clicked off the phone, then absentmindedly placed it near a pile of mixing bowls.

"So do you think your sister's gonna fire me?" Tiffany asked.

"Tiffany, would you please stop worrying. She won't fire you."

"I really like working for you two. My job is more like visiting family instead of going to work. And I get to do fun things like this."

"Don't worry," Felicia reassured her.

"It's hard not to. You know I have rent, a car payment, and Tyrone just needs so much stuff," she said, her voice quavering a little.

Felicia turned to Tiffany and gave her a quick hug. "It'll be okay. Trust me, it will be okay," Felicia promised.

Twenty minutes later they were finished. One table was brimming with tapas, cutlery and plates. And three trays of Felicia's homemade brownies and ice cream covered a second table.

"This is beautiful," Tiffany said, awed. No matter how many times she assisted Felicia, she was always astonished. Felicia's assignments always looked like a piece of art. Starting with the food, then the presentation. "You always do such an awesome job. Girl, you really should think about doing this full-time."

"Yeah, it would be nice," she answered wistfully, thinking how much she would love to be a full-time caterer.

Suddenly Prince wailed. "Oh, it's Aisha." Felicia automatically reached to her waist for the phone, but she came up empty. "Tiffany, I can't find my phone. Have you seen it?"

"I hear it but I don't know where it is. You just had it. It can't be too far away." They moved toward boxes and frantically pulled out cloths, then rummaged through cutlery and dishes. Felicia stepped over to a pile of bowls, then happened to glance down, sitting in the middle of one of the mixing bowls was her phone.

"Is this where I put it?" she asked no one in particular before snatching it up, but then it went silent. "Oh well. I'll call her back later. Let's take one last look to make sure everything is perfect. Those women are going be coming in here hungrier than a three-hundred-pound lady on a liquid diet."

Felicia and Tiffany stayed a discreet distance away while the ladies lunched. They occasionally replenished a platter or cleaned up a spill, which gave them an opportunity to overhear some of the positive comments made by the ladies. Diana strolled by and gave them a thumbs-up.

At least she's happy, Felicia thought. God this has been a long day—even my bones are hurting. The image of her garden tub filled with hot water and bath beads looked pretty good.

Two hours later the tables were bare. "Let's start with the cleanup," Felicia instructed as soon as the last person walked away cradling a brownie covered in ice cream. She glanced at her watch. "Whew, it's late."

"I know the time sure flew by. It's a good thing you got that grant out of the way first."

Felicia froze. *Shit! The grant.* The last thing she remembered was placing it on her coffee table. Tiffany saw Felicia's face crumple like a soufflé.

"Oh shit! You didn't mail it, did you?" Tiffany asked, although the look on Felicia's face gave her the answer. "Aisha's gonna have a heart attack. Oh shit! Oh shit! Oh shit!"

"Yeah, oh shit!"

"We're going to go out of business."

"Shut up! And let me think!" Felicia snapped. She looked frantically around the room. *What do I do? What the hell do I do?* Her eyes stopped on her carry-all bag and a huge grin spread over her face. She sauntered over to her purse, pulled out the grant and triumphantly held it over her head. Tiffany shouted excitedly. Felicia shook her head with relief and amazement. "I can't believe I had forgotten. I stuck it in my bag last night, right before I went to Wal-Mart."

"Yahoo! Girl, you scared me. I just knew we were out of a job. Thank you, Jesus," Tiffany said. She glanced at her watch; it was almost three o'clock and the post office closed in another two hours. "I can finish up here if you want to go to the post office," Tiffany offered and picked up two pitchers of water. She needed to dump it out in the restroom across the hall. The cleanup was nearly complete.

Felicia smiled gratefully at Tiffany. "Thanks so much, girl. I'll go mail this grant, which shouldn't take long, and by the time I'll get back all we have to do is load everything up in my car."

"Sounds like a plan," Tiffany called over her shoulder as she practically ran across the room. She was almost at the exit.

"Be careful!" Felicia yelled at Tiffany's back. "Don't be spilling any water on this carpet." She leaned over to pick up her carry-all, slung it over her shoulder and headed toward the door. She was right behind her friend when Tiffany decided to turn around.

"I'm not going to—" She turned and smacked into Felicia. Water sloshed over the pitcher, drenching the grant. Tiffany's and Felicia's eyes widened with horror.

"Oh no!" Felicia wailed. The grant had soaked up the water faster than a sponge.

"I'm so sorry," Tiffany cried. "I didn't know you were behind me. I didn't know."

"Hush! And let me think," Felicia said. She glanced down at the waterlogged papers. "We can make this right. I know we can," she said, and began pacing while Tiffany set down the half empty pitchers and sat down on the floor.

Felicia walked to the window and leaned against it. She looked up at the sky. "God, please help me. You know I don't ask for help very often, and when I do it's a biggie. But please clear my head so that I can think of a way to make this right. Please," she begged.

It was then that "Let's Go Crazy" reverberated through the room. Her and Tiffany's eyes met. "It's Aisha."

"I know," Felicia mouthed, her eyes wide with fear.

"Aren't you going to answer it?"

Chapter 25

It was Thursday evening, and Felicia still hadn't told Aisha about the grant. She wanted to tell her sister what happened when she called. But she didn't. She wanted to tell Aisha as soon as she picked her up from the airport. But she didn't. And she also wanted to tell her during dinner. But she didn't. It wasn't until they were home and Aisha was relaxed that Felicia had worked up enough nerve. Felicia sliced up a loaf of banana bread and placed it on the serving dish with a dollop of honey butter on the side. Taking a deep breath, she picked it up and stood on the threshold of the living room and studied her sister. Aisha sat on her couch, with her feet tucked underneath her and a glass of wine in her hand. She looks calm, Felicia decided. It's now or never.

"Here you go!" Felicia eased into the living room and placed the bread on the coffee table.

"Thanks," Aisha said before picking up a piece of bread and slathering it with butter. "Mmm, this is delicious. You make even the simplest dish mouthwatering," Aisha said as she reclined on the couch. "It's so good to be back home. And I know what else would be good."

"What?"

"If you would oil my scalp. I didn't get a chance to do it while I was gone."

"Sure."

Felicia went into her sister's bedroom for some moisturizer and a comb. By the time she got back to the living room, Aisha was already sitting on the floor. Felicia settled on the couch behind Aisha and hugged her with her legs.

Felicia parted her sister's hair and heard her let out a low moan. "Man, that feels so good. Can you massage it when you're done?" Aisha asked.

"Hey, you gonna pay me? Some people get paid fifty dollars an hour for what I'm doing for you."

"Tab it," Aisha ordered.

Felicia laughed. "So is this the same tab you've been running since you were six years old?" Aisha nodded. "Dang, you owe me enough money to buy a mansion."

Aisha smiled. "How's Tarik?"

"He's fine. I'll see him later this week."

"Have you told him yet?"

Felicia blushed. "I will when I see him. I'm so scared."

"Girl, don't be. Tarik's a good guy. He won't do anything to hurt you."

"I hope so. I just like him so much. I want this to work."

"It looks like you might get your prince after all," Aisha teased.

"You'll get yours too," Felicia said knowingly.

"Whatever."

They were silent for a couple minutes while Felicia sectioned and oiled Aisha's hair. "I was just thinking, are grants really important?" Felicia asked nonchalantly.

"They're very important! They're free money. So of course they're important."

"Oh!"

"Whassup?"

"Nothing. Just wondering," she answered. They were silent while Felicia moved the comb though her sister's hair. Aisha groaned softly. "I guess somebody would be considered stupid if they don't take advantage of it, huh?"

"Yep. It's a good thing we made it before the deadline. Like I said, I think we have a good chance of getting the money. We should be hearing something in about twelve weeks. I think we should implement your suggestion."

"Which one?"

"Conducting free seminars. I think they would be pretty lucrative in the long run. Don't you?" The comb was poised over Aisha's head. "Don't you?" she repeated.

"The application was damaged, and I couldn't mail it," Felicia blurted out.

Aisha pulled away from her sister and whirled around to face her. "It got what?"

"The grant application, got damaged."

Aisha craned her neck at her sister, then decided to get up. She paced across her living room. "How did this happen, Felicia? All you had to do was review it, stick it in the *already stamped and addressed envelope* and mail it. How did you mess it up?"

"I had taken it to a catering job and it had gotten drenched with water," she answered, omitting Tiffany's part in it.

"None of this would have happened if you hadn't gone to

that catering job. That's your problem! You're focusing too much on catering!" she snapped.

"No I'm not. I give each about the same amount. As a matter of fact, I probably give FAACS a lot more."

"Yeah, right. It's like you have a catering event every night. When you should be coming up with ideas and implementing them, you're baking cookies."

"I'm the one who came up with the seminars."

"Yes you did," Aisha reluctantly agreed. "But you dropped the ball. I haven't heard a word mentioned about it until I said something two minutes ago. If you were into FAACS like you were supposed to be, you would've already had the program developed, maybe a place to hold it. But you don't."

"You're right," Felicia sighed. "I dropped the ball. If I could've run out to Wal-Mart, then come home to prepare the food, I could've mailed the application and not brought it to the catering site. I messed up."

"Felicia. Yeah, you messed up. You messed it up for me and Tiffany. Because of you we might lose the company."

Felicia's eyes widened. "Because of me? Because of me? We wouldn't be standing here right now if you were able to keep your panties on. But no. You go around tasting dicks the same way people sample chocolate. We're here because of you!"

"What did you say?"

"Yeah, I said it," Felicia said, then jutted her chin at her sister. "You caused all this. Just because you couldn't keep your legs closed. You got poor Tiffany all worried about her job. She was panicked. You saw her face—I thought the poor girl was going to faint with fear."

"I was waiting for that," Aisha hissed.

"What?"

"The Lance thing. For you to blame everything on me. Yes, I take partial responsibility for our losses. But five months from now, when FAACS closes its doors, it's going to be your fault."

"I don't care," Felicia said.

This time it was Aisha's eyes that widened. "You don't care?"

"I do care, I care about what happens to you, but I couldn't care less about FAACS," Felicia admitted.

"You don't care about the business?"

"I *cared* about the business. But I don't love it the way you do. You nurtured it, you grew it into a reputable company. I don't have that passion for it."

"So what are you telling me?"

"I want to cater full-time. That's my passion. I love to cook, I love the smell of food, I love to create. I don't feel that way about FAACS," she said sadly.

"So all this time you were unhappy?" Aisha asked, staring at her sister as though seeing her for the first time. "I never knew, I never knew," she repeated softly.

"Aisha, I'm sorry."

"All you had to do was tell me."

"I didn't want you to think that I was abandoning you."

"Instead of abandoning me, you chose to destroy FAACS in some passive-aggressive ploy."

"No, Aisha." The realization of what her sister said hit her with a force. "This isn't the way it was supposed to happen."

"Get out!" Aisha said quietly.

"Aisha," Felicia pleaded. "Let's talk." She ran over to the computer. "I bet if we reprint the application we can send it in. Don't you know someone there who could pull some strings?"

"It's over Felicia. It's over," she roared. "Because of you, we're going to lose FAACS. I just want you to leave."

"Maybe I don't want to leave," Felicia said, then crossed her arms over her chest.

"If you don't get your ass out of my apartment, I'm going to throw you out," Aisha responded in a deadly manner.

Felicia looked at her sister. She had never in her life seen her so mad. Her hands were clenched into fists, her eyes narrowed, and she was poised on the balls of her feet like a tiger ready to pounce at the least provocation. " 'Isha, I'm sorry."

"Save your sorries for someone who'd believe them. Just go, Felicia," she said quietly. "Just go."

Felicia trudged to the door, opened it, then glanced back at her sister. "I'm sorry. I'm really sorry." Felicia walked through the door. As soon as it closed, she heard a loud wail. Moments after that Felicia mirrored that sound.

Chapter 26

"Whew! That was tiring," Felicia said as she and Tarik stepped into his new apartment. Both were loaded down with bags from IKEA, T.J. Maxx and Bed Bath & Beyond. They had done enough shopping to last five lifetimes. Hopefully it'll add some life to this place, she thought as she surveyed his apartment. Nestled in a corner of Atlanta's affluent community of Buckhead, it looked about as lived-in as a recent divorcé's bedroom. He had the staples—a fifty-two-inch TV, a black leather sofa with a matching ottoman and an end table to rest his beer on. After he had broken his engagement with Tara, it had taken him less than two weeks to locate an apartment and move.

"That was. I never realized that shopping could be an Olympic sport."

"Well, I would definitely get a gold medal in wrestling. Because those ladies sure made a sistah fight for some of this stuff," Felicia joked. "Did you see how that lady almost killed me for these throw pillows? I almost had to beat her down."

"You should've let her have them. What am I supposed to do with throw pillows? I'm a guy, for Pete's sake. No red-blooded man cares about this froufrou stuff."

"No red-blooded man would use the word *froufrou* in a sentence correctly," Felicia teased. "Besides, it'll make the place look nice and it'll add that special touch."

"I guess it's a woman thing because Aisha would say the same thing."

Tarik, who was punching the pillows, looked up just in time to see Felicia's face cave in like a Cabbage Patch doll.

"Aw shit! I'm sorry. Are you okay?" Tarik asked.

"I'm cool," she said nonchalantly, then: "Not really. I miss her so much. It's like a piece of me has been cut away," she answered, her eyes tearing up. "We haven't talked in almost a week."

"How do y'all work together?"

"We haven't. We've been corresponding via e-mail or she's been having Tiffany call me. Well you know how stubborn she is. I showed up at work as usual with all her favorite foods . . . I spent the whole night cooking it. Believe me when I say that my sister barely looked at it. She barely looked *me* in the eye. I had to leave, I couldn't take it anymore," Felicia admitted with a teary voice.

"Damn, don't you think she's overreacting?" Tarik asked as went into the kitchen for some tissues. Experience had shown him that it would be a good idea to have some close by.

Felicia shook her head. "Yes and no. I should've known better. Aisha loves FAACS like a baby. But she did have a part in its demise. I mean, you just can't sleep with someone and walk away. I know that . . . but that's how Aisha is. Sex to her is like a meal, for sustenance only. There weren't any feelings involved. So she thought she could make her rules and Lance was supposed to follow them. And if that didn't work, cut it loose. But I should've known better. I should've mailed that grant information out. There's no excuse for that. I have to be responsible for my part in the situation."

"Just remember that it wasn't all your fault," Tarik stressed.

All Felicia said was, "I should've known better."

"Well what are you going to do?" Tarik asked.

"I don't know," Felicia sighed. "Let's start doing some decorating," she said, trying to lighten the mood.

Two hours later the windows were topped with valances, the bed was covered with a leopard skin bedspread and pillows, the bathroom sported black and white accessories, and the kitchen cupboards were filled with plates, cups and saucers.

"This is beginning to look like home," Felicia said to Tarik's back. He stood on top of a ladder with a hammer in one hand and a picture in the other. Her eyes roamed up his backside. *Maybe I should tell him how I feel.* "Tarik?"

"Yeah," he asked around two nails sticking out his mouth.

"I want to talk to you about something."

"Whassup?"

"Well, I can't talk to you while you're hammering," Felicia protested.

"Hold on. I have one left." Felicia nervously waited while Tarik finished banging in the nail and hung up the picture. Once satisfied that it was secured and straight, he plopped down on the ladder. Four feet above her.

Felicia craned her neck up at him. "Come on down here. I feel like I'm talking to the Jolly Black Giant."

"Well you know what they say about black men, we're all *big*," Tarik joked as he hopped off the stepladder and plopped down on the floor. Felicia sat next to him. "What's on your mind?"

Felicia looked into Tarik's eyes and suddenly she felt like she had a mouthful of stale bread. "Are you hungry? Or thirsty?"

"Naw, I'm straight."

"Your place is beginning to get that homey feeling," she said.

"It's getting there. Is that what you wanted to talk about?"

Felicia shook her head. Her tongue suddenly felt as heavy as a rock. "I really like hanging out with you."

"Me too. You're good people."

"Thanks," Felicia replied, chuckling nervously, then: "I just wanted you to know that I like you."

"I like you too. You're cool."

Felicia grabbed Tarik's hands. Surprised, he pulled away. Felicia's lips fractioned up into a small smile. "I'm not going to hurt you." She grabbed his hands again and held them firmly. "I really like you," she said, then more slowly: "Not like a sister but like a girlfriend. I want for us to be more than friends."

"What did you say?" Tarik asked, his hands slipping from Felicia's.

"I don't know where these feelings came from. I mean, when we shared our bubble gum back in kindergarten I never thought we'd end up here." Tarik simply stared at her as though she had a leg growing out her neck. "Are you okay?"

"I'm just shocked. You sure know how to throw a brother a curveball," he said giving a shaky laugh.

"So how do you feel about me?" Felicia asked eagerly, relieved that her feelings were out in the open.

"Huh?"

"How do you feel about me?"

Just as Tarik opened his mouth to answer, his cell phone rang and he hurried into the living room for it. She was on his heels, then perched on the arm of the couch and carefully scrutinized his face while he talked. After several umms and mmms, then "What hospital are you in?" she knew it wasn't good news. He was halfway to the door even before he clicked the phone off.

"Who was that?" Felicia asked.

"Tara. She's just been admitted into the hospital and she wants me there."

"And you're going?" Felicia asked, incredulous.

"Yeah, she needs my help."

"She needs you? You're running to the lady who cheated on you more times than Elizabeth Taylor was married. Doesn't she have a family member or a good friend?"

Tarik shrugged. "I'm sure they're on their way . . . in the meantime, she wants me there with her. Besides, she's still my friend."

"She's playing you again."

"How is she playing me? The girl is in the hospital. She can't be faking that."

"She might not be faking, but she could've called someone else." A thought suddenly came to Felicia. "You're not over her, are you?"

"I am. Maybe. Look, she and I share a history."

"*You and I* have history."

"Yeah, but I was going to marry her. Not you." Felicia

opened her mouth but nothing came out. "I'm sorry. I didn't mean to say that," Tarik said.

"You're telling the truth. I'm just someone who taught you how to get out of going to sewing class. I showed you the difference between a lady and a ho. I was the one whose shoulder you cried on when Bridgette McDaniels broke your heart in the twelfth grade. And I was the one who helped you arrange your mother's funeral. You're right, the history you share with Tara is so much deeper," she said contemptuously. "I guess she was by your side during all this and more."

"No, things are different when—"

"When what?"

"When you're having sex with that person."

"Oh."

"Let's talk about this later. I need to get to the hospital."

"Sure, I'll call you."

"Lock up when you leave," Tarik instructed, and was out the door before Felicia could respond.

Things are different when you're having sex with that person, rang in Felicia's ears. "So, Tarik, how am I gonna get us in the sack?" she wondered.

Chapter 27

"I'm glad you're here," Felicia said.

"I'm glad that you called me," Mia answered as she kissed Felicia's shoulder. "I missed you."

"Yeah, same here. I don't want you to think . . ."

"I don't," Mia reassured her.

"You don't know what I was about to say."

"I knew it was going to be something self-deprecating."

"Was not," Felicia protested.

"Well what?"

"I didn't want you to think that I was using you. I'm sorry."

Mia quirked an eyebrow at her. "What makes you think *I'm* not using *you?*" she joked.

"You're not," she answered, thinking back to Mia's declaration of love.

"You know me so well."

"Not really. I never suspected," she said softly.

Mia laughed. "Can you not stand the irony of our situation? After years of being your friend and lover I fall in love with you—"

"And I fall in love with Tarik. How weird. You never know when love decides to look your way," Felicia said. "So what's going to happen to us?"

"What do you want to happen to us?"

Felicia smiled at her friend. "I want for us to remain friends."

Mia winked. "Is that all?"

Felicia noticed the longing that flashed in Mia's eyes. She gulped. "I like being with you, but I can't offer you anything else," she said, and suddenly her eyes widened.

"What?"

"I'm a female Tarik. He said almost the same thing to me when I told him about my feelings. Oh crap."

"It's okay," Mia said as she began rubbing her friend's shoulders. Felicia shrugged her off.

"No it's not. I don't want to lead you on and I'm not into mind games."

Mia leaned down and gently kissed Felicia's shoulder. "You're not leading me on."

"You're sure." Felicia shivered with desire.

"I'm positive. I'm a big girl. Maybe you should get undressed."

Felicia vigorously shook her head. "Aisha might come in."

"No she won't," Mia answered while pulling her top over her head. "I thought she was pissed at you."

"Yeah, but the sky might turn purple and she'll come over with an apology," Felicia said, and her mouth went dry when she saw Mia's breasts.

"I doubt it." Mia kicked off her jeans. "And even if she does we'll hear her when she opens the front door."

"You think," Felicia said as she began unbuttoning her blouse.

"I *know*. Why are you worried now? You never cared about us getting caught."

"I guess that I'm not ready to tell her about us and have to explain our relationship."

Mia pulled down Felicia's skirt and tugged her friend to her. "What is our relationship?" Mia asked against her lover's neck while Felicia tore off her underwear.

"You know what it is," Felicia moaned. "We just talked about it."

"What?" Mia led Felicia to the couch. Felicia reclined and Mia fell on top of her.

"Just two ladies enjoying each other."

"That's what I like to hear. And I'm so enjoying you," Mia said as she kissed her way down Felicia's naked body right down to her clit.

Felicia splayed her legs and tilted her pelvis up, allowing Mia better access. "I love you enjoying me." She ground her mound against Mia's mouth. Mia shifted down and began nipping at the inside of Felicia's thighs. "Why did you stop?" she protested. "I'm so close to coming."

"You were? I didn't know," she said, feigning innocence.

"You knew," Felicia accused while she wiggled closer to Mia's mouth. Mia teased her by sliding backward.

"Kiss it," Felicia begged.

"I guess so," Mia said, then kissed her way back to Felicia's clit.

"Oh, girl. That feels so good," she sputtered. "Don't stop." Mia kept her tongue on Felicia's clit while she slipped a finger in Felicia's hole. She slowly finger-fucked her and Felicia let out a pleasure-filled scream.

Aisha burst through the front door. "Hey, Felicia, I just want to tell you that I'm sor—" At the sight of seeing Mia between her sister's legs, Aisha froze in place.

Chapter 28

"Are you gonna tap it?"

Tarik eyed his friend. He had just told him Felicia's confession. "This is crazy coming from a man who knocked up a stalking-needs-to-be-committed-crazy-lady. You should know better. The dick should stay anonymous until you have a chance to do a psychiatric evaluation—that should be a rule in the game."

"Two totally different things, man . . . totally different."

"True, dat! But Felicia is my girl. Even kissing her would seem indecent, almost incestuous. I can't even think about jumping into that territory."

"You'll forget all that as soon as you see her lying beside you without any clothes," Derrick chuckled.

"I can't do that to Felicia. Besides, I don't want to ruin our relationship. Well, what's left of it. She's not returning any of my calls."

"Why you sweating her?"

"'Cause we're deep. And she's my hanging partner."

"I thought I was your partner?"

"Yeah, yeah, but she and I can shop for hours. Sometimes she wears *me* out."

"What do you think we're doing now?" Derrick said as his eyes skimmed row after row of cribs. "Do you think this crib will do?" Derrick asked, looking at the mahogany bed as though it was a spaceship.

"Looks good to me," Tarik answered with glazed eyes while standing in the middle of an ocean of baby beds. So far they had looked at half a dozen different ones and they were all beginning to look the same to him. "Where's that saleslady?" he asked while peering down the aisle for the woman who as soon as they walked into the store had clung to them like a bad case of dandruff.

"That's just like them. They're all up in your face as soon as you step into the store, but when you take your time and browse they're ghosts."

Tarik shook himself out of his daze. "Maybe you should go to the customer service desk. I bet you can find someone there."

"Bet. See you in a few," Derrick promised before trotting off.

Derrick returned two minutes later with a clerk, and thirty minutes later he had the baby's bedroom suite picked out.

"You did a good job," Darla said as she walked around the furniture. Derrick had moved his computer and desk into his bedroom. He had one of his friends transform the office into a baby wonderland. Giraffes, lions, elephants and hippos decorated the caramel-hued room. Miniature throw pillows, comforters and a dust ruffle decorated the crib. Rust, gold and off-white striped wallpaper cocooned the room in warmth. "This is kind of boyish. What happens if it's girl?" Darla asked. She gave her stomach a rub.

"It won't be."

"It could be. There's a fifty-fifty chance it could be a girl."

"I don't make girls," Derrick answered cockily.

"We'll see," Darla answered. "I'm really glad that you're sticking to the contract."

Derrick snorted. "I'm not doing this because of your so-called contract, I'm doing this because I take care of mine."

"So do you want to take care of me? I used to belong to you," Darla whispered. Ever since she had waddled into Derrick's apartment she couldn't take her eyes off him. Memories of the years they spent together flooded her.

"Excuse me?" Derrick asked, although he clearly had heard Darla and didn't mistake her intent. Blood rushed to the tip of his penis. He liked the pregnant Darla. The six-month bulge in her stomach made her look like she swallowed a small watermelon. The soft mound made her curvier. It looked like her breasts had already increased a cup size. Boy, I would love to touch those cantaloupes, he thought, almost drooling.

Darla sidled up to him and gently stroked his arm. "I've missed you. I'm pregnant and I'm horny. I haven't been with anyone since you. And I really need some sex."

Derrick couldn't take his eyes off Darla. "What do you need?" Derrick asked, gazing at her hypnotized.

"You." She reached down between his legs and smiled to herself when she felt his hardness.

Derrick instinctively did what any man in his shoes would, he closed his eyes and pressed against her hand. A small groan slid between his lips and Darla's smile grew.

"Just like old times, huh?"

"Yeah, you got skills. You should be giving lessons."

"I can think of something else I should be giving lessons in." Suddenly Derrick felt her hands slip inside his pants and pass the elastic waistband of his underwear. Reason sliced through the haze of his desire; he snapped his eyes open, then swatted her hands away as though they were mosquitoes.

"Whoa! Hold up. We're not going down this road again."

"Close your eyes and enjoy. I'll make you feel *real* good."

"No, Darla!" he barked, and she stepped back as though he had slapped her.

"You used to like it."

"That's right, I *used* to. This isn't going to work between us. Let's just focus on being good parents to the baby. It's all about him now, not us."

"Why do you have to be so difficult? All I want is for us to enjoy each other like we did in the past. No strings attached," she whispered seductively, studying him. He couldn't meet her eyes. "Aha! You've met somebody! You've met another woman and you're screwing her! You're screwing another woman!" she ranted.

"Oh shit!" he mumbled. The last thing he needed was an over emotional pregnant lady. "Darla, listen, I'm not seeing anyone."

Darla snorted. "I know you. You enjoy sex just as much as Japanese like sushi. So I'm not believing you . . . not for one second."

"It doesn't matter if I'm seeing anyone or not," Derrick replied, exasperated. "We're done. That part of our relationship is over."

"I can't wait to see who you're screwing. I'll be the first to tell her exactly what you are."

Derrick frowned. "What am I, Darla?"

"You're a user, you're a fucking—"

"I think you need to go," Derrick said. He had had enough of her. He moved closer to her. Darla took the opportunity to wrap her arm around his waist. Gritting his teeth, he ignored the grip on his waist and edged her toward the front door. As soon as they reached it, Derrick pulled it open.

"You know," she began, her voice sly.

"What?"

"I just decided that I'm moving back to Chicago."

Derrick slammed the door shut. "You're what?"

"I want the baby to be raised near its relatives. I don't know anybody down here."

"You're not taking my child back to Chicago!"

"I just think it would be a good idea. The baby will be close to my parents. They're excited about being grandparents and they want to do all the grandparenting stuff."

"They can always visit Atlanta," Derrick said, his voice low.

"But they won't like it here."

"They haven't even visited."

"I know that they won't. There isn't anything for them to do."

"You already told me that they would love it here and that your brother could go to Morehouse."

"Well, I thought about it and decided that I was wrong. See, I made a mistake. See how easy it is for me to admit it?"

"Darla, you'd better not take my baby away."

Darla sneered at him. "Oh, your baby can stay here."

Derrick's heart resumed beating its normal way. "Now you're talking sense."

"Am I? Ask me how I'll let him stay. Ask me, Derrick. Aren't you curious?" she taunted. "Aren't you gonna ask me?"

Chapter 29

Aisha stepped into her aunt Hattie's house and faltered. No matter how many times she told herself it wasn't going to happen, it did, and no matter how many times she braced herself for the shock, it didn't work. It came at her like a sledgehammer, leaving her breathless. Looking at her aunt Hattie was like looking at her mother. It'd been six years since her mother's death, and although the pain had numbed to a dull throbbing, it flared like someone poking an open wound whenever she saw her aunt Hattie, her mom's identical twin.

They both had long thick hair, the color of black licorice, thick legs that black men loved, faces that could easily grace the cover of any magazine and personalities that made Jamie Foxx look shy. Whenever they went out together people flocked to them as though they were celebrities.

That's where the similarities ended. Where her mother had walked, her aunt zoomed through life in a state-of-the-art wheelchair threatening to flatten anyone who crossed her path. Ten years ago while walking home from the park, she had been hit by a drunk driver, crushing her pelvis and making her legs into bone soup. Where most people would wither away after being sentenced to a life of being eye level to stomachs, she lassoed life like a renegade cowboy and held on tightly.

Aisha leaned down and hugged her aunt. She stifled a gasp of surprise at the strength in the arms that wrapped around her shoulders.

"I've missed you so much."

"Well if you would stop by more than once a year, you wouldn't have that problem," Aunt Hattie replied good-heartedly.

Aisha pushed down the complaint. She tried to see her aunt twice a month and she knew Aunt Hattie wished it was more. "I love you," Aisha said simply.

"I love you too," her aunt responded. Her auntie pressed a lever forward and before Aisha could blink she was halfway across the room. "I'll be right back. I need to check on something in the kitchen," she called over her shoulder.

"You need my help?"

Hattie slowed to a stop, then turned around, but not before letting out a laugh that had Aisha's ears ringing. "Honey, I need your help like a hooker needs a cop. Sit down and read a magazine." She chuckled to herself before whooshing into the kitchen. "Like she even knows what goes on in the kitchen," Aisha heard Hattie mutter.

"Whatever," Aisha mumbled.

Her aunt's southwest Atlanta home was purchased before the area had turned into a place where black folks earning six figures moved. Her modest three-bedroom home sat a mere stone's throw away from million-dollar homes, where cars that cost more than what she paid for her house dotted their driveways.

Aisha made herself comfortable on Hattie's couch. She glanced around the room, it hadn't changed a bit from when she was a little girl.

"Auntie could fix this place up a little. I feel like I've been flung back to the eighties," Aisha grumbled while taking in the old mirrored tiles glued to the wall that were shaped into an inverted box, reflecting the gold crushed-velour love seat, chair and matching couch. A shag rug the color of muddy water spread throughout the house like a bad virus. She ran her hand over the threadbare furniture. The only peek into the twenty-first century was the flat-screen TV that hung on the wall across from the couch.

"I bet I could hook this place up for her. Hey, Auntie!"

"Yeah, baby," she said while zooming into the living room.

"You really need to come into the twenty-first century."

"I'm already here."

"Your house isn't," Aisha quipped.

"It works for me," she answered, looking around.

"But don't you want to come home to a spa-like room? Picture a room filled with lush plants, comfy furniture, hard-wood floors and bright paint."

"That does sound nice."

"I can do it for you. I like decorating."

"How much are you gonna charge me?"

Aisha quieted. She hadn't thought about getting paid.

"I don't know." She shrugged.

"You don't know. You're a businesswoman."

"But I've never done this before. I can do it for free."

"For free? For free?" Hattie asked incredulously. "Girl, don't be giving nothing away for free. People don't appreciate anything unless they have to pay for it. Besides, that drunk driver may have left me without legs, but he also left me with a seven-figure gift."

Aisha blinked. "Seven figures? You're a millionaire and never told anyone?"

Hattie nodded. "I am, and why should I announce my financial status to the world? And especially to my family. They'd be all over me like ants on a picnic. They'll be sniffing after my money so hard that they'll probably end up needing a nose job."

"Our family isn't like that. At least I'm not. Come on, Auntie. I *want* to do it for free. After everything you've done for my sister and me, it would be mean of me to charge you. Let me do it for you," Aisha insisted softly.

"I don't take any handouts," she grumbled.

"Auntie!"

"Okay, okay," she relented. "I'll be right back." After rocketing off for a second time, a few moments later her aunt called her. "Come on into the dining room, baby."

Aisha walked into the next room and gaped at the table. No matter how many times she'd seen one of her aunt's spreads she was always pleased. Even though it was just the two of them, her table was filled with more food than a Piccadilly buffet. And she needed it. Ever since she and Felicia stopped talking she hadn't had a home-cooked meal. She was fiending for something that didn't come in a Styrofoam container. Smothered pork chops, twice-baked potatoes with melted cheese, bacon and chives, with a bowl of sour cream on the side, string beans swimming in fatback grease, strawberry shortcake for dessert and a half dozen covered dishes that Aisha couldn't wait to see what they held.

Aisha inhaled deeply. "Ooh, I'm in heaven," she said, moaning.

"Go on," Hattie encouraged her. "Help yourself. I cooked this all for you. And whatever you don't take home, I'll pack it up and send it over to the church."

"Thank you, Auntie. Thank you, thank you," Aisha sang as she rounded the table faster than a speed skater in the winter Olympics, filling her dish with food until it almost spilled over the edges. Aisha placed her plate on the table. "Would you like me to fix your plate?"

"Naw, I got it. Thanks." She was right. It took her less than three minutes to wheel around the table to fill her plate before settling at the head of the table. She quickly blessed the meal.

"What's this I hear about you and your sister fighting?" Aunt Hattie asked after swallowing a forkful of string beans.

Who told you? was on the tip of Aisha's tongue. But knowing her family, it could have come from anybody. "You know we separated because we thought our lives were getting too entangled. Now that we're no longer talking our lives are like dead vines."

"How poetic," Hattie drawled. "I'm sad for you. But what really happened?" she deadpanned.

"We both messed up. Plain and simple," Aisha said sadly.

"So what's wrong? There's equal culpability in this situation." Aisha's eyebrows shot up to her hair. "What? I know more than two-syllable words."

"I know," Aisha chuckled, a little ashamed of her reaction. "But I didn't see it at the time. I was so mad that I couldn't see straight. Now that I had some time to think about it, everything made sense."

"Tell her."

"I tried to," she protested, almost telling her aunt about seeing Mia cleaning Felicia's clit.

"Well, try again."

"I can't."

"Can't? Or you won't?"

"I can't," Aisha insisted while fiddling with her fork.

"Why not?"

"I said the meanest things to her. I wouldn't accept my own apology."

"You know your sister isn't like that. She has one of the biggest hearts. And I bet hers is hurting just as much as yours. Don't be too prideful. You know that's one of the seven deadly sins."

"Yes ma'am."

"You can't go around thinking that you're everybody's world."

"But I was her world and she was mine. That's not pride, that's just how it is! I can't deny that."

Hattie sighed. Then: "You know, your mother and I had a big fight once."

"No, y'all didn't," Aisha protested, thinking of the special bond she had witnessed between the two sisters while growing up. They were closer than the Jackson clan after a Michael Jackson trial. They had always finished each other's sentences and they always knew what the other wanted even without them requesting it. The psychic link between them was amazing.

"We did," Hattie continued. "We had a hair-pulling-fist-throwing-face-scratching fight."

Aisha's stomach clenched. "What happened?" she asked, horrified. "I bet it was over some man. I know it had to be something really important for y'all to fight like that."

Hattie chuckled at the memory, then: "A doll," she admitted.

"Y'all almost killed each other over a doll? A doll?"

"Yep. We were five. For Christmas Daddy had given Mattie a doll and me a chalkboard with chalk. He didn't know any better. If he had taken Momma shopping with him he would've known to get us both the same thing. But I think he was trying to force us to be different."

"I guess it didn't work, huh?"

"Oh no. I wanted that doll. Your mother spent the day dressing it and combing its hair. When she went to the bathroom, she set it down and I grabbed it. All I wanted to do was play with it, I really did," she added as though still trying to convince her sister of her true intent. "When she found out what happened to her doll she ran across the room and pushed me so hard that I fell, then she jumped on top of me, bit me and pulled my hair out. I swear there's still a chunk missing," she said, patting her head. "Momma and Daddy had to pull her off me."

"Wow! So how long did you two stay mad at each other?"

Hattie laughed. "Not long. Until supper. I apologized for destroying her doll."

"And you guys didn't have an argument after that?"

"Of course we snipped at each other once in a while, but everything rolled off our backs. We wouldn't fight if we didn't love each other. But nothing like you and your sister. If your mother was alive . . ."

"I know."

Hattie cupped her hands around her niece's face, forcing eye contact. Aisha shivered. It was almost as though she was looking in her mother's eyes. "You're a smart young lady. Felicia told me what happened. And she's hurting. People make mistakes. I'm not saying who's wrong because in your heart you know the truth." Aisha began crying and her aunt Hattie thumbed her tears away. "Now you can be one of those people who walk around with their pride, never wanting to make the first step. Or you can be an adult and loving sister and talk to Felicia. Tell me, which one are you going to be?" Hattie asked. Aisha's tears flowed down her face and over her aunt's hands. "Which one, girl? Which one?"

Aunt Hattie's question reverberated through Aisha's head while she drove home. "I'm really going to have to decide what I want to do." After making a couple of stops, she headed home. Inside the house, she paused at Felicia's door and lifted her hand to knock. Just then Derrick barreled through the front door and her hand fell to her side. She glared at him.

"Hey!" he said, smiling.

Aisha rolled her eyes. She hadn't seen him since they had made love. "What do you want?" she snapped as she turned on her heel, unlocked her front door and stepped inside her apartment. *I'll talk to Felicia later.*

Derrick winced. He knew she was pissed . . . but this. "I wanted to talk to you . . . you know . . . about what happened. May we talk in your apartment?"

"Nope."

"Well, I don't like announcing my business to the whole neighborhood."

"It's not the whole neighborhood. So what do you have to tell me?"

"The whole baby situation isn't what you think."

"The baby situation," Aisha softly repeated. "You're not

talking about a traffic jam, you're talking about a baby. A baby is *never* a situation."

What-the-fuck-ever was on the tip of Derrick's tongue. "You're right," he said instead. "Why don't we go out to dinner and talk about it?" he asked with a smile.

Aisha looked him in his eyes and her nipples hardened. She immediately crossed her arms over her chest before refocusing her gaze on a spot above his head. *Remember, don't look directly at him.* "No."

"Come on," he cajoled. "We can take a drive right around the corner to that new Japanese restaurant. Their sushi is so fresh it'll bite you," he joked.

"Listen to me, Derrick," Aisha hissed. "Until you man up to your responsibilities I don't want anything to do with you. Men like you make me sick, going around making babies without giving a second thought about being a father to them," and before Derrick could defend himself, she slammed the door in his face.

Chapter 30

Felicia glanced around her kitchen. "Now this looks like a caterer's kitchen." Mixing bowls, oversize spoons and pans of different shapes were scattered throughout her kitchen. A variety of spices dusted the counter. And aromas wafted through the air, tickling her nose.

Felicia happily diced a tomato, then an onion. "This is so perfect." Since focusing on catering full time, she had more jobs than she could handle. "The salsa is looking good," she said. With flawless precision she diced some garlic and chiles. "I just wish Aisha was here," she mumbled sadly. Her sister didn't even answer her knocks. Felicia had been forced to slide her letter of apology and resignation under the door. "I'm a big girl, I can deal with it," she said with determination before turning back to her work order.

"I love this salsa," Tarik said before sticking a tortilla chip in the dip and scooping up a mountain load.

"I see," Felicia answered.

"This is the bomb. I'm so glad you stepped out and went full time."

"Yeah, because you know that I'll give you my leftovers."

"True, dat," Tarik said with a laugh. They were sitting in his apartment watching DVDs. They had a *Mission Impossible* marathon planned. Aisha popped into Felicia's head. She and I used to have movie night, she thought sadly.

"I miss her," Felicia mumbled, her good mood gone. Aisha had been avoiding her like she was a bill collector.

"Miss who?" Tarik asked.

"Aisha."

"Call her. Crash her crib."

"I called her a million times, but she never calls me back. And I knocked on her door so much that I swear my knuckles started bleeding."

"Naw! That's some serious knocking."

Felicia nodded. "A couple of weeks ago, I didn't even have to knock. But that was before I caused her to lose her business."

"It wasn't *all* your fault."

"No. But I was the one who—excuse my French—shitted on her parade," she said with a wince.

"Come on, forgive yourself."

"I'd feel better if I could talk to my sister," Felicia said tearfully. "I'm sorry," she said, swiping a hand across her face. "We were having a good time and I'm not about to ruin it." She forced a laugh that sounded like a cross between a bark and a cough. "I'll be right back," she said before trotting off to the bathroom. "You'd better get it together, girl," she ordered her reflection. "You have a plan tonight, so stick with it.

You can deal with Aisha later." She tossed some cold water on her face, then dabbed it dry before walking back into the living room, wearing a huge smile that took up half her face.

"Feeling better?" Tarik asked, and Felicia nodded. "Anyway, this is the last time I spend my money on this cheap beer," he said with a grimace as he slammed down the bottle.

"You shouldn't be so cheap," Felicia said. "You knew that stuff was going to taste like camel pee. What did you expect with a name like Homeymeister? I bet it does taste horrible."

"Would you like to try it?" Tarik asked with a gleam in his eye. He picked up the bottle and inched toward Felicia.

She gave a wail and backed up to the arm of the couch. "Don't you dare!" she said while eyeing the bottle, then Tarik, who grinned at her.

"So do you want to wear it or drink it?"

"Tarik!" Screaming, Felicia rolled off the couch with Tarik right behind her. They gazed in each other's eyes. "Is this awkward or what?" Felicia whispered.

Tarik looked up at her, his eyes slowly stroking her face. "A little." He gulped deeply. "But not at all unwelcome."

"I'm glad." Felicia smiled as her heart jumped at his words of encouragement. "Normally people in this position kiss," Felicia said.

"Oh really?" Tarik whispered.

"Yeah."

"Well, I don't want to be an oddball," Tarik said. Cupping the back of Felicia's head, he pulled her face closer to his. He gently grazed his lips over hers and his body shuddered as though struck by lightning. Felicia pressed her mouth against his. "You taste so good."

This is what I've been waiting for so long, Felicia sang to

herself as Tarik's tongue slowly entered her mouth, and she sighed softly. Her arms slipped around his neck and her hips moved against him in a primitive way she didn't know they could. Tarik's hands roamed down her back before encircling her rear end.

Tarik pulled off her clothes. "Stay right there!" he instructed.

"I'm gonna have crazy rug burns on my ass," Felicia mumbled to herself, but a smile wide enough to light Atlanta crossed her face. "Finally!"

Tarik skidded into the living room with a condom in his hand. In less than a minute he was by her side, wrapped and ready to go. Spreading her legs, he positioned himself between her legs, and acting as if his penis was searching for gold, began poking at her.

"What are you doing?" Felicia yelped, while backing away from him.

"Trying to have sex with you."

"Um, haven't you heard of a thing called foreplay?"

Tarik grinned sheepishly. "Sorry. You got me so excited. I'm not thinking right."

"Yeah, I want to get excited too."

"Let's try to rectify the situation. Turn over on your stomach," Tarik said softly, and Felicia opened her mouth to protest, but Tarik cut her off. "Just do it," he commanded softly. Suddenly she felt a warm breeze on the nape of her neck, and she shivered.

Tarik smiled to himself, so she liked that. He tenderly rained kisses on her shoulders, down her back, over the slope of her behind and the backs of her thighs. Felicia moaned.

"Is that a frustrated moan or a happy moan?" Tarik whispered.

"Happy. Definitely happy."

"You wanted foreplay . . ."

"You're doing a good job."

In response, Tarik tenderly nipped at the backs of her thighs and calves before retracing his trail to the small of her back, where he lightly sucked at her skin. Felicia gasped with surprise, which quickly turned to a low groan when Tarik's hand slipped over her cheeks to stroke her mound.

"You're flowing."

"Only for you," Felicia panted while she moved her hips to keep up with his hand. "If your lovemaking is just as good as what you're doing with your hand, then I'm going to die."

"I'll try to hold back," Tarik teased while his finger slid into her moist folds and caressed her clit.

"Oh, don't stop, stay right there," Felicia begged as her hips picked up their pace. Her mouth went slack as a tingling began in her core and spread to her hips. "Oh God!" she panted as wave after wave of pleasure washed over her. She shuddered, then went limp.

"Are you ready for me?" Tarik asked with a smile.

Felicia giggled. "Of course. C'mere," she said with her legs spread open.

"I'm coming."

"Not yet, I hope," Felicia laughed. "Do me!" Tarik nodded before complying. "Ah, the perfect size," Felicia groaned as Tarik slid into her.

"What does that mean?" Tarik gasped as he moved in and out of her.

"Exactly like I said. You're the perfect size, not too big and definitely not too small."

"Not too big?" Tarik asked, frowning, then slowed his stroke.

Felicia smacked his behind. "Hey, pick up the pace."

"You called me small."

"I did not. I said that you weren't too big, there's a difference."

"That still means that I'm too small," he said, almost pouting.

"You're not. I can handle a lot. What I meant was you're not some freakishly big thing."

Tarik thought a moment, then: "Oh, okay." He resumed his movements.

"You feel so good," Felicia whimpered against Tarik's chest while gripping his behind, pulling him closer to her.

"How good do I feel, baby?"

"*Real good.* Keep that stroke, you're hitting my clit."

Suddenly Tarik felt Felicia's mound tighten around his cock. "Oh yeah, baby!" he shouted as his orgasm washed over him and Felicia lay quivering under him.

"That was good," Felicia said, and giggled as she snuggled into Tarik's bed. They had moved to the bedroom after the couch had gotten too small.

"Yeah, especially the second and third time. It just got better."

"And it wasn't weird. I thought it would be weird," Felicia admitted.

"Weird how?"

Felicia glanced over at him. "Because we've never kissed before, not even as a joke. Be honest, didn't you think it would be weird?"

"I did," Tarik confessed.

"I always thought of you as my best friend. You don't kiss your best friend."

"If you're lucky you do," Tarik replied.

Felicia nuzzled Tarik's neck. She slowly traced over his muscled bicep with her forefinger. "So do you want to go to the High Museum this weekend? They have an exhibit I want to see. There's one all about chocolate, it looks really interesting." She was met with silence. "Did you hear me?"

"I did," Tarik mumbled.

"Well?" Felicia laughed, then gently nudged him in his ribs.

"I'm not sure if I can make it. I might be traveling."

"Oh," Felicia answered. Her face scrunched with disappointment. "What about a movie tomorrow night? Will Smith's new movie is out. My treat."

"Ummm, I'll let you know. Derrick said something about going out after work for drinks."

"Well, you're not going to be drinking all night. I can meet you at the movies. What part of town are you going to be in? Probably downtown," she said, answering her own question. "I think that's where Derrick works. If that's the case, I can meet you in—"

"I'm not ready for this," Tarik announced abruptly.

"Not ready for what?"

"I'm not ready for a relationship."

Felicia stopped her movements, raised up and stared at her best friend and lover of two hours. Damn. *Our relationship didn't last as long as Jennifer Lopez's marriages.* "You're not ready for a relationship?" Felicia croaked while seeing images of her and Tarik married explode.

He shook his head. "I'm sorry, baby, but I need time. I want to date more."

"You mean you want to *fuck* more!"

"No, that's not it!" Tarik protested. "I need to figure out where I went wrong." Felicia shot him a look. "With Tara," he explained at Felicia's gaze.

"I know what happened. You were thinking with the wrong part of your body."

Tarik snorted. "That might be the case. But I want to figure that out for myself, and the best way for me to do that is to just date."

"*Just date?* Where does that leave us?"

Tarik squirmed nervously under her gaze. "We don't have to change."

"Let me get this straight. You're telling me that we're still going to sleep with each other, but you can still date other women?"

"You can date other men if you want," Tarik offered lamely.

"Forget it!" Felicia shouted. She flung back the covers.

"Shit!" Tarik mumbled under his breath. "Where are you going?" he asked louder. Felicia glared at him, then stomped out to the living room. Tarik hopped out of bed and followed her. She began scooping up her clothing. Tarik grabbed her arm. "Just stop it. Let's talk about this." He nodded to the couch. "Let's sit down."

Felicia perched on the edge as though ready to bolt at any second. Tarik settled back on the cool leather. "So what do you want to talk about?"

"Us."

Felicia rolled her eyes. "I think everything was said in the bedroom."

"You're my best friend. I don't want to lose that."

"I think we already did."

"We don't have to. And we don't have to sleep together anymore. We can go back to what we were, platonic friends."

"We can't undo what just happened. Life doesn't have a rewind and delete button."

"No, it doesn't . . ." Tarik mumbled.

"I'm not a freakin' robot. It's not like I'm programmed to forget shit."

"Just think about it," Tarik pleaded. "Will you do that for me?"

Felicia held his gaze.

Chapter 31

Aisha stared at the computer screen while sipping wine. Her eyes were dryer than a Republican's sense of humor. For the last four hours they had been glued to the screen. The only time her gaze shifted was when she refilled her wineglass.

"FAACS is so far into the red that we're bleeding. There's no way it can continue like this. I need to stop the blood. Oh Lord," she moaned as though she was actually bleeding. "Which means I'm going to have to cut people. I'm sorry, Tiffany."

At that moment her cell phone rang and "That's What Friends Are For" reverberated through the apartment. Two weeks ago she would have instinctively reached for the phone. A week ago she had actually held the phone and cradled it like a baby. Today all she did was stare at it longingly.

For the last two weeks, Aisha had stationed herself in front of her bay window to watch Felicia's comings and goings. It afforded her the only time to see her sister. As soon as Felicia had parked her car and made her way up the stairs, Aisha had backed away from the window, sliding into the shadows.

Suddenly a small smile played across Aisha's lips and her fingers began flying over the keyboard. "What about if I cut this expense, then put that extra money into this program?" The numbers barely moved. "Gosh, it's like trying to absorb a leaking dam with a Q-tip. If I keep FAACS running all it's going to do is bankrupt me. There's nothing left I can do. Let me send Felicia an e-mail, updating her." Aisha quickly shot off an e-mail to her sister and wasn't surprised when two minutes later she got a response.

She quickly pounced on it. Her eyes became shiny as she read the simple message: *I support you one hundred percent.* "Thanks, girl," she whispered. "I just hope Tiffany is that forgiving." Sighing, she grabbed her purse and keys before heading out the door.

The sun was setting by the time Aisha neared her destination. She made her way down a street lined with apartment complexes, and every other one had the names Peachtree, Plantation or River. She glanced over at her doors to ensure that they were locked.

This part of Atlanta had three rules: 1) Don't stare too hard, 2) Watch your back because somebody already is, 3) If you suspect criminal activity, it probably is, so don't stare too hard, and watch your back.

Craning her neck to peer over the steering wheel for the apartment complex made her feel like an old lady or, worse, a tourist lost in a bad neighborhood. She was about to turn around when she saw it: The Pines at the River. "This is it," she said before pulling into the complex. "Gated community my ass," Aisha snorted while cruising through the open fence.

Something told her that the gate was open more often than it was locked.

The complex was a mixture of two-story town houses and Cracker Jack–size apartment buildings. Tiffany had a one-bedroom apartment in the back of the complex. Aisha rolled up to Tiffany's building and turned off her engine, but sat glued to her seat. A beach-ball-size lump of dread bounced around in her stomach. "I am so not looking forward to this."

She rang Tiffany's doorbell, then waited a heartbeat before pressing it again. She knew Tiffany was home because she heard the TV going. Moments later Tiffany opened the door.

"Aisha, what are you doing here?"

I was in the neighborhood almost came out, and *I wanted to stop by to say hi* was a close second. But instead she spoke the truth: "I need to talk to you."

Alarm caused Tiffany's eyes to stretch as big as carnival-size lollipops. "About what?" she asked before slumping against the door.

"May I come inside?"

"Oh sure. I'm sorry." Tiffany pulled herself up and opened the door wide enough for Aisha to come through.

"Auntie 'Isha!" Tyrone yelled as soon as she stepped into the apartment.

"Hey, baby," Aisha said before leaning down and giving him a hard hug. *I'm sorry. I'm so sorry.*

Tyrone pulled out her arms. "Are you okay?" he asked solemnly.

She shuddered as though shocked. Little kids are so intuitive, she thought, awed. Aisha smiled sadly. "I'm fine."

Tiffany placed her hands on her son's shoulders and

steered him toward the bathroom. "I think it's bath time. Go run the water and I'll be in in a little bit."

"I'm old enough to take a bath without you watching me," he pouted.

"I know you are. But I just want to make sure that you put enough soap in the bathwater." Tiffany forced a smile on her face before turning back to Aisha. "Whassup?"

"I'm sorry," Aisha said.

"I knew it the moment I saw you at the door." Tiffany dropped down on her new leather couch. She had gotten it with the bonus Aisha had given her.

"I just can't afford to keep you anymore. With the loss of KBS and not getting the grant, I'm barely making enough money to support myself. And I'm thinking that the few customers that we have left might be leaving us soon."

"What am I going to do?" Tiffany asked.

"You'll be fine," Aisha assured her. She reached into her purse and pulled out an envelope and handed it to Tiffany. "Hopefully this will help some."

"Mom, I'm ready!" her son called from the bathroom.

"Hold on. I'll be right there."

"But I'm cold!" he protested.

"Sit on the edge and put your feet in."

"Okay," he sang.

"Just your feet!" Tiffany slid a nail under the flap and lifted it. Inside was a check. She glanced at Aisha before pulling it out. Almost immediately her mouth turned into a small *o*. "Thank you!" she cried as soon as she saw the amount. She raced over to Aisha and threw her arms around her. "Oh, thank you so much!"

"Hopefully it'll help you."

"How can you afford this?" Tiffany asked, shaking her head in amazement. The check was close to three months of her pay.

"We did have some reserve. And I have enough to keep me going for a while. I still have contacts in corporate America who can hook me up with a job."

"This is so nice. I wasn't expecting this," Tiffany said while wiping tears off her face.

"You're family to us, girl. I wasn't going to kick you to the curb like that."

"Thanks again," Tiffany said gratefully. "Speaking of family. Did you and Felicia make up?"

"Nope."

"I know that this business was your life, but Felicia is your sister. You need to call her," she scolded. "You know, I used to be so jealous of you two."

"Why?"

"Because you guys can say more with your eyes and gestures than most people can with words. Your bond was so tight that you didn't need words. I've never had a connection with anybody like that."

"Sure you do," Aisha said, smiling.

"Who?" Aisha nodded toward the bathroom. "That's true. That little man can give me such a look of love that'll melt my heart. But you have the same thing. What are you going to do about your sister? You can't stay mad at her forever."

Chapter 32

Felicia hugged the mixing bowl to her chest as she whipped the ingredients into a creamy froth. Most people preferred using the blender to make their frosting, but she liked using a little elbow grease. And it showed—her frosting always turned out to be the lightest and fluffiest of anybody's. The aroma from baking a chocolate-banana cake filled her kitchen. She glanced forlornly out the window. It was storming. Jagged bolts of lightning sliced through the night, rain pelted the window as though it was punishing it, and the wind whipped the tree branches until they were howling. On a night like this she and Aisha would be giving each other manicures and pedicures while stuffing their faces with anything containing more than two hundred calories.

"Oh well," Felicia muttered. "I've called her more times than a bill collector and she's never called me back." She glanced up at the flickering lights. The way they were blinking it looked like they were going to go off at any minute. "I hope this cake gets done before the power decides to go out."

Felicia opened the oven door and stuck a toothpick in the center of a baking cake; it came out clean. "At least these are done." After putting on her oven mitts she pulled the three cake pans from the oven and set them out on the counter to cool. "This is going to be so delicious. It will be perfect on a night like this. Maybe I should call Aisha." She reached for the phone, then stopped herself. "You can only set yourself up to be hurt so many times."

Felicia meandered into the living room and turned on the TV. She surfed the channels until she found an episode of *Good Times*. Tucking her feet underneath her, she curled up on the couch, and five minutes later she was fast asleep.

Across the hall Aisha was sitting at her desk working on one of the few client accounts she had left. She glanced out the window and smiled. The last time it stormed like this Felicia and I braided each other's hair, then ate blow pops until our tongues turned purple, she mused. Her aunt Hattie's voice echoed in her ears. "You're right. I need to make the first move, but as soon as I finish this. If I don't, then I'll be moving in with you," she chuckled.

Aisha refocused and moments later her fingers were zooming over the keyboard. She was still typing when a bolt of lightning angrily cut through the sky and hit a tree, cutting it in half. One half fell on the power lines and the other fell on an unfortunate family's roof.

In the blink of an eye, her computer screen went black as well as her apartment. "Oh crap! A power outage." Living in the South had its advantages, but its thunderstorms were ferocious. "I hope I remembered to save my work." Easing up from her chair, she stuck her hands out in front of her and touched her way to the kitchen, where she found a flashlight. Aisha turned on the flashlight and was rewarded with a spray of light. She walked over to the window and peeked out, and was met with darkness. It looked like every house on the block had lost power. Looking off into the horizon she discovered that downtown Atlanta had survived the power outage. The lights of Atlanta winked back at her, teasing her. "I guess now would be a good time to go see Felicia."

Five seconds later she stood in front of her sister's door, her face tight with worry. What do I say after all this time? she mused. Knocking lightly, she nervously swung her flashlight. She didn't get a response. She knew her sister was home because she had seen her come in. Using the end of the flashlight, she banged on the door. "If she didn't hear this—"

"Who is it?" Felicia called.

"It's me, Felicia!"

"Me who?" Felicia called.

"Your sister, Aisha. Look through the peephole."

"I am, but it's too dark to see."

"Hold on." Aisha stood back, then held the flashlight up to her face. Seconds later she heard the door being unlocked.

"Hey."

"Hey."

"What happened?" Felicia asked.

"I guess there's a power—"

"I know that. I meant what happened to *us*?" she asked softly.

"Oh. May I come in?"

"Sure." She held the door open for her sister. "Just be careful where you're walking. Don't want you to hurt yourself."

"Thanks." Aisha used the flashlight to carve out a path for

her and Felicia. Aisha sat on one end of the couch and Felicia on the other. Aisha shined the flashlight on her face. "I'm sorry. I'm sorry for all the mean things I said about you. I'm sorry for not letting you live your dream. And I'm sorry for being such an asshole."

"It wasn't all your fault. I should've mailed out the grant. That way Tiffany would still be working."

"You knew about Tiffany?" Aisha asked, and Felicia heard the surprise in her voice.

"Yep. She called me as soon as you left. But you know Tiffany—our girl always got something going on. But at least she can help me out more. I have jobs coming out of the woodwork. Oops!" She clamped her hand over her mouth. "I didn't mean to say that."

"Stop it. Say what you want to say. I'm not jealous. I'm not," she insisted. "I'm happy for you. There's nothing more exciting and meaningful than getting up every day and living your passion. Besides, I take sole responsibility for the demise of the company. If I hadn't been thinking with what's between my legs, we still would've had the KBS account."

"You don't know that."

"Sure I do. Lance likes to test people and I failed. It's as simple as that. I thought I could separate sex from business and my feelings. But I couldn't, and it was an expensive lesson. So can we put this all behind us and be sisters again?"

Felicia nodded, then flew into her sister's arms. "I never stopped being your sister. And no matter what you do, I never will. We're stuck for life."

"Why didn't you tell me?" she asked gently, still dazed and shocked by what she had seen. The image of her sister and Mia kept looping through her head.

There was no need for Felicia to ask her sister what she was talking about. "I didn't think it was such a big deal."

"Not a big deal? Felicia, I walk in on our friend polishing her teeth on your clit and you're saying it's not a big deal?"

"I don't mean to be so glib. I mean, it happens, women make love to each other."

"Yeah, other women but not my sister. How the hell did this happen? *When* the hell did it happen?" Aisha asked.

"Let me answer the *when* first. It happened in our sophomore year in college. Mia and I had gone out one night. I think you had a date and couldn't come with us. Anyway, we had gone out clubbing, drank a little too much and ended up in bed together."

"So she got you drunk? Is that what happened? She seduced you?"

"No. It just happened. I think we both were horny after seeing all the fine men and were feeling good from the drinks. One thing led to another . . ." Felicia's voice drifted off.

Aisha skeptically eyed her sister. "So are you gay? Or bi?"

Felicia shook her head. "Neither. I hate to label things. But if you're so intent on labeling it, just label me happy."

Aisha snorted. "Have you been with any other women?"

"Nope, just Mia," Felicia answered, and Aisha stared at her as though she had just smacked a rainbow sticker on her forehead. "I connected with her," she offered as an explanation. "Sex with her is much more spiritual than it is with a guy. With a man there's always that pressure to come, to perform—it's not there with a woman."

"Maybe you haven't met the right man!" Aisha retorted.

"Oh, I have. He can't make up his mind," she said, thinking of Tarik.

"So all those times Mia stayed overnight, you guys were doing it?"

"Sometimes yes. But not all the time. I mean, we didn't do it *all* the time, sometimes we just hung out. She wasn't my girlfriend or anything, she was my lover."

Aisha wrinkled her nose. "So what's the difference?"

"*Girlfriend* implies that we were in a relationship, which we weren't. We were lovers."

"You and Mia?" Aisha said, still stunned. "I still don't believe it."

"Are you shocked because it was Mia and me or because it was a woman and me?"

"I don't know. A little of both. I feel like I've been deceived," Aisha said, while eyeing her sister suspiciously.

Felicia saw their fragile bond beginning to unravel and went over to wrap her arms around her sister. "I'm so sorry, I'm so sorry," she crooned into her hair.

Just then the flashlight started flickering. "Oh no. Don't tell me that *this* is going out."

"I hope not, because I don't have any other batteries for my flashlight. I'll turn it off to conserve the batteries." Felicia turned the flashlight off and they were covered in inky blackness. "Oh, what are we going to do? I don't want to sit here in the dark."

"I know where there might be some light."

"Where?"

Aisha hesitated, then said, "Derrick. He has a fireplace."

"Fine, let's go to Derrick's," Felicia announced; she didn't ask her sister how she knew about the fireplace. I'll ask her later, she decided before grabbing her sister's hand. "Lead the way!" she demanded.

Chapter 33

"You lost, mothafuckas," Derrick gloated as he pressed down hard on his controller.

"In your fucking dreams!" Tarik shouted as he tackled his friend's player.

"You think you're gonna win, you ain't. You haven't won a series yet."

They were at the end of an all-day Madden NFL marathon. The games were tied—whoever won this would be the champ.

"If my boy makes this play, it's all over," Derrick gloated. "Your ass is going down."

"It's not gonna be that easy," Tarik said, his brow furrowed in concentration and his fingers moving over the control panel almost faster than the lightning that filled the Atlanta sky.

"Got you now," Derrick almost crowed.

"Like hell! I'm going to—"

"What the fuck!" The lights had suddenly gone out, taking the game with it.

"Shit!" Tarik said, and dropped the controller. It fell to the floor with a hard clanking sound.

"Hey, be careful with that. Break it and your ass bought it." Derrick stood up and stretched. The eight-hour marathon had taken a toll on his body—he felt like he had just uncurled his body from a trunk. He walked over to the window and saw what his downstairs neighbors saw and what the rest of the neighborhood saw: a sea of blackness. "I'd better light the fireplace. That'll give us some light." He turned and walked toward the fireplace and his knee connected with something hard. "Ouch!" he shouted, and rubbed his knee. "Hey, toss me the flashlight," he instructed Tarik, who had made it to the kitchen unscathed. "It's on top of the refrigerator," he said before Tarik could ask.

He stood still until Tarik walked over with the flashlight. "Hold that until I get this lit." Tarik held the flashlight while Derrick piled in wood, then lit it. "This is good," Derrick said, admiring the flames.

"I'm starving, what's in the fridge?" Tarik asked. They had ordered two pizzas four hours ago and had demolished both of them, each having one.

"Yeah, we might as well eat—otherwise it might spoil." Derrick strolled toward his kitchen. "Bring the flashlight," he called over his shoulder.

Tarik stood behind him and shined the flashlight into the refrigerator, making it easier for Derrick to rummage around.

"I have some sushi, wine, brie, crack—"

"Aw, man, what's up with the sissy food?"

"Not sissy food, pussy food," Derrick answered, and laughed out loud. "This is my seduction food. It's different from what the other brothers are feeding their ladies. This food is sophisticated, different, and most of all healthy. As soon as a lady sees this little spread, it's on. The clothes are coming off faster than at a visit to Hedonism."

"Well, believe me, I'm not trying to get in your drawers, so give me some real food. I know you got a steak up in here," Tarik said as he pulled open the freezer door and saw a freezer filled with hot dogs, steaks, pork chops, chicken and some salmon. But he ignored the fish and reached for the steaks. "Damn, holding out on a brother," Tarik mumbled. "You've been knowing me too long to be holding out on me like this."

"I thought you were looking for a snack."

"Snack my ass," Tarik grumbled while pulling off the plastic wrap from the steaks and seasoning them and rewrapping them in aluminum foil. "Real men don't eat snacks . . . they eat full meals. Let's go put these on the fire." Tarik and Derrick walked back to the fireplace.

"Shit!" Derrick blurted out, realizing they had a problem. "Let me run out to the balcony for the grill." He was back in less than a minute with the grating from his grill. He placed it on the logs and Tarik put the steaks on.

"So," Tarik started as he settled on the couch. "Whassup with you and Aisha?"

Derrick shook his head. "Nothing. She wouldn't talk to me even if I was the last black man with a job."

"So it's that bad, huh?"

"Yeah."

"Let's hope that she doesn't find out about your and Darla's agreement. If you think she was mad then, I think she'll kill you."

"She won't find out. I'm keeping that way on the low low."

"I can't believe you're still sexing Darla."

"That's all it is, partner, sexing. There's no love or at this point like involved."

"But to sleep with her just so she'll stay in Atlanta and you'll see your child. That's wild."

"It's what I have to do, man. I don't want her to take my child away. He's already a statistic. And I want to be totally involved in his life. So if that means that I have to sleep with his crazy-ass momma to do it, then . . ."

"What happens if she changes her mind?"

"She won't."

"But what happens if she does?" Tarik insisted.

"But she won't."

"Just suppose she does."

Derrick exhaled sharply. "Then I'm in some deep shit, aren't I?"

Suddenly there was a knock on the door. "Who the hell can that be?" Derrick asked as he strolled to the door. He opened it to find Felicia and Aisha on the other side.

"May we come in?" they sang.

Chapter 34

Derrick's eyes roamed over Aisha. "So you want to come in?"

Aisha met his gaze with a defiant stare. "We wouldn't be knocking on your door if we didn't," she retorted.

"Well, you're not going to get into Derrick's Bar & Grill with that attitude," he joked.

"Hey Felicia!" Tarik called from the couch.

Felicia froze before peering into the semidark apartment. "Tarik?" she squeaked.

"Yep."

Felicia took an involuntary step back. Aiy-yi-yi. She turned wide panicked eyes to her sister.

"Hold on," Aisha said to Derrick before tugging her sister away from the door and down the hall for privacy. "What's wrong?" she asked while shining the flashlight in her sister's face.

"Get that thing away from me. I feel like I'm being interrogated by someone on *Dragnet*," Felicia fussed while swiping at the offending object.

"My bad." Aisha set the flashlight down on the floor, making it look like a mini torch lamp. "Tell me what's wrong."

"I can't go in there. I'll go back downstairs to my apartment. Just give me the flashlight."

"How come you don't want to hang out? It's just Derrick and Tarik." Suddenly, despite the dark, she was able to see the situation crystal clear. "It's Tarik, isn't it?" Felicia nodded. "What did he do to you? Don't have me go in there and kick his ass." She turned on her heel, but Felicia grabbed her hand.

"Stay here!" she ordered before continuing, "He did hurt me," she admitted and quickly squeezed her sister's hand when she felt Aisha's body tense and position to run. "But not physically. He broke my heart."

"You told him how you felt?"

"Yep. Not only that, but we bumped pelvises. Then after it was all said and done, he said he wasn't ready for anything serious. Then he asked if he and I could still hang out."

"Whaaat? Did you tell him to kiss your black ass?"

"Well, I would've if he hadn't already done it ten minutes before that."

"Oh damn, girl," Aisha said before bursting out laughing. "Now listen, we can go back downstairs and sit in our dark apartments or we can hang out up here. Did you smell that food? I think I saw some steaks grilling in the fireplace."

"I know. But I'm not ready to see Tarik right now."

"You're gonna have to see him sooner or later. Now I'm not saying to forgive him. Because his shit does stink. He shouldn't have done what he did. But play him like he played you. Don't let this man control you. Deal?"

"Well," Felicia answered. "I don't know what to—"

"It'll come to you. Deal?"

"Deal."

"Cool. Come on." Aisha and Felicia retraced their steps to Derrick's apartment. *How can I take my own advice?* Aisha mused to herself.

Two hours later and after eating four steaks between them, they glanced at one another. "So what do y'all want to do now?" The combined light from the flashlights, candles and a lantern provided enough light for them to play a couple hands of spades and bid whist.

"We can play strip poker," Derrick offered.

"I bet you would love that," Aisha muttered.

"Of course I would," Derrick said with a wink. Aisha's heart jumped but she looked away.

"Let's play truth or dare?" Felicia suggested.

"So we're in high school again?" Derrick asked, and Aisha rolled her eyes.

"No, but we don't have anything else to do."

"I can think of something," Derrick offered.

"Keep dreaming," Aisha snorted. Then: "Don't we need a bottle or something?"

Felicia laughed. "That's spin the bottle."

"That's even more fun," Tarik quipped.

Aisha rolled her eyes. "Let's just go around the room. I'll start." Taking a deep breath, her eyes flitted from her sister to Tarik, then rested on her ex-lover. Even in the shadows of the flashlight she could see them all nervously shifting, the playful banter gone. "How do you feel about being a daddy?"

"Like a man who was blindsided by a seven forty-seven."

"That's harsh!" Aisha exclaimed.

"Just keeping it real." Derrick shrugged. "Come talk to me

the next time a woman shows up at your door telling you that she's pregnant with your child. Come talk to me then."

"First of all that won't ever happen. And second, you should've been more careful. Dudes always act like pregnancy is some fairy-tale shit. Like the women are sprinkled with some magic powder and they suddenly turn up pregnant. And they mysteriously forget their part in it."

Derrick shot up. "You trippin'. I never said I wasn't the father," he hotly denied as he glared down at her.

Aisha sniffed as though something stunk. "That's what it sounded like."

"All I'm saying is that the whole situation caught me by surprise."

"You don't remember screwing her?"

"No I don't," Derrick vehemently denied.

"What?" Aisha and Felicia exclaimed at the same time.

"It's true, I don't remember. I was so drunk that night that I probably couldn't remember my name if someone had asked me."

"Oh wow!" Aisha said, and broke out laughing. She laughed so hard that her body shook. Tears ran down her face.

"It's not *that* funny," Derrick almost growled. Tarik punched Derrick in his shoulder. "Yo dawg chill. Why don't you get a beer? We still need to drink them, since the refrigerator is off."

"Beer doesn't spoil, man," Derrick said, then sat down.

"Hey, other people are playing, let's keep it moving," Felicia said. "It's your turn," Felicia said, turning to Derrick.

"Do you regret the night we spent together?"

"What?" Aisha sputtered. In the artificial light, Derrick could see her nervously fidgeting.

"You spent the night with Derrick?" Felicia squealed. "And you didn't tell me?"

"Yeah, like you didn't tell me about Lawrence *and* Mia."

"Oh wow! How did you find out about Lawrence?"

"Who the fuck is Mia and what about Lawrence?" Tarik shouted.

"Nobody!" Aisha and Felicia said simultaneously.

Derrick cleared his throat. "You still didn't answer my question," he taunted, suddenly enjoying the game.

Aisha shot her sister a look that said she'd talk with her later. Then she turned her attention to Derrick. "Hell yeah, I regretted it," Aisha lied. "Not because it wasn't the best night of my life—I've had better—but because I should've been home painting my toenails. I really should start being more discriminating about how I spend my time," she said. "And now I have to use the bathroom," she announced before standing up and finger-touching her way to the bathroom.

Derrick was waiting for her when she stepped out. "What do you mean that you regret the night we spent together?" he hissed in her ear. He felt himself go hard. Just being so close to her turned him on.

"Just like I said," Aisha replied airily.

He tried to scrutinize her in the candlelight. "So you regretted this?" Derrick asked as he bent down and grazed her lips with his.

"Yes."

"And you regretted this?" he teased as he gently took her earlobe into his mouth.

"Yes," Aisha squeaked as his warm breath sent waves of desire through her body, making her legs wobbly as Chinese noodles. She leaned into him for support.

"What about this?" he asked as he slipped his hand under her butt and pulled her against him. Aisha felt his cock press into her stomach.

"Maybe," Aisha breathlessly answered.

Derrick softly kneaded her behind. What he really wanted to do was to pull off her pants and lick it all over. "What about this, baby? Did you regret this?"

"Derrick!" Aisha weakly protested.

"What, baby?" Derrick asked as he cupped her butt and lifted her petite body. Aisha's legs automatically wrapped around his waist. "Did you regret this?" They gazed into each other's eyes. Aisha was the first to look away. Derrick caught her chin and turned her face toward his. "I know you didn't regret this," he said before putting his mouth on hers. He softly glided his lips over hers and Aisha trembled.

"I don't," she mumbled before opening her mouth wider to allow his tongue in. She hungrily attacked it.

Derrick pulled back and swiped her mouth with his thumb. "Maybe we should take this to the bedroom."

"Forget that, let's do it right here," Aisha answered.

"Here?" Derrick asked, incredulous.

"Yeah, here." She nodded toward the toilet. "Put down the lid."

With Aisha's legs still wrapped around his waist, Derrick backed into the bathroom and Aisha immediately slammed the door shut. Derrick closed the lid and Aisha straddled him.

He reached in between her legs, pushed her G-string to the side and gently caressed her folds. "You're hot, baby."

Aisha nodded, too dazed to speak. Heat shot through her body; every inch of her body was sensitive to his touch. She pressed her crotch into his hand. "Stick your finger in," she moaned.

Derrick nipped her neck. "Happily," he breathed, and quickly obliged.

Aisha clung to his neck as she rotated her pelvis on his hand. Her soft whimpers filled Derrick's ear. His hand moved in and out of her with precision. He knew exactly where to touch her and the exact pressure to apply. Aisha began working his finger like it was his cock. Her eyes closed as she found her rhythm.

Derrick's fingers were slick with Aisha's juices. She shuddered against him and licked his fingers.

"Take off your clothes," Aisha instructed. Before the words were out her mouth, Derrick was out his sweatpants. They lay in a puddle next to the bathtub.

Derrick pressed his mouth against hers, then in one fluid movement he lifted her and impaled her on his penis. Aisha sucked in a breath of air.

All of a sudden Aisha froze, her body went as still as a block of ice. "Where's your condom?" she asked, panic rising in her voice.

"You want me to stop *this*? Aw, baby, you feel too damn good to stop now," he groaned, clutching her ass and moving it up and down as he pumped in her. Aisha's concerns were forgotten, she screamed with pleasure. "Shhh, baby, or your sister might think I'm doing something to you," Derrick said.

"Oh, baby, you are," Aisha panted as her fingers dug into Derrick's thighs and leaned back. "You are!"

Derrick bounced her up and down, plunging himself inside her.

On the other side of the door, Felicia and Tarik sat in the

dark living room. The sounds of Derrick's and Aisha's love-making floated to them.

Tarik laughed uncomfortably. Damn Derrick. But he grew hard thinking about his and Felicia's lovemaking.

"It sounds like they're breaking things," Felicia nervously joked when it sounded like the medicine cabinet had crashed to the floor. "Um, want to go down to my apartment?" she asked, and felt Tarik stiffen. "I don't want us to do anything," she hurriedly explained. "But I used to live with her and I'm tired of having to hear her sexapades. I love her, but it's gotten old."

"At least you two are talking again."

"I know. I feel so blessed. So . . ."

"What are we going to do in your apartment?"

"I have a cake to frost." Suddenly they both heard a series of loud grunts.

"Let's go," Tarik said, already halfway off the couch. They each grabbed a flashlight and headed toward the door.

"Do you think we should tell them we're leaving?" Felicia asked while looking at the bathroom door. Just then Aisha let out a scream.

Tarik grinned. "I really don't think they care."

"You're right. Lead the way."

"I hope the frosting is okay. Hopefully it didn't get too soft," she babbled as she nervously fumbled around in her kitchen. She hadn't expected to have Tarik so close to her.

"I'm sure it'll be fine," Tarik reassured her. "And even if it wasn't you'd make it work."

"Thanks," Felicia said quietly before she scooped up a

spatula full of frosting and patted it onto the cake. She bowed her head in concentration as she moved the frosting around.

Tarik was shining his flashlight on the cake for her. "I'm sorry about what happened," he stated quietly.

Felicia continued frosting the cake. "Why are you sorry? 'Cause it happened? Or 'cause it was good?"

Tarik thought for a second, then answered, "That it happened I guess. I didn't want it to. Our timing is all off. I'm not ready for what you want."

"What do I want?" Felicia asked, pulling her gaze away from her cake. She cocked her head, waiting for his reply but trembling on the inside.

"Come on, girl. You've told me time and time again that you want to be married and have a couple crumb snatchers." Felicia nodded. "And I'm not there yet. I can't give you all that. I know that I want it . . . just not now," he answered. Felicia heard the frustration in his voice.

"Come on. Let's sit on the couch." Tarik eyed the cake. "Is it your chocolate-banana?"

"Yep. You'll get some later. I promise." She grabbed his hand and pulled him to the couch. "Now, when do you think you'll want it?" Felicia quietly asked as soon as they sat down.

"I don't know." Tarik shrugged.

He looked like the little boy she had grown up with. She exhaled a breath of air, then wrapped her arms around him and pulled him to her chest. After a few moments she felt him shift. "Is this uncomfortable for you?" Felicia murmured. Tarik nodded. "Here, let me do this." She leaned back, fully reclining on the couch, and pulled Tarik on top of her. Tarik's eyes widened when he realized the position he was in. "Is this better?" she asked, staring up at him, watching the emotions run across his face.

Felicia reached up and tenderly caressed his face. "I understand what you're saying. And I respect it. I just want for you to be happy," she whispered before kissing one of his muscled biceps.

Tarik groaned. He leaned down and tenderly glided his lips over Felicia's. She reached up and brought his mouth closer, crushing his mouth against hers. "Felicia, I don't think we should be doing this," he said, suddenly pulling back, and Felicia pushed down a scream of frustration.

"But I want to," she protested. "I really do," she gazed into his eyes. "No strings attached, okay?" Tarik swallowed deeply, indecision washed across his face. "Let's just kiss," Felicia murmured.

Tarik nodded his agreement before bending down and catching her lips. Felicia's eyes fluttered closed as their mouths touched, she groaned softly before gently suckling his lips.

Tarik rained kisses over her face and Felicia smiled softly. "Why are you smiling?"

"Because this feels so right. I could fall in love with you." This time Tarik pushed himself up before Felicia could catch him. "What's wrong!"

"I don't want to do this. I can't do this."

"It'll be okay. I'm a lot stronger than you think."

"No you're not. We're not even friends anymore."

"Sure we are," Felicia offered lamely.

"Like hell. We don't hang out anymore. You don't let me test your food anymore, and we don't talk on the phone like we used to."

"I've been busy. And this thing with Aisha really messed me up."

"True, dat. But we're not as tight as we used to be."

"I guess there's a little truth to what you're saying."

"There's a lot of truth. Listen, I fucked up one time but I'm not going to do this again."

"Never?" Felicia asked as she reached up and gently stroked his face. "Or maybe there's room for negotiation."

Aisha relaxed against Derrick, waiting for her heartbeat to return to normal.

"Can you please grab the flashlight?" she asked Derrick. "Then shine it on me," she instructed. Using her personal spotlight, she turned to the vanity mirror, fussed with her hair and splashed water on her face. "Do you think they heard us?"

Derrick cocked an eyebrow at her. "I think the whole block heard us," he answered.

"Shit!"

"We're all adults," Derrick said. "Now put your G-string on and let's get out of here." Aisha picked up her Scotch-tape-size underwear and slipped into them, then picked up her clothes and took her time dressing. By the time she was halfway dressed Derrick was fully clothed and had his hand on the doorknob.

"Don't leave," Aisha blurted out.

Derrick's hand dropped to his side. "Whassup?"

"Don't you think our *relationship* is kinda strange? I mean, we barely know each other, both of our front doors are turn-stiles, and we're both aggressive as pit bulls."

Derrick chuckled. *I could fall in love with this lady.* "Our relationship is cool. And I'm ready to sit back and chill with you . . . no one else."

Aisha felt her lips go up in a grin, but forced them into a scowl. "Oh really? You think you can just stop the blood flow to that thing?" she gestured to his crotch.

"This *thing* is under control. Believe it or not, I do have willpower."

"Just not when you're drinking, huh?" she quipped.

"Funny. So are we gonna make this happen?"

"Maybe, maybe not," Aisha answered slyly.

"Don't sleep on me. I might end up changing my mind," Derrick arrogantly replied before stepping out the bathroom and sauntering into the living room. Aisha was close behind him.

Felicia and Tarik were sitting on the couch with the cake on the coffee table. A big chunk of it was gone.

"Anybody ready for dessert?" Felicia asked.

"I think they've already had theirs," Tarik joked.

"I did work up an appetite," Derrick said. "A piece of cake would be good."

"Sure. Would you like some?" Felicia asked her sister.

"Just a little piece."

Derrick stuck some of the cake in his mouth, then groaned. "This is off the chain, girl. You really should go into catering full-time."

"I am. As of a couple weeks ago I'm a full-fledged, full-time caterer."

"You are!" Aisha squealed. "You told me about your new clients, but I didn't know you had taken it to another level. I'm so happy for you. And if I could see a little better, I'd get up and give you a hug."

"You owe me one as soon as the lights come on."

"I tell her all the time that she's good enough to have her own TV show on the Food Network," Tarik chimed in.

"I bet she'll have one one day," Aisha said confidently.

"Thanks, girl." Felicia beamed. She was so happy that she felt like her heart was going to burst.

A hard banging on the door made them all jump. "Who the hell's banging on my door like they're the po po?" Derrick sauntered to the door. "Who is it!"

"It's me."

"Me who?" Derrick called.

"Stop playing, Derrick. It's me, Darla. It's our sex night. Open the door, baby."

Chapter 35

At six o'clock in the morning Aisha bolted out of bed and ran faster than Flo Jo to the bathroom. She made it to the toilet just in time to empty her stomach. Not that there was a lot. Last night she felt so queasy that she was barely able to eat any of the dinner Felicia had prepared. Aisha hugged the cool porcelain until she felt like she had hacked up a lung and kidney. On wobbly legs Aisha pulled herself up and used the sink for support. She splashed cold water on her face and looked at her reflection in the mirror. Her face looked like a deflated balloon and her eyes were flat pennies. "I don't know where this bug came from," she grumbled as she wiped her face off. "But I don't have time to be sick. I have to meet with a new client today."

During the meeting Aisha bolted once again to kiss the toilet bowl and was poised for a second trip when the wave of nausea rolled back.

After her meeting Aisha drove twenty minutes out her way to go to a Kroger where she was certain no one would know her. Inside the store, she eased over to the pharmacy department, where she stopped at the pregnancy tests. "There are too many to choose from." She reached out and snatched up the one she had seen on TV that promised to confirm your pregnancy three days before your period.

Back at her apartment, Aisha stared at the stick, her jaw dropped with astonishment. "I don't believe this. I don't fucking believe this." Stunned, she stumbled into the kitchen and pulled open the refrigerator door. "I need something to drink." Her hand automatically reached for the wine. It wasn't until she had her hand around the bottle's neck that she remembered why she wanted to drink. She snatched her hand back. "That's so off limits." She picked up a bottle of juice. Twisting off the cap, she gulped it down as though she hadn't had a drink in years. Pulling her shoulders back, she marched toward the bathroom, where a second pregnancy test sat on the vanity. "Let me try this again."

Aisha squinted at the stick; the word *pregnant* dominated the little screen. She scooped up the kit and dropped the whole thing into the garbage. "This can't be right. The test is defective. It has to be giving me a false positive. I need to try another one." Two hours and three different tests later, the results hadn't changed. She was knocked up.

Felicia and Aisha were in Felicia's apartment, sitting at her dining room table. Half-empty take-out boxes were forgotten as the sisters caught up with each other's lives. Aisha's eyes were dull and her hair was sticking up as though she had moussed it in a meth-induced spell.

"I'm pregnant," Aisha announced nonchalantly, as though she had just said that she had put on black socks.

"You're pregnant?" Felicia asked. "What do you mean 'you're pregnant'? You're what?" she croaked.

"I'm pregnant."

"No you're not."

"Yeah, I am."

"You're not!"

"I am."

"You can't be," Felicia protested as she stared at her sister as though she had just discovered after all these years she was a man in drag.

"Why can't I? I'm a woman who sleeps with men. It's bound to happen. Condoms get forgotten."

"Oh my God!" Felicia said. "Do you even know who the father is?" she blurted out, and immediately felt bad.

"Of course I do!" Aisha hissed.

"Of course you do. I'm sorry. Who is it?"

"Derrick," Aisha mumbled.

"Who?" Felicia asked, leaning forward to hear.

"Derrick," Aisha answered, louder this time.

"Derrick? Tarik's boy Derrick? That Derrick?"

"Yep! That Derrick," Aisha answered.

"*Darla's* Derrick?"

Aisha bristled. "He's not Darla's Derrick."

"Isn't she having his baby?"

"Yeah," she said glumly.

"Aren't they still sexing?"

"I guess."

Felicia's eyebrows arched with skepticism, but she let it go. "What are you gonna do? Are you having it?" Felicia held her breath. She would love a niece or nephew.

"There isn't any question about what I'm going to do. This

isn't what I had planned for myself. I always imagined that when I got pregnant I would be married, but I guess He had another idea. But I'm definitely going to keep it. Just because it doesn't fit into my schedule I can't get rid of it. I just can't do that," she said adamantly while shaking her head.

"Congratulations!" Felicia rounded the table and threw her arms around her sister. "I'm so happy for you, girl." They hugged tightly. "Ooh! I don't want to hurt my niece or nephew," Felicia teased. She liked the way it sounded. "So how many weeks are you?"

Aisha groaned. "About seven. And I feel like shit. I puke at least three times a day. I don't know why they call it morning sickness, because it happens at all hours of the day. It's horrible. There's nothing worse than driving on the interstate at eighty miles per hour and the urge to throw up takes over."

"Oh no! What do you do?"

"I zip across three lanes of traffic, put the car in park and crawl over to the passenger seat, open the door and just hang my head out."

"Poor baby," Felicia murmured.

"I'm scared, Felicia," Aisha admitted, sounding on the verge of tears. "I don't know if I can do this by myself."

"You thought that you were going to do this by yourself?" Felicia asked, astonished. "Oh hell no. You're not going to do this by yourself. I'm here for you, girl. You know that," she said passionately. "I'll always have your back. I'll even move back in with you if you want."

"Thanks. That's exactly what I needed to hear," Aisha admitted as tears began streaming down her face.

"What's wrong? Why are you crying?"

"I don't know," Aisha wailed. "The silliest things make me

cry. Hand me a tissue." Felicia got her sister a cold washcloth. "Ah, this feels good," Aisha said while dabbing her face.

"Hmm—so I'm assuming that you haven't told Derrick?"

"Not yet," Aisha admitted.

"So you are going to tell him?"

"Yeah. I just don't know how and when. It's not like I can just show up at his door and announce that I'm pregnant."

"I heard that's exactly what Darla did."

"Well, Darla and I are two different people. I've got to approach him the right way."

"No matter how you package it, girl, all he's gonna hear is that you're pregnant and he's the daddy. So when are you gonna tell him?"

Aisha worried her bottom lip, then shook her head. "I'm not."

"What did you say?"

"I said, I'm not going to tell him. Do you have a problem with that?" Aisha asked, glaring at her sister.

"Aisha, not two seconds ago you said that you were going to tell him. So what made you change your mind so fast?"

"What you said."

"What did I say?" Felicia asked exasperated.

"That he's going to think of himself as my baby's daddy and not the father of my child. So I don't think that he'll want anything to do with my baby."

"That's silly. You don't know how he's going to think. And it's unfair of you to make that decision for him."

"Well, I've made it," Aisha decided.

"It's stupid. I think you should tell him."

"I'm not going to tell him and you'd better not either," Aisha hissed.

Chapter 36

Aisha spooned chicken broth into her mouth and sat back against the cushions.

"You're looking a lot better," Felicia told her before grabbing a triple cheese burger and taking a huge bite from it. A mixture of catsup and mustard dribbled down her fingers onto her hand.

"Yuck! You're gonna make me sick," Aisha said. The condiment mixture looked like something she had thrown up two hours ago. "This is all I can eat. I already lost ten pounds making my stomach poke out like I'm five months pregnant instead of three," Aisha moaned.

"I heard your appetite will return."

"Don't tell me that. I have six more months to go. I'm going to gain so much weight that they're going to have to roll me into the delivery room."

"Par for the course, my dear. Par for the course." Felicia picked up a french fry, dipped it in hot sauce and popped it into her mouth. She cut her eyes at her sister. "So have you run into Derrick yet?"

"Oh God no! Thank goodness. I wouldn't even know what to say if I did. How can I explain this?"

"So you're going to tell him?"

"No—yeah—maybe. I just don't know."

"I see," Felicia laughed. "You really need to put yourself in the baby's shoes. Would you want the baby growing up without knowing her father?" Aisha shook her head. "Well then, what's up with all the secrecy? Why don't you tell Derrick, he deserves to know."

"I agree," Aisha moaned. "I guess that I'm so ashamed. I'm almost thirty years old and I got knocked up. Hell, I should know better."

"Dude's of legal age too, and *he* should've known better. To make it worse, he already has a baby on the way. So he should've had his thing triple wrapped."

"True."

"I think you should put away your pride and tell him. That's all I'm saying."

Derrick tossed his briefcase onto the couch, kicked off his shoes and clicked on the TV. ESPN blared through the room, soothing his nerves like a magical balm.

"What a fucked-up day!" He strolled to his kitchen and opened the refrigerator. He was met with four empty grates, even his pussy food was gone. "Shit! It just got worse." He slammed the door shut and spied the phone number of his favorite pizzeria on a magnet stuck to the refrigerator door. It took him less than five minutes to order a large pizza smothered in cheese, heavy on the pepperoni and sausage sprinkled with onions.

Twenty-five minutes later he was wearing nothing more

than his sweatpants and a wifebeater when the doorbell rang. "Man, they are fast," he said as he reached for his wallet. He was glad, his stomach had begun rumbling louder than a runaway train. He pulled open the door. "You guys are—" The words stuck in his throat. Standing behind the pizza delivery man was Aisha. She was still as if caught with her hands in the cash register. Derrick's eyes automatically roamed over her body, they drifted over her stomach then quickly retraced their route. Damn, she looks like she spent too much time at an all-you-can-eat Chinese buffet, Derrick mused.

He absentmindedly shoved a twenty in the delivery man's hand, who happily strolled off.

He nodded toward her small mound. "What happened to you?"

After two months of playing hide-and-seek, she was found out. At twelve weeks, her normally flat stomach looked as though she had swallowed a honeydew melon. She jutted her chin out. "What do you think happened to me?"

"You don't have to be so tart with me. You want to talk about it?"

Aisha sighed, then nodded. Derrick held the door open and she stepped through. "Whassup?"

"We need to talk," she said quietly. And Derrick, who was walking behind her admiring her butt, stumbled. In the past whenever he heard those words he knew he was in trouble or it was close behind. He straightened up and braced himself.

"Sure," he answered smoothly, motioning toward his couch. Aisha quickly sat down.

Taking a deep breath of air, she prayed for calmness. Having to utter two words that she had never said to a man before made her want to crawl under the sofa. She closed her eyes and Derrick watched her lips move as she mouthed a prayer. Her eyes fluttered opened, then: "I'm pregnant," she announced quietly.

"I know. I can see."

"I'm pregnant," she repeated.

"Congratulations!"

She gave him a pointed stare. "*I'm pregnant.*"

"And you're telling me because?"

Aisha pressed her lips together, then forced out: "I'm telling you because—" The phone rang and Derrick answered it. He paced around the living room while throwing glances in her direction. She heard snatches of the conversation and knew that it was a female. It sounded like he had forgotten their date, and she wasn't hearing his apology.

Aisha stood up to leave. *I'll see you later,* she mouthed to him, and before she could make the five steps to the door Derrick was off the phone. "Sounds like you're in trouble," Aisha joked.

"She'll be okay," Derrick answered. "Sit back down," he instructed. They both resumed their seats on the couch. "You were trying to tell me something before the phone rang. Whassup?"

"I-um-wanted-to-tell-you-that-I'm-pregnant," Aisha said, fumbling for words faster than a rookie cop does for his gun on his first day on the job.

"Well, you kinda told me that already."

Aisha unconsciously placed her hand on her stomach. "I am pregnant," Aisha said slowly, then: "And you're the father," she whispered.

"What did you say?" Derrick asked. "I didn't hear you."

"You're the father," Aisha declared, a hair louder, but it was enough for Derrick to hear.

"What did you say?" Derrick asked, a feeling of déjà vu washing over him. It was warm inside his apartment, but suddenly he felt clammy all over, as though he had plunged into ice water.

"You're the father," Aisha announced strongly.

"I'm the father?" Derrick asked stupidly, and Aisha nodded her head. "I'm the father?" he repeated.

"Yep." A grin the size of Georgia grew on her face. But Derrick's next words turned the smile to a frown the size of California.

"Oh, you're tripping now. I'm not the father!"

Aisha tilted her head and quirked an eyebrow at him. "The hell you ain't! Derrick, we did it so many times without a condom that I can't even count."

He narrowed his eyes. "How many other men did you fuck without protection?"

"I didn't *fuck* you. And you were the only man I've been with in the last four months."

"Lance? Didn't you do him *and* me on the same night?"

Aisha's mouth gaped open in shock. "Screw you! Yes, Lance and I were together, but we used protection. And it wasn't that night. Our baby was conceived the night of the storm. The night Darla came over looking for her dick on demand."

"Oh, that night!" Derrick quickly replayed that night in his head, smartly editing Darla out. "Oh fuck!" he moaned, then: "Are you sure it's mine? You've always been kind of free with the goods," he snapped, thinking of the incident on her porch.

Aisha popped up off the couch and stalked to the door. She twirled around to say something, but everything went topsy-turvy. She reached out to catch her balance. "Oh no . . ." she cried, before falling to the floor.

"I'm so happy that you're here." Aisha almost wept as she clutched her sister's hand. It took Felicia less than forty-five minutes for her to get to the hospital after Derrick called her.

"Always. I'll always be here for you. So what did the doctor say?"

Aisha nodded at the tubes that extended from her wrist. "I'm dehydrated. I've been throwing up like I walked by a crime scene."

"So how long are you going to be here?"

"The doctor said overnight."

"That's wonderful." Felicia looked over her shoulder. "Where's Derrick? He was just here."

"He left."

"What? He left you by yourself!" Felicia shouted. "What a jerk."

"I told him to leave."

"Why?"

"I was telling him about the baby, he didn't believe it was his. I didn't feel like talking about it anymore."

"He still should've stayed," Felicia said. Just then an orderly came into the room pushing a wheelchair. Behind him was a nurse.

"You ready?"

Aisha nodded.

"I thought you were okay!" Felicia said, her voice filled with panic.

"I am. But the doctor wants me to have an ultrasound just to make sure the baby is okay."

"You think something's wrong with the baby?"

"Don't worry. The doctor just wants to be sure."

The orderly and nurse half carried Aisha into the wheelchair.

"May I come with her?"

"Sure."

Felicia followed the small entourage to the ultrasound room, where the technician slathered her sister's rounded belly with gel.

The technician studied the screen. "There's the baby," she said, and pointed to a small blob on the screen. "Oh wait!"

Felicia and Aisha stared at each other. "What's wrong?" Felicia asked.

"I hope you have a big house," the technician said.

"Why? Am I having twins?" Aisha joked. She felt much better since receiving the fluids and Felicia coming.

The technician nodded. "Yep!"

Chapter 37

"I'm glad you're okay," Felicia said before wrapping her arms around her sister. Ever since her night in the hospital, she had been sticking to her sister like static cling. They were doing their favorite thing, shopping. Unfortunately they had decided to go during the lunch hour and the food court was filled with low blood sugar office workers.

"Are you sure you're up to shopping?"

Aisha nodded. "Yeah, the doctor okayed it. I'm cool as long as I take regular breaks. Now that I'm having twins," she whispered as though she had been issued a death sentence.

"It won't be that bad," Felicia answered as she gently rubbed her sister's shoulders.

Aisha teared up. "What am I going to do? I'm going to be a single mother to twins. How am I going to handle two babies?"

"I'll help you."

"Who'll help me with their feedings? I'll never sleep at night because I'll be up feeding them all the time," Aisha moaned.

Felicia bit her tongue. Now wasn't the time to tease her sister about karma. It wasn't too long ago that Aisha was keeping her from her sleep. "I'll help you," Felicia said instead.

"Who'll help me with their diaper changes? I bet they'll go through twenty diapers a day," Aisha said, her voice frantic.

"I'll help you," Felicia quietly repeated.

"And I can't afford *babies*. Maybe one . . . but not two. I'll need twice as much formula, diapers and clothes. I'll end up in the poorhouse taking care of them," Aisha wailed as she began crying.

Felicia pulled her distraught sister into her arms. "It'll be fine. I'll help you," she calmly reassured her. "My business is doing really well. It won't break me to contribute to your baby fund. And I'll move in with you."

Aisha sniffled and swiped her hand across her nose. "You will?"

"Here." Felicia handed her sister a napkin. "I will. We'll raise a new generation of Goodman women."

"Thanks. I feel so much better," she sniffed, and Felicia felt her sister's body tighten.

"What?"

"You won't be getting much sleep."

"Oh, I think I can deal with it." Felicia smiled, then: "Mia should be here soon. I told her that we'd meet her in the food court."

"Mia's coming?"

"Yes, Mia will be here," Felicia said firmly. "I don't want you to get yourself stressed out about all this."

"I don't like what she did to you!" Aisha fumed, feeling like her old self.

Felicia laughed. "Mia didn't do anything to me. For the record, she didn't seduce me, she didn't trick me into anything and she certainly didn't turn me out," she said reassuring her sister. "So please don't stress yourself out," she gently pleaded.

"I'm sorry, sis, but I still can't get used to the fact that my sister had a female lover."

"You jealous?" Felicia teased.

"What?" Aisha sputtered.

"Because I did something freakier than you."

"How do you know I've never been with a lady?"

"Because you haven't."

"How do you know?"

"Because if you had been, you'd put it on a billboard."

"Why? Because I'm sexually creative?"

"Is that another word for freak?" Felicia joked. "You'd put your business all out there because your ass likes to show off."

"You're right," Aisha laughed. "But a billboard is a little bit extreme. I'd just keep pictures in my private collection." She smirked.

"You have a sex collection?" Felicia asked. "It wouldn't surprise me," she said shaking her head. "Oh, here comes Mia."

"Hey, girl," Mia sang as she pulled Felicia into her arms, giving her a big hug. She turned to Aisha, who stood stiffly in her friend's arms. Mia patted her shoulder. "You look so cute, Aisha."

"I know, I just told her that," Felicia gushed, Aisha rolled her eyes. "Let's try to find some baby clothes. Let's try Nordstrom first. I heard they're having a sale."

Felicia began walking and Mia grabbed Aisha's hand, gripping it tightly. "Are we cool?"

Aisha strolled along with Mia, matching her stride. She narrowed her eyes at her former friend and Mia calmly held her gaze. "About as cool as an ice cube on a hot Bahamian beach."

Mia chuckled. "Why all the drama 'Isha? Your sister and I were lovers, big deal."

"Why did you pick her?" Aisha asked quietly.

"What?"

"Why my sister? I mean, everybody knows how I am."

"Is that why you're mad at me? Because I picked your sister and not you?" Aisha nodded. "Well, because e*verybody* knows how you are."

"What?" Now it was Aisha's turn to be confused. "What are you talking about?"

"There wasn't a man within a ten-mile radius of Howard who hadn't seen the inside of your legs."

"That's not true!" Aisha protested.

"Oh yeah it is. And there's nothing wrong with that. You got your groove on. But Felicia—"

"Was more discriminating?"

Mia nodded. "Yeah, but she's also sensitive, gentle and sweet. All the qualities I look for in a woman."

"Are you two coming?" Felicia called.

"We're coming," Mia yelled.

"So you weren't attracted to me because I was a slut?"

"I never said I wasn't attracted to you. I didn't pick you because you scared me. You would've been too much to handle. For the record, would you have done something with me if I'd asked?"

Aisha simply smiled and waddled toward her sister.

"I'm going to be a single mom," Aisha announced. "Do y'all realize that? I'm going to be raising my babies all by myself." After shopping they went to Ruby Tuesday for dinner.

"I'll help you," Felicia offered for the millionth time.

"What happens if they're boys? I don't know anything about raising a boy," Aisha said, her voice filled with panic.

"You'll be the perfect mommy no matter what sex they are," Mia reassured her.

"Why does Derrick have to be such an asshole?" Aisha blurted out.

"What?"

"Why can't he just act right and fall in love with me?"

Mia and Felicia hooted with laughter. "It's not that simple, crazy girl," Mia said with a giggle. "From what your sister told me you two have enough heat between you to burn up California *and* Alaska."

"That's true, he sure had my fire going," Aisha said with a laugh. "But he comes across as a brother who won't commit to one lady, even if she's having his baby."

"Are you sure you're on point? You might be unfairly persecuting that man."

"I don't know," Felicia said, shaking her head. "I know that he cares about you, especially after you fainted in his apartment. He rushed you to the emergency room and when I got there he looked so stricken that I thought you had died."

"That was fear on his face. He was worried that he might have harmed the baby," Aisha quipped.

"I don't think so."

"Maybe he's acting the way he is because he knows that you think men are like a buffet line, and you enjoy sampling," Felicia suggested.

"I doubt it," Aisha protested.

"Remember that you two do live in the same apartment

building and he could see who's coming in and out," Mia reminded her.

Aisha blushed at the image of her alfresco lovemaking on her porch. "Well, I'm not a saint," she huffed. "Nobody is."

"Do you like him?" Mia asked.

Aisha nodded. "I like him a lot," she admitted. Felicia reached over and rubbed her sister's back.

"I really hope that everything works out between you two."

"I do too," Aisha softly confessed.

"But you hardly know the man!"

"I know enough about him to know that I'm very close to falling in love with him. That's why this whole thing is so crazy. After years of avoiding a real relationship, I end up with a male version of me."

"Let me ask you this." Mia leaned in toward her friend. "Suppose Derrick comes correct and says that he loves you and wants to take care of you and the babies. Would you forgive him?"

Chapter 38

Felicia slathered a piece of bread with hummus, then groaned softly. "Mmm, this is heaven. I feel so guilty for playing hooky. I have a whole day to do whatever I want. No ripping and running." The windows were open and Atlanta's warm early spring air poured into her living room, and the sunshine spilled in. "I really should be out enjoying the weather. But it's so nice to just chill." She took another hummus-coated chunk of bread and reclined on the couch. So far today the most strenuous physical activity was walking to the bathroom. All morning long the TV had gone nonstop, giving her a chance to catch up on the talk shows and all the Court TV shows. She had long since turned off the TV. Now her attention was focused on reading. *So You're Gonna be an Aunt?* lay open in front of her.

Tucking her feet under her, she immersed herself in the book. Her head was still bowed as she read when two hours later her doorbell rang. She set her book down and walked to the door. Stepping on tiptoes, she looked through her peephole and her eyes grew as wide as the doorknob when she saw who was on the other side. She backed away from the door as though he had X-ray vision. What is *he* doing here? she wondered. Their last meeting left her more frustrated than an eighty-six-year-old man on his wedding night.

Well, you won't find out unless you open the door, she thought before throwing on a big smile. "Hey," she sang to Tarik. "What are you doing here?"

"I brought you some Chinese food," he said as he held up two plastic bags filled with little boxes. I took a chance that you were going to be home."

"Cool. Come on in. You brought enough to feed the whole neighborhood," she joked. "Let me take these."

"Nope," Tarik answered as he put them out of reach. "I'm going to serve you. I would've cooked for you, but I had a closing today that went over." Tarik motioned to the dining room table. "Sit down while I get everything ready."

Felicia eyed him suspiciously as he moved around her kitchen, pulling out dishes, eating utensils and wineglasses. He still hadn't told her why he'd showed up at her front door. "Yummy," Felicia said when Tarik piled her plate with an assortment of rice and lo mein dishes. Felicia let Tarik finish his first plate and was on his second when she decided to open the floor. "So whassup?"

"Nuthin'."

Felicia took a deep breath, then: "Why are you here? Not that I don't enjoy having you. But really, why are you here?"

Tarik let his fork drop with a clang. "I want to talk to you," he said, his voice serious.

Felicia set her fork down. "Sure."

"I want to ask you something first."

"Okay."

"Whassup with you and Mia?"

"It wasn't as serious as everybody made it out to be. Yes, she and I have a connection, but it's so fluid it can be sexual or spiritual. And right now it's spiritual."

"Is it over?"

"Of course."

"Will you two have a repeat performance?"

Felicia shook her head. "She and I talked. She already found someone."

"A man?"

"Why does it matter? Do you want her?" Felicia teased.

"What about both of you? I would love a ménage à trois."

"Yeah, right."

"So this thing between you is over?"

"Stick a fork in us, because we're done."

He nervously cleared his throat. "Um, I'm not feeling our new relationship. I want something more."

"You want something more," Felicia repeated. "What does that mean?" she asked calmly. This is exactly what she wanted to hear.

Tarik reached for Felicia's hand and gently stroked it with his thumb. "I want you to be my lady."

Felicia snatched her hand away. "You want me to be your lady? You want me to be your lady?" she repeated, her voice escalating to megaphone level. "First you said that you weren't ready for a relationship, then you said that you didn't want to ruin our friendship by having sex. Then we did have sex and you rejected me. Now all of a sudden you want us to be together? What kind of BS is this, Tarik?"

"It's not BS. Trust me on this."

"Then what is it?"

"It just took me a while to realize what I had."

"Oh, so you realized that there aren't too many women out there who would spend the day shopping with you, going to a basketball game with you and cooking you gourmet meals. Is that it?"

"Naw, it's not like that," Tarik said.

"Well, what is it like?"

"I admit I had to get some things out my system."

"You mean you had to let your dick free?"

"Honest?"

"Of course."

"Yep. How can you expect me to jump into another relationship so fast? I needed some time to regroup and figure out what I wanted."

Felicia rolled her eyes. "So now you know what you want?"

"I do," he said softly as he began stroking her arm. This time Felicia didn't pull away.

"What do you want?" she whispered.

"You."

"Me?" Tarik grinned, then nodded. "Why?"

"Because you're a generous, giving woman who has a heart the size of the moon. You genuinely care about what makes me happy, and you're thoughtful and considerate. And I'm sorry that it's taken me this long to see it."

Felicia batted back tears. These were the words she had wanted to hear when she opened her heart to him. "How do I know if you really mean it or if you're just jealous of Lawrence and Mia?"

Tarik grazed his thumb over her bottom lip. "I admit I got a little green when I heard about both. Hell, to be honest, I was surprised about Mia. But you explained that whole thing to me."

Felicia pulled away from Tarik's caresses. "Is that all you have to say?"

"I'm sorry. Just give me one chance and after that if you don't want to have anything to do with me, then I'll leave you alone. Please," he begged. "You won't regret it. Just say yes."

Chapter 39

Sprawled across his bed and sound asleep with the sounds of jazz floating around the room like a soft mist, Derrick snored softly. Lying next to him was Francesca, a lawyer he had met last week at a mixer. Her long legs were crisscrossed with his, making their legs look like two pairs of scissors.

The ringing from his phone woke him up.

"Yeah," he answered sleepily as he automatically sought out the alarm clock. It read four o'clock in the morning. He was met with silence. "Hello!" An anguished moan filled his ear. Suddenly he sat straight up and Francesca quickly mirrored his action.

"Darla?" he asked while jumping out the bed and blindly reaching around on the floor for a pair of sweatpants he knew he had thrown there earlier. Francesca clicked on the bedside light that was closest to her. With narrowed eyes she watched him scramble around the bedroom searching for clothes.

"Derrick," Darla groaned.

"Are you okay?" All he heard was panting. "Where are you?"

"I'm in the hospital," Darla uttered painfully. "The baby's coming," she cried out.

"Which hospital? Take a deep breath and tell me which hospital you're at," he asked, hating himself for not writing down the information when she had offered it to him a month ago.

"I'm at Piedmont Hospital," she answered in a voice that sounded as though someone had reached into her throat and twisted her vocal cords.

"Are you okay?"

"I'm having a baby, what do you think?"

"What? It's four o'clock in the morning," Derrick said stupidly.

"It's not like it has a clock or something."

"Give me thirty minutes. Don't let anything happen until I get there."

Darla yelled loudly and every hair on Derrick's body stood to attention. "I don't have any control over this," Darla said while gasping for air. "Just get here as soon as you can. Bye."

"What's going on?" Francesca asked.

Derrick looked in her direction and blinked. He had forgotten she was there. "Darla," he answered simply.

"Okay, who's Darla?"

"She's having my baby," Derrick admitted. He snatched up a T-shirt, and threw it on, and put a jacket on over it.

"You were in bed with me while your girl—"

"Ex-girlfriend," Derrick corrected her while zipping up his jacket. "Ex!"

"If she's your ex, why are you going to the hospital?"

Derrick looked at her and slowly shook his head. Where

do I find these heartless women? he wondered. "She's having *my* baby. But I don't have time for this conversation. I want you to get up, get dressed and leave. If you want to talk about it, call me tomorrow—otherwise peace out."

Moments later he trudged to the bathroom. It took him less than ten minutes to get ready and hurry out the door. A fully dressed Francesca marched out right behind him.

"Push!" Derrick coached Darla. Her normally pretty face was scrunched into a grotesque mask of pain. By the time he got to the hospital the doctor was all ready to send her off to the delivery room. He had enough time to let her know he was there before being rushed off to scrub up for the birth.

"I can't. It hurts too much. I want some more drugs. Can somebody please just knock me out!" Darla yelled.

"Just don't think about the pain. Just do it."

"Don't think about the pain?" Darla shrieked. "How the hell am I not supposed to think about a fifty-pound alien ripping me apart?"

"Can't you give her something stronger for her pain?" Derrick asked warily. The two hours he had been at the hospital felt like twenty. And the stench of the room was making him sick. It was a mixture of medicine, piss and shit.

The nurse shook her head. "She just got the epidural, let's give it some time to work. We didn't think she was going to dilate so fast—first-time mothers usually don't. Otherwise we would've administered one earlier. It's important that you get her to focus on delivering this baby. The doctor will be here any minute."

No sooner did she finish than the doctor arrived; sauntering into the room as though he was attending a cocktail party and not a child's birth.

"So are you ready to have that baby, Miss Darla?"

Darla made a sound that sounded like yes.

Derrick nodded. He glanced down at the mother of his child. She looked like a lady going through heroin withdrawal. Sweat poured off her face, her hair was plastered to her scalp, and her lips were pulled back in a grimace that scared him.

"Honey," Derrick whispered, cutting through Darla's moans.

The endearment acted as a painkiller, causing the groans to stop. "Yes."

"Look at me," he instructed.

"I don't want to," she protested.

"Look at me!" Derrick demanded, and Darla's eyes immediately popped open. "Look at me. When I tell you to push, you push."

"I can't. It'll hurt," she whined.

"You're a strong lady."

"No I'm not."

Derrick racked his brain for an example. "What about the time you ran the Chicago marathon and the time you interviewed President Bill Clinton? Not everybody can do that. That took a lot of balls and strength."

"It did, didn't it?" Darla panted.

"Yep. You can do anything you set your mind to."

"I guess," Darla said, her voice full of doubt.

"You can."

"I'll try," Darla answered.

"No, you're not going to try. You're going to do it." He glanced at the nurse, who gave Derrick two thumbs up.

"Push," the nurse instructed.

Derrick touched Darla's chin, forcing her to look him in the eyes. "Push!" Darla let out a scream that cut Derrick to the bone before she bore down.

"Good job!" The nurse said. "Give me another one of those pushes."

Darla's eyes never wavered from Derrick's face as she wailed, then pushed.

"You're doing awesome, Darla. The baby's crowning. I see the head."

"What is it?"

The doctor chuckled. "We can't tell the sex by the head."

"Oh," Derrick mumbled, feeling stupid.

"Don't feel bad," the nurse quickly reassured him. "I've heard worse."

"Yeah," the doctor agreed. "We could probably write a book on what goes on in the delivery room."

"Give me another one," the nurse commanded.

"Go ahead," Derrick said to Darla.

"Terrific!" The nurse motioned to Derrick. "Come see your baby. The head's all the way out."

Derrick stepped to the end of the table and went breathless. Staring up at him was a little human being, his baby, his child. The rush of feelings that overtook him made him light on his feet. "Take a deep breath," the nurse instructed. She had seen the same reaction from hundreds of new fathers.

"Okay, Darla, give me one little push." A second later a screaming, pale baby popped into the doctor's hands.

"It's a boy!" the doctor announced, and tears flowed down Derrick's cheeks.

"Would you like to cut the cord?" the doctor asked, and Derrick eagerly grabbed the scissors.

After the baby was weighed and prints were taken of his feet and hands, he was placed in Darla's arms.

"He's beautiful and *big*," the nurse called from the doorway. "Have you two thought of a name?"

Derrick's eyes shot up in surprise. He hadn't even thought about a name.

Darla stopped cooing at her son long enough to answer. "Derrick Tolbert, Junior," she said softly.

"Thank you."

A look of awe and admiration crossed Derrick's face as he watched Darla and his son. Tears glazed his eyes. Suddenly he knew what he needed to do. "Darla, I want to talk to you."

Chapter 40

Felicia and Mia walked out of the movie theater and into the night air. They had just seen the latest Sandra Bullock movie. "That was a good movie, huh?"

"It was okay. Sandra is so adorable," Mia responded.

"That's true. So how's your job?"

Mia stopped in her tracks and turned to Felicia. "What's up? You've been acting funny."

Felicia averted her eyes. "I'm fine."

"Did I do something to you? If I did I'm sorry."

"No, you didn't." Felicia sighed. "Come on." Felicia led her friend to her car. Once inside, Felicia grabbed her hands. "I'm sorry I've been in such a funky mood. I just don't know how to say what I have to say."

"Come on. You've never been scared to tell me anything before."

Felicia glanced outside and saw a man and lady strolling by, holding hands. "I'm in love with Tarik," she confessed.

Mia laughed. "Oh, is that all? I thought you were going to

tell me I got you pregnant. I knew about you and Tarik. You knew that."

"I know."

"Then, what's wrong?"

"I'm going to miss you," Felicia admitted.

"You're not going anywhere, are you? We're still going to be friends, aren't we?"

Felicia nodded. "I'm going to miss making love to you and our connection."

"We'll always have our connection. As far as making love, that's up to you and Tarik," she answered with a smirk.

"Oh yeah, he would love that. He already mentioned it."

"So you're going with Tarik after everything he put you through?" Mia asked for clarification.

Felicia nodded. "I'm in love with him."

"And I can't change your mind?"

Felicia furrowed her brow. "What? We've already had this discussion. Besides, I thought you were seeing somebody."

Mia stroked her lover's face. "I am. But I'll drop him in a heartbeat for you. I love you. I always thought that you would be around. Now that you're not . . ."

Felicia grabbed Mia's hand. "I will always love you. You brought out a side of me that I never knew existed. But I love Tarik and I'm going after him."

Mia grinned. "Well, a girl gotta try."

"So you're really cool?"

"I'm cool," Mia answered. "Look out, Atlanta, a gorgeous bi is on the prowl!"

Chapter 41

Aisha stared at the stack of FAACS business cards in her hand. Her eyes misted as she plucked half a dozen from the bunch and tossed the remaining cards into the garbage. With the exception of a couple of clients who still needed her services, FAACS was officially closed.

Aisha rubbed her stomach. "Hey babies, Mommy is taking a leap of faith. I'm going to open another business. What kind, you ask? It's going to be interior design, I'll be decorating houses. I've already done your Great Aunt Hattie's. I can't wait for you to see it. And you know that I'm in school, you've probably heard the instructor talking. Mommy's smart . . . but not that smart—I'll need someone to fill me in on everything that I don't know. So what do you guys think? Is this a good idea?" Suddenly she felt a rush of movement in her stomach, and she gasped. "Either that was two thumbs up or you two are fighting to tell me to get a regular paying gig. Knowing my babies, I bet it's two thumbs up," she decided, then plopped down her newly printed bright pink business cards.

◆ ◆ ◆

"You look awesome, girl!" Felicia said to her sister.

"Thank you. Thank you very much. Since I'm past that horrible first trimester, I no longer throw up. Now I'm at the cute stage," she bragged.

"You're adorable," Felicia agreed. Her sister's eyes shone and her skin glowed. At six months, she was at the stage where pregnancy was cute. Her stomach had blossomed to the size of a big beach ball—only her profile would give away her pregnancy. "I hope I look as cute as you do when I'm pregnant."

"Thanks, girl. And I can eat anything I want."

"I see," Felicia drawled, eyeing her sister's plate. She had decided she wanted pizza. In front of Aisha were two slices of pizza loaded with everything and bigger than any personal pan pizza. "That's definitely a two-hander," Felicia said.

"I know," Aisha agreed as slices of pepperoni, chunks of sausage, and strips of onion and green pepper dripped onto her plate. "But I'll get it up."

"So have you heard from Derrick?" Felicia asked cautiously.

"Indirectly."

"Huh? We live in the same apartment building. What is he doing, sliding notes under your door?"

"Kinda," Aisha snorted. "His lawyer contacted me."

"What? When? Why didn't you tell me?" Felicia shrieked.

"Would you calm down! All this drama isn't good for the babies."

Felicia rolled her eyes. If she heard that excuse one more time . . .

"It all went down yesterday—that's why I didn't get a chance to tell you but I was. Dude had his lawyer draw up a contract stating how much he plans on paying in child support and visitation rights."

"What! He did all this without consulting you?" Aisha shrugged. "I thought he didn't believe the babies were his."

"I guess he got some sense."

"Wow! That's awesome. I guess you don't have to worry about child support."

"I guess not," Aisha agreed. "But I'd take him over the money," she whispered.

"Oh, I'm sorry," Felicia said. "Well, go talk to him. Tell him what you want."

"No, that won't work," she said, then after a heartbeat she added, "He and Darla are back together."

"Huh? I know that I'm out of the loop sometimes . . . but huh?"

"Yeah. She moved in with him. I saw him bring her and the baby home from the hospital. It's a boy . . . he has a boy."

"I think you're wrong. I can't see him going back to that woman. I think he despises her."

"Oh yeah. So you think that he despises the woman that he sexed on the regular?" Aisha asked sarcastically.

"I think you got it all wrong."

"How can I get it wrong? I saw her hobbling into his apartment, he had a suitcase in one hand and the baby in the other. I don't think she was coming for a visit."

"But if he was back with Darla, Tarik would've told me."

"So you're with Tarik?"

Felicia ducked her head and smiled sheepishly. "No, but we're going out on a date, a real date. Not one of our hanging-out get-togethers. He said that he planned something really special for me and for me to wear something that would make Jermaine Dupri's tongue hang out. Do you think I should go?"

Aisha considered her sister's question, then: "First of all, why would he want some other man drooling after you?"

"You know how men are, they like to have the best—the best job, the best car and the best lady."

"Well, he'll certainly get the best lady," Aisha said with a smile. "And second, I think you should be careful. I like Tarik and everything, but that man is more indecisive than a five-year-old. It seems like he changes his mind faster than the weather. Just be careful," she reiterated.

"I am. My heart is right here," she said, holding out a clenched hand to her sister. "And this won't open until Tarik proves himself. I'm not falling again. Call me stupid once but slap me silly the second time."

"I'll be sure to slap you into next week," Aisha laughingly promised. "Just be sure he says I love you first."

"Oh, I will, believe that!"

"What about Mia? She suddenly did a disappearing act."

"We're okay. She and I always knew we weren't permanent."

Aisha shook her head. Felicia and Mia still surprised her. "Well, as long as you two are cool."

Felicia continued to munch on her calzone. The crust was a little doughy and the sauce thinner than she would use. Felicia smiled to herself.

"You're critiquing your food, aren't you?" Aisha asked.

"I'm no—" Then: "Yeah, I am," she admitted, a little embarrassed.

"Don't be embarrassed. So how would you rate it?"

Felicia looked around before answering. She leaned in close to her sister, then said, "On a scale from one to ten, I'd give the calzone a six."

"That's pretty good, coming from you."

"Yeah, I like the sausage and the vegetables are fresh. The sauce is a little thin but it's tasty."

"Go on, girl. I am so glad that I'm doing something that I love. After FAACS I thought I would die. I never thought that I would find a job that I loved as much as FAACS."

"How's the decorating going for you?"

"Phenomenal! Just phenomenal! Business is crazy. I just love it. Oh, here," she said, then reached into her purse and pulled out a stack of bright pink business cards. "Give one of these to everybody you meet."

Felicia studied the card, then: "Aisha's Interior Designs. I love it. Simple, but it says it all."

"I think so," Aisha responded. "I can't believe I've done so much already. I'm in school for interior design and I have customers. You know, there's nothing like walking into a room and transforming it to a showplace for my customers."

"I'm so glad that you're happy again. How's school?"

"Crazy . . . good. But it's something that I need. I have the magic touch. I can transform any room into something beautiful. But I'm learning how to read a blueprint, and understanding flammability and toxicity standards."

"Wow! And all this time I thought it was all about knowing which colors and fabrics look good together."

"Well, that's part of it," Aisha said modestly.

"But how did you get so many clients so far?" Felicia asked. Even though her sister wasn't licensed yet, she was busy with clients.

"Well, I used Aunt Hattie's house as a before and after."

"Her house is off the chain. I love how the whole room is centered around the plasma TV and the colors are delicious. I never would have put purple and yellow together. Amazing!"

"I love it too. So her living room is in my portfolio as well as my apartment. Those are enough to get me customers."

"And I know you're persuasive as hell."

"You know it!" Aisha said, and they both broke out laughing.

"Ugh!"

"Ugh what?" Aisha said, trying to follow the direction of her sister's eyes.

"Lawrence just walked in."

"The one you used to date?"

Felicia nodded. "I'm not in the mood to talk to him. We didn't end on the best of terms. Hopefully he won't see me. God, please don't let him see me."

Chapter 42

Derrick stood on the threshold of his living room and shuddered. "What the hell was I thinking?" Darla's words came back to haunt him: *Life is gonna sucker punch you so hard that it's gonna turn you inside out.* "Well, Darla, you got a kick-ass aim, 'cause my life is crazy."

Moving Darla into his apartment was the biggest mistake he had made in his life. Well, second, he decided. Getting her pregnant was his first. Gone was the organized chaos of his home; in its place was Hurricane Darla. It had been two days since the birth of his boy and he had asked her to move in. Her items were strewn everywhere. Open suitcases lay in the middle of the floor, bottles of lotions and shower gels cluttered his bathroom, and his kitchen looked like it was turned upside down and shaken. Since he had relinquished his bed to her she had turned his room into a department store during Christmas season. Clothes were hung from every free space, even his ceiling fan, and over two dozen pairs of shoes with three-inch heels, which reminded him of colorful ice picks, were scattered over his rug.

He had negotiated with his boss to work from home for the next two weeks. Darla strolled through the apartment with her cell phone superglued to her ear, oblivious to the clutter. This was her third call to her parents today—he knew because every time they were on the phone Darla insisted that he update them on the baby. Her parents, sisters and aunts were scheduled to be in Atlanta within the week. But he wasn't sure if he could take her that long. The two days she had been living with him felt like an eternity.

"I don't know why I'm doing this." Suddenly his son's cry echoed throughout the apartment. "That's why." He sprang forward. "I got him!" he called out. He hurried across the living room and gently pulled him from his bassinet. His little head, which was the size of a coconut, was scrunched so tightly that even his scalp wrinkled. "It's okay, little man." As soon as D.J., short for Derrick Jr., heard his father's voice he began whimpering. Derrick cradled his son in his arms and a surge of love enveloped him so quickly he had to lean against the couch for support, otherwise he knew for sure that his legs would buckle. "I think I know this cry, it's the hungry one." He sidestepped several pieces of luggage while he made his way to the kitchen.

"What are you doing?" Darla asked sharply. She had hung up the phone and trailed Derrick into the kitchen.

Derrick sighed deeply and bit back a retort. She was getting on his nerves worse than Simon from *American Idol*. "I'm getting ready to feed him."

"How do you know he's hungry?"

"Because it's been two hours since his last feeding. And I know his cry."

"He might be wet."

"He might be. But I'm going to feed him. Then I'll change him."

"Well, maybe he—"

"When will your family be here?" Derrick asked while cradling his son on one arm and reaching into the refrigerator for a bottle. He pulled one out and stuck it in the microwave.

"In a couple of days. They can't wait to see you again."

"You did tell them that this was only temporary, didn't you?"

Darla averted her eyes. "Yeah . . . I did," she mumbled.

"So you told them that you're moving back to your apartment as soon as they get here?" Derrick asked as he pulled the bottle from the microwave and tested it. Perfect! It took him only a moment to readjust D.J.'s head and give him the bottle.

"Yes, Derrick, I told them. We'll be out your way."

"Oh, *he's* not in my way," Derrick said while admiring his son. Suddenly an image of Aisha popped into his head. *I'm going to be the father of two children under the age of one.* The thought shocked him. Never had he imagined he would be the creator of a baby triangle.

Darla watched Derrick and D.J. "I really like us being together."

"It's all right."

"Maybe we should make it permanent."

"Like getting married?" Derrick asked as he restrained the urge to laugh.

"We don't have to get married right now. We could live together, then we could get married . . . maybe next year."

Derrick sighed. "Darla, listen to me, we are *not* getting married. And as soon as your parents get here you're *going back* to your apartment with them. Our arrangement was only temporary."

"You're an asshole," Darla hissed.

"And this, D.J., is why your mother and I aren't together," Derrick said as he glanced down at D.J., who was hungrily slurping. "Look at him eat. He's gonna be big," he said proudly.

"Yeah, he's greedy. You should see the way he attacks my breasts, like he hasn't eaten in ages."

"Thanks for that image," Derrick said dryly. "I have some papers for you to sign," he said nonchalantly.

"What type of papers?" Darla asked, her eyes narrowing suspiciously.

"About my son." He had a lawyer buddy who specialized in custody cases draw up papers detailing their custody arrangement. "It's something that we need to discuss. But I'll let you read the document first, then we can talk."

"You're not taking my baby!" Darla shrieked.

"I'm not taking the baby away," Derrick replied calmly. "I want us to share him."

"Well, he's not a piece of gum. I don't believe you. I think you want me to sign something giving my baby away."

"Hold up! Step back and take a deep breath. You're talking crazy. Just listen to me. I want what's best for the baby. I want to ensure that his future is stable. That's all I'm doing. Besides, you said that if we have sex you'd let me see D.J. whenever I want."

Darla snorted. "You fell for that?" she asked, and laughed nastily. "That was the only way for me to keep you in my bed."

"I knew that, that's why I had the document drawn up."

"My document is just as good," Darla shot back.

"You haven't even seen mine. So take your time and read it over. Maybe we can incorporate some of your points into mine."

"Yeah, all of them. I want to see this document," Darla demanded.

"Let D.J. finish his bottle."

"I want to see it *now*."

"The terms aren't much different from what you wanted me to sign. But this is a real legal document. Not something that some night school lawyer developed," he added, not being able to resist a jab at her document. "Give me another minute."

"Now!"

Derrick looked at Darla, not sure if he wanted to strangle her or kick her out of his home. He passed his son over to Darla. "Wait right here. I'll go get it."

Chapter 43

"This is an awesome building," Aisha said to herself in a state of awe. "Just beautiful." Her eyes drank in the lobby, everything about it screamed money, high class and good taste. The concierge stood discreetly to the side, hidden but ready to jump on command. The uniformed valet watched her with a smile as though he was ready at the drop of a dime to do her bidding. But it was the interior design that left her breathless. White marble gleamed throughout the room, rich cherrywood warmed up the lobby. The complete effect made her feel like she was stepping into a five-star hotel instead of an apartment building.

Aisha stepped into the elevator and laughed when she noticed a seventeen-inch flat-screen TV. Bling-bling. This is *that type* of neighborhood, she mused. A couple of blocks down was the building where the late great Coretta Scott King had lived and where Elton John currently stayed. Even Shaq and Janet Jackson had apartments in the neighborhood.

Aisha absentmindedly watched CNN as the elevator

whizzed her up to the thirtieth-floor penthouse. "I wonder who this mystery client is. This would be a once-in-a-lifetime decorating assignment."

Tiffany had made the appointment for her. All Tiffany knew was that the client was male and that he promised to pay her big bucks. As soon as her interior design business started making money, she had hired Tiffany back on a part-time basis.

Aisha stepped off the elevator and gasped—it looked like she had walked into paradise. The penthouse was over five thousand square feet with a view of Atlanta that made her feel like she was sitting up in the clouds. "Man, I love this."

A fireplace big enough for her to walk into commandeered the living room. She meandered down the hall to find three bedrooms, each of which were large enough to hold a king-size bed. She peeked in two and discovered that each had a private bath.

"This must be the master suite," she said as she eased into a room large enough to hold her living room two times over. "These closets are bananas. They're bigger than my bedroom."

She stepped into the master bath and inhaled sharply. It was like walking into a spa. Different shades of green, pink and beige graced the room. A sudden urge to drape herself in a plush towel and stick cucumber slices on her eyes overcame her. "Fabulous, just fabulous."

Aisha turned and found herself in front of a floor-to-ceiling mirror. She gawked at her reflection. She was still unused to seeing the beach-ball size bump in front of her. Turning to the side, she tilted her head and studied her profile. With the exception of the lump in front she still looked the same. "I can't believe that there's two babies in me and that I'm going to be a mommy. Thank you, God," she whispered, then rubbed her stomach.

Moving away from the mirror, she looked at the Jacuzzi, which looked like it could hold four people.

"Reliving some old memories, baby?"

Aisha jumped so high that she almost fell into the Jacuzzi. She caught herself just in time to keep from falling in. She hadn't heard the elevator door open. Whirling around she found Lance and Koi standing at the bathroom door. "What are you doing here!" she hissed before marching toward the living room; Lance and Koi were behind her.

"This is my condo. You're here to help me decorate it," Lance answered.

"This is yours?" Aisha asked while nervously studying him. He still wore the same smug expression that he'd always worn.

"Yeah," Lance drawled. His eyes roved over her body. "Looks like you've been having a little fun." Aisha shrugged. "It isn't mine, is it?"

"Aw hell naw! And thank God. I won't be responsible for creating another devil on earth."

Lance smirked. "Come on, now, it wasn't all that bad. You got trips, jewelry and even a chance for some freaky sex. Girl, you did shit that people only read about."

"That's over and done with. How the hell did you find out I was decorating houses?" Aisha asked sharply.

"From my boy Julius. I saw how you hooked up his crib, it was tight."

Aisha pursed her lips. "Shit! Atlanta is too small. I didn't realize you and Julius knew each other."

"Yeah, we go way back. He's even close with Koi, ain't that right, baby?"

Koi had moved to the window. "Yeah. Me and him and a good time," she answered.

"Hey, baby, go into the kitchen and get the stuff out the refrigerator for me."

Aisha's eyes narrowed. "What do you have? I hope it's not drugs. You don't have drugs, do you?"

"I'm just high on greed," Lance quipped.

Aisha rolled her eyes. This coming from the man who could smoke enough blunts to make a Rasta man look normal. "I think I'd better go. I don't ever want to work for you again. You're an asshole and you truly showed yourself when you kicked me out of the car on that rainy night."

Just then Koi sauntered in with a tray of chocolate-covered strawberries, grapes and slices of chocolate cake.

"Perfect," Lance murmured. "There should be a bottle of champagne right next to it. Bring the glasses."

Aisha vehemently shook her head. "I'm not drinking champagne. That's what got me into trouble the first time I met you. Besides, I'm pregnant, enough said."

Lance reached over and stroked her cheek. "You can have a sip."

"Fuck you, Lance! You're sick. I don't know why you think you can treat people like little wind-up dolls and expect people to come running back to you when you beckon."

"Because they do," he said simply. He gestured toward Koi. "Isn't that right, baby?"

Koi smiled and nodded her head, then gave Lance a glass of champagne before trying to hand one to Aisha. "Are you deaf? Didn't you hear me say that I wasn't drinking champagne?" Koi simply shrugged, then brought the glass up to her mouth and gulped half of the contents down.

"Would you like some strawberries, Aisha? I remember that you liked for me to rub them over your body and lick the juice off. But I think Koi would love to have the honors this time."

Aisha wanted to scream. She felt like she was in an episode of the *Twilight Zone*. "Why don't you just leave me alone? There's a lot of women in Atlanta—hell, the state of Georgia—for you to stalk. Why can't you let me go?"

"'Cause you're fun—you got fire, and you got balls. Things that people around me do not have."

Under normal circumstances she would be flattered having a multi-millionaire say those things about her, but coming from Lance they made her feel dirty. "Why thank you," she replied sarcastically. "I feel a whole lot better knowing that's how you feel about me. But I really need to go."

"Why leave? Koi had something planned for you." He nodded to Koi. "Go ahead."

Koi slowly began undulating her hips. Aisha watched wide-eyed as Koi reached up and slipped her finger under the strap of her blouse and seductively pulled it off her shoulder, then moved to the other shoulder, and her blouse fell to a puddle at her feet.

"This is sick. This is so sick. I really have to go."

Lance snapped his fingers and Koi immediately stopped dancing, then pulled on her blouse. "So let's make this happen."

"What!" Aisha sputtered. "Let's make this happen. This is coming from the man who got mad at me because I wouldn't sleep with his toy, then bankrupted me. Let's make this happen? This coming from a man who thinks that showing me some lady's titties gonna make me come running. Hell naw! You've fucked with me for the last time, Lance." She turned on her heels.

"Aisha!" he called. She continued her march across the room. "I'll pay you a quarter of a million dollars, cashier's check, to decorate my condo. I trust you, so you'll have total control over the project. You won't even see me, I'll stop by at night to check on the progress. Is it a deal?"

Aisha stopped in the middle of the floor, turned slowly. *A quarter of a million dollars?* she mouthed. "Oh shit!"

Chapter 44

Derrick wandered around his apartment, the silence weighing down on him like a heavy quilt. "It's so quiet without D.J." His son's sleeping area reminded him of a ghost town. The crib lay unused and the Baby Gap outfits with the matching hats and shoes that he and a cute salesclerk picked out were folded on the dressing table.

As soon as Darla's parents got into town he had her packed up, dressed up and prettied up before handing her off to them.

It took him only a day to get his apartment back to its original chaos. But it took a little more time to stop looking down at the floor when he walked—there's nothing worse than stepping on a stiletto heel. He glanced at the clock—it was time for D.J.'s feeding. "At least I have him this weekend." Once Darla had gotten a chance to read the legal document outlining child support, visitation rights and custody, and she had seen how much child support he was willing to pay, she had signed it faster than a meth addict. She even consented to the alternating weekends and the two weekdays clause.

Derrick strolled out to his balcony and peered over the railing and sighed with disappointment. Not that he had expected to see anybody, but there was a little part of him that hoped that he would. Wild horses wouldn't drag him to Aisha's apartment. Especially after the way he had treated her. He had been avoiding her like she had the bubonic plague. "I'm such an asshole," he murmured to himself before returning into his apartment.

Just then his doorbell rang and Derrick hurried to it, eager for visitors. Even a Jehovah's Witness would be welcome.

Wearing a smile the size of Georgia, Derrick swung open the door and the smile melted off his face. "D-Dad? I mean Phil," he stuttered. "What are you doing here?" he asked as a sense of déjà vu enveloped him. His last pop-up from Chicago didn't come bearing good news.

"To see you," he answered in his typical no-nonsense manner, then strolled into the apartment before Derrick had a chance to invite him in. Derrick's hand tightened on the doorknob as his father plopped onto the couch as though he and Derrick were old friends. If the doorknob had been made of glass it would've shattered in Derrick's grip. Closing the door, Derrick turned and studied his father.

The time he was able to understand what the words *fuck* and *whore* meant was the same time he learned that his father was always closely associated with them. Phil was the biggest player in the neighborhood. And as soon as he found that out, he lost all respect for his father.

Sitting on the couch, his father looked more like a retired schoolteacher than a man who broke up more marriages than crack cocaine. He had more gray hair and wrinkles than he remembered, but his six-foot-two body was still lean. *My father's getting old.* The thought shocked him. He had never thought evil grew old.

"You want a beer or something?" Derrick asked, fumbling for words. He vaguely remembered that his father liked to drink rum and Coke. But he had neither.

His father shook his head. "None of that. Juice or water will be fine."

Derrick sauntered into the kitchen for a bottle of water. He barely handed the drink to his father before the words came tumbling out. "What are you doing in Atlanta?"

His father eyed his firstborn. "I came to see you," he confessed.

"You could've called."

"I had to say this in person."

Derrick's eyes narrowed, the sense of déjà vu grew stronger. "What?"

"You're a young man, a young black man, who has the world within walking distance, within his grasp. Ruby told me about the car you just bought. Sixty-five thousand dollars." He gave a low whistle. "That car cost more than mine and Ruby's house. And you're doing things that was unheard of when I was coming up."

Derrick shifted impatiently on his feet. "I know you didn't come to Atlanta to talk about the good old days."

Phil shook his head. "You're right. I came to talk about you." He fixed his son with a pointed stare. "You have the world by its balls. Don't loosen your grip."

Derrick's brow furrowed. "Why are you talking in riddles?"

"You're fucking up."

Derrick's relaxed stance immediately turned rigid. He was

so still that he looked like a banana popsicle. "What did you say?"

"You're fucking up," Phil repeated calmly.

"How the hell am I fucking up?" Derrick asked, his voice rising in anger. "I have a job making six figures. I'm looking to buy a half-million-dollar home, I drive a sixty-five-thousand-dollar car, I wear custom-made suits. I'm going to make partner—"

"You're making babies," Phil thundered. Startled, Derrick stepped back. "I know about Darla and Aisha. Ruby told me. I don't want you to end up like me," Phil said, his voice sad with regret and a touch of shame.

"That'll never happen. You can smell pussy three miles away. If it's within sniffing distance, you're on it like white on rice. I'll never be like you," Derrick vehemently denied.

"You've gotten a good start. Two babies by two different women? And the kids will only be months apart? They used to call me Fill 'Em Up Phil. And boy did I live up to that name," he chuckled sadly at the thought of all his children. "It looks like your nickname should be Derrick the Dick. So who does that remind you of?"

Derrick thought back to his half brother, with only four months separating them. "I only have two. You have enough kids to make a fucking basketball team," Derrick spat, ignoring his question.

"*Only five,*" Phil spat. "Three kids by two different ladies and then you and your brother. That's still three too many."

"You keep reminding me of that. Why are you here? To absolve yourself of your guilt?"

"What guilt?" Phil asked.

"What about being sixteen years old and finding out that

you have a half brother that you had no idea existed? And you two are the same age? What about learning that your father wasn't the hardworking man you always thought. You were working sixty hours a week, but you were someone who couldn't keep his dick in his pants! What about hearing Momma cry every Saturday and Sunday night because you never came home on the weekends? That guilt."

Phil's face suddenly sagged, making him look like a crumbling graham cracker, and Derrick was afraid that he was about to cry or collapse. He fixed his face, then: "You have two children with two different mothers. Don't follow in my footsteps. Stop this cycle. Please stop it," he pleaded.

"There's no *cycle*. I just made a couple mistakes."

"That's what I thought too. I thought it all the way up till your mother and I went to counseling. I knew that I had hurt Ruby and I apologized a million times over to her. But I never knew how much I hurt you." Phil's eyes became shiny, but he continued talking. "I'm sorry. It took me over twenty years to say it, but I'm very sorry for everything I've done to you." They were both silent, then he shifted gears. "Now you know black folks don't like counseling, especially black men, but I went—I didn't want to regret away my golden years."

Derrick simply nodded, still stunned by his father's apology.

"I'm not going to lie and say that counseling was all easy. It was hard. There were some days that I could barely walk out the room, because my legs were trembling so much. It was so emotional. The reverend dug and dug until he got to the core of my problems. And I slipped a couple of times. I slept with women whom I would never even speak to if I were to pass them on the street. But I'm a project in progress. I know that I'll be okay," he said proudly.

"Good for you. Maybe you should be awarded some type of gold-plated dick. For every month you keep yours in, you're given one for your efforts of restraint," Derrick said sarcastically.

"I've changed," Phil said. "I'm changing," he hastily corrected himself.

"Yeah, that's what Momma keeps telling me. But I don't believe it. A leopard never changes its spots, it just changes colors. I don't believe you changed. And this counseling thing—why didn't you man up and tell me?"

"I didn't want the embarrassment of finger-pointing and I-told-you-so's. Not for me and certainly not for your mother. I'm sorry. Can you forgive me?"

Out of the blue Derrick's mouth went dry, his nose and ears began to itch and before he could figure out what was going on, his eyes watered and tears ran down his face, surprising him and his father. Derrick slumped against the wall as years of anger and resentment poured down his face. When he felt as though he had cried himself out, Derrick went to the bathroom, where he threw cold water on his face and toweled it off. He stared at his reflection. "Man, you're turning into a punk. Crying is for sissies," he scolded himself. But he felt undeniably lighter and freer.

Derrick strolled into the kitchen and pulled a beer out of the refrigerator. He stood at the counter and surreptitiously studied his father. He had picked up his latest copy of *Sports Illustrated* and was nonchalantly turning the pages. Derrick gulped down his beer, then walked into the living room.

Phil grinned as soon as Derrick returned to the living room. "You okay?"

Derrick nodded, avoiding his father's eyes. "I'm straight. I didn't know what happened."

"You're human," Phil said, then nervously cleared his throat. "I want to ask you something."

I can't take any more of this. "Go ahead," Derrick said in a calm voice.

"So how do you feel about your old man now? Can you forgive me?"

Chapter 45

"This is so classy, Tarik," Felicia said, awed. Her eyes were wide as she stared around the backseat of the stretch limo. Tarik could tell that she had never been in one before the way she touched everything as though it wasn't real. "When you said you wanted to do something special for our first date, you really meant it."

Until an hour ago, when Tarik showed up at her door wearing an Armani suit and carrying a bouquet of tulips, her favorite flowers, she had no idea that she was going to be pampered like a princess.

"You deserve it, baby. I've been such a jerk. I have so much to make up to you."

"You've gotten off to an awesome start. And I love this dress," Felicia said, running her hand down the black Tracy Reese dress. Tarik had surprised her with it, along with a pair of strappy sandals in the back of the limo. It took her only a few minutes to race back to her apartment to change. Felicia looked out the window, watching Atlanta whiz by. "So where are we going to dinner?"

"You'll see when we get there. I think you'll enjoy it."

Felicia began naming off several restaurants whose checks could easily total over two hundred dollars.

"Just wait and see."

Felicia stuck her tongue out at him. "Spoilsport," she teased. Suddenly they stopped at Centennial Park. "Oh, this is cool. They have a seafood restaurant down the street that's off the chain. I know the owner."

Felicia stepped out of the luxury on wheels and began walking. "Where are you going?" Tarik asked.

"To the restaurant."

"We're here," he said softly.

The driver got out of the car, rounded it, and pulled out an oversize picnic basket and blanket.

"We're having a picnic?"

Tarik nodded. "Kind of."

The driver pulled out a square item that was two-thirds the size of a card table and set it up, a crisp white tablecloth, bud vases with more tulips, sterling silver cutlery, china dinnerware, crystal stemware, linen napkins. By the time Tarik lit the candles tears were streaming down Felicia's face. "You did all this for me?"

"You deserve it," Tarik said tenderly. He cupped Felicia's face in his hands and gently kissed her lips. Felicia's arms wrapped around his neck as she deepened it.

"Thank you," she murmured against his mouth.

"You're welcome, baby. Let's eat."

Felicia's mouth watered at the food Tarik pulled from the picnic basket. Grilled salmon, rice pilaf, baked potato and a pasta salad filled their plates. They quickly blessed the meal. "This is good. What restaurant is this?"

"Chez Tarik," he quipped.

Felicia almost dropped her fork. "You did this? You made all this? Naw! You're joking, right?"

Tarik laughed at her amazement. "I cooked it all. Remember I told you that I wanted to cook for you one day? So I took some cooking classes. It was brutal, they had a brother making croissants and stuff. But this was my favorite dish and I knew that you would enjoy it."

"I'm so impressed," Felicia said. "This is so much better than a restaurant." She glanced up at the twinkling stars. "It's almost magical."

They ate in silence, each enjoying the food and occasionally having to stop to be congratulated by passersby who thought the whole affair was romantic.

"Let's walk off this food," Tarik said as soon as Felicia took the last forkful of food.

"Don't we have to clean up?" Felicia asked as soon as Tarik grabbed her hand and led her away from the table.

"Sam got us covered."

"So he does it all—he drives, sets up the tables and cleans up. Good deal."

"I only get the best for you." They strolled along quietly, each enjoying the sights and sounds of downtown Atlanta. "So are you still seeing Mia?"

"No. I told you that before," she said, lightly scolding him. "We still hang out together, but we're friends. Nothing's ever going to happen again."

"How can you be sure?"

"It takes two. And I'm not interested," Felicia said firmly.

"Why?" Tarik persisted.

Felicia stopped, forcing Tarik to halt his steps. She looked into his eyes. "I love Mia and I always will, she has a piece of my heart. *But* I want to be with you. I've made that choice and she respects it."

"Do you think you'll miss it?"

Felicia arched an eyebrow. "It?"

"You know . . . pussy?"

"Well, I got along without it when she and I didn't see each other, I think I'll be fine. Besides the sex, it was about the person. I loved her as a person. The sex part was extra."

"Do you love me as a person?" Tarik asked shyly.

"I totally adore you as a person." Felicia grabbed his hand and placed it against her cheek. Tarik's heart fluttered.

"What about Lawrence?"

"Nope. Aisha and I saw him at a restaurant a while back. Fortunately he didn't see me. As soon as I got a chance, I ran out of there like the po po was after me. I am so over that man."

"Why that man got you running from him? What did he do to you?"

Felicia hesitated, then: "He hit me. Right after he found out I was leaving him, he smacked me."

Tarik wrapped an arm around Felicia's shoulder. "Oh shit! He's a punk. Nobody but a punk hits a woman. He'd better not let me see him, 'cause I'll be glad to give him a taste of his own medicine. I'll have him crying for his momma and daddy."

"Look at you being all protective," Felicia teased. "I like it."

"I protect what's mine," Tarik said solemnly.

Felicia smiled shyly at him. "So I'm yours now?"

"Yeah, um, but not like one of my pieces of property, um, like—" he stuttered.

"What are you trying to say, Tarik?" Felicia asked bluntly,

her mouth dryer than a thousand Q-tips. And her heart felt like it was going to burst through her chest.

Tarik nervously cleared his throat before squeezing her hands. "It means that I love you and that I want you with me always," he said quietly.

Felicia suddenly swayed from side to side.

Tarik gripped her shoulders to steady her. "Are you okay?"

Felicia nodded, then stilled. She gulped deeply, then asked, "Are you proposing to me?"

"Would you like me to?" Tarik whispered.

"No. Yeah. Well, I don't know. This is all so fast. You don't seem to know what you want," Felicia said, then turned on her heels and resumed walking. In two steps, Tarik was at her side again. He was silent as he took her hand and gently steered her back to the limousine.

When they were inside the palace on wheels he picked up their conversation. "I always knew what I wanted. I just didn't want it when you wanted it. Our timing was off."

"So now we're in sync?"

"I guess you can say that." Tarik grinned and he began nibbling on Felicia's ear.

"Hey, haven't you had enough to eat?" Felicia joked.

"Haven't you heard? Always save room for dessert," Tarik said before pulling Felicia into his lap.

"Tarik!" she squealed playfully.

"This backseat looks big enough for us to stretch out."

"Ewww, I can't do anything with the driver looking at us."

"He can't see us. Besides, if he could I'm sure he's seen more than his share of people frolicking in the limo."

"*Frolicking?* I should turn you down just for using that

word," she said with a giggle. "I just feel so uncomfortable with him so close."

Tarik's hand slipped up her thigh and under her dress. He was met with bare skin. Felicia winked at him when his mouth widened with surprise. "You've been walking around all evening without any underwear?" Felicia nodded. "And all this time this was easily accessible," he said as his hand slipped farther between her legs and he slid a finger into her mound. Felicia groaned loudly as Tarik slowly moved his finger in and out. In one swoop Tarik had Felicia on her back with her dress bunched around her waist. Felicia tried to unclasp his pants. "What about the driver?" Tarik joked.

"What?" Felicia asked as she pushed Tarik's pants down over his hips.

"Nothing," he said as he kicked off his pants.

"Okay, I'll marry you," Felicia announced.

"What?" Tarik asked, then pulled away from Felicia.

"So you weren't serious? Then I wasn't either. Ha-ha!"

"No, I was serious. You caught me off guard by throwing it out there like that. You were so nonchalant about it, as if you said: 'Okay, I'll take the green one.'"

"So . . ."

Tarik moved away from Felicia and began fumbling around.

"What are you doing?" Felicia asked, watching as Tarik squirmed around in the back of the limo in his underwear, jacket and shirt.

"I'm trying to get something out of my pants . . . and I'm having the hardest time."

"I was trying to get something out your pants," Felicia muttered.

Suddenly Tarik let out a triumphant shout.

"I guess you got whatever you wanted out of your pants," Felicia said dryly.

"I did, baby," Tarik said as he straightened up. "Here, sit up." He grabbed one of Felicia's hands and pulled her upright. He looked in her eyes, then he nervously cleared his throat. "I want to tell you something."

"Okay. But can't it wait until *after* we finish?"

"I would prefer to tell you before we get started."

"Okay," she said, then with a wave of her hand said, "The floor is yours."

He pushed a button and the interior side panel lights came on. Felicia's eyes slid over to a blue jewelry box, then two seconds later her eyes zipped back. She gasped. Her mouth went dry and she stared at the box as though it was a live grenade.

"You know that we've been friends for a long time."

"Yes we have," Felicia answered with a shaky voice.

"And during that time I've confided in you and told you things that I haven't told anybody."

"Yes."

"And you've always been there to listen to me and to kick my ass when I needed it."

Felicia nodded as her eyes glistened.

"I never knew what I had until I lost you. It's a cliché but very true. I thought that I knew love before. But I didn't. I can't think of anybody else who I would want to spend the rest of my life with. Grow old with me, baby." Tarik opened the blue box to show a huge Tiffany ring. "I love you. Will you marry me?"

Tears raced down Felicia's face as she nodded. "Of course I'll marry you."

Tarik pulled the ring out the box then slipped it on Felicia's finger.

"It's so beautiful. I love you so much!" she exclaimed before she leaned in for a kiss. "This whole evening has been a dream," she said once she and Tarik separated. "Here I was thinking that all I was doing was going out on a date with a friend. I started off with a friend and ended up with a fiancé. I love it." They were silent for a minute, then, "Is it bigger than Tara's?" Felicia asked while admiring her ring.

Tarik chuckled. "Does it really matter?"

"No, not really. I'm just curious. I mean, it doesn't look as big," she said, trying to visualize Tara's engagement ring.

"Yours is bigger, a whole lot bigger—try a karat bigger."

"No!" Felicia said, shocked but happy. "My ring is bigger than Miss Snotty Tara's? I love it!"

"Hey, do you love me or the big-ass ring I got you?"

Felicia pretended to mull over the question. "Well, I do like the ring . . . but I love you. I truly do."

"So when do you want to get married?"

Felicia shrugged. "I don't know," she answered, then giggled.

"What?" Tarik asked.

"I feel so grown up. I'm getting married. I don't believe it."

"Well, believe it."

"I'm glad. At least you don't try to change me and always tell me what to do."

Tarik pulled her closer and began blowing in her ear. "I have something I want you to do for me."

Felicia pulled back, her eyes suddenly wary. "What?"

"Take off that dress and show me how much you love me, baby."

"I'll do that for you any day."

Chapter 46

Derrick strolled to the flower shop and stopped on the threshold. His father's visit torpedoed him into taking a deep look at himself. And he didn't like the image he saw. A young, intelligent, gainfully employed black man with two different women mothering his children, neither of whom was his wife. "I'm about to rectify that," Derrick muttered to himself. "I love Aisha. That lady has everything I'm looking for in a woman and then some. And I'm going to get her."

Squaring his shoulders, he walked into the shop. Bright colors and the sweet smell smacked him in the face, nearly causing him to back up and retreat. Floral shops weren't for men, they were for dreamers, little old ladies and people who had way too much time on their hands. He stepped in and immediately felt more out of place among the flowers than Britney Spears at Buckingham Palace. He picked up some roses and little white things.

"Hi, I'm Millie, the owner, may I help you?" He found himself looking down into the face of a small lady who barely came up to his chest and who looked like a freeze dried Nicole Richie.

"I kind of know what I want. I'll just keep looking."

Millie eyed the two roses and baby breaths he clutched. *Pitiful, just pitiful.* She pointed to the counter. "I'll be right over there if you need me. Don't be shy about asking for help, that's why I'm here," she said, her voice a mixture of Southern drawl and honey.

"Sure, thanks," Derrick answered absentmindedly. He continued wandering around the small shop sniffing, touching and bunching flowers together until his head hurt.

"I can create a brief that can save a client millions of dollars but I can't pick out flowers to create a bouquet," he mumbled to himself.

Millie kept an eye on Derrick but didn't bother him until his eyes got glassy and he moved around the store using small robotic steps. "He's ready to talk to a professional," Millie whispered to herself, then chuckled. She saw it every day. Men who usually ordered flowers over the telephone or Internet decide that they want to take a hands-on approach but end up looking like deer in headlights.

"That's a nice start," Millie lied. His arrangement looked like something a two-year-old would stick together.

"I want some flowers. But I don't want the typical roses," he was quick to say.

"So what's the occasion?" Millie asked while gently tugging the flowers out of Derrick's hands.

Derrick wanted to ask her if there were special flowers to give a lady after getting her pregnant and practically ignoring her for most of her pregnancy. Suddenly the thought of flowers seemed so insignificant. How can flowers make up for his behavior? A sudden urge to turn around and walk out the door overcame him, but Millie's voice stopped him.

"Sir, what's the occasion?" she repeated.

"Ummm, I'm sorry. I need to apologize for being the biggest ass—I mean jerk—in the world."

"Okay, do you want a mini garden or a bouquet of flowers?"

Derrick thought about it. He loved the idea of a garden so that she could have something that reminded her of him, but he also wanted the bouquet of flowers, something to brighten up her day. "What about both?"

"Follow me," Millie offered. Derrick was her shadow as she moved around the store. In the fifteen minutes it took for Millie to arrange a bouquet, he learned more about flowers than he ever thought he would. "I think she'll enjoy both of these arrangements. They're beautiful, some of my best work," Millie said while ringing them up.

Derrick studied the finished projects. "I just hope she thinks so too."

"Hopefully this will get you on her good side."

I've seen her good side, and I loved every minute of it, Derrick wanted to say. "Just say a little prayer for me."

Aisha waddled up the front steps to her apartment. A bag filled with potato chips and three pints of ice cream, three different flavors, banged against her leg. All day long she'd had a craving for something sweet *and* salty, and her usual trail mix wasn't hitting it. "What a day, what a day!" The day was spent at a decorators' warehouse rummaging through bins of fabric remnants, browsing through knickknacks and sitting on and poking enough furniture that by the end of the day all she had to do was eyeball the couch to know whether it was comfortable. "At least I got a lot of unique stuff. I think Lance will be happy." The warehouse had promised to deliver the items to his penthouse by tomorrow afternoon.

Suddenly she felt a jab against her stomach. "Whoa!" Aisha said, laughing. "Keep it down in there. The ice cream and chips are coming ri—" She froze in her steps. Standing at her front door was Derrick. "What do you want?" she snapped.

His response got stuck in the back of his throat. Her beauty stunned him. Gone was the short hair he'd last seen her wearing. It had been replaced by a head full of long sexy braids, which flowed over her shoulders and down her back. Derrick couldn't take his eyes off her face. She was glowing with contentment and peace that he hadn't seen before on a pregnant lady, not even Darla.

"I'll take these," he said, finding his voice, and he grabbed the grocery bag away from her before she could protest. As soon as the door opened, Aisha did what she always did when she got home—she rushed to the bathroom. Her bladder had shrunk to the size of a lima bean. By the time she came out Derrick had three bowls of ice cream sitting on the coffee table and a bowl of chips sitting next to it. "I wasn't sure if you wanted these in the same bowl or separate ones," he said nervously.

Aisha eyed him suspiciously. She hadn't talked to him since the baby was no bigger than a pea. Ever since then he had acted as though she didn't exist.

"I'll be right back," Derrick said, then raced out of the room.

Aisha stared after him a moment, then shrugged. She sat

down and began eating her ice cream, occasionally scooping it up with a potato chip.

"Heavenly," she moaned. She was so engrossed in her treat that she had nearly forgotten about Derrick—that was until he knocked softly on her door. "Come in," she called. Derrick came in and presented her with his gifts.

"I bought these for you," he said, offering her the flowers.

"Thanks," Aisha said, barely giving them a glance.

"I picked them out myself."

"That's nice," Aisha answered before returning her attention to her ice cream.

"I've never done it for any woman before," Derrick said, exasperated. Most women jumped up and down when they got flowers, or at least smiled.

"Well, I guess it was a good experience for you."

"Is that all you got to say?"

"What do you want me to say?" Aisha demanded. "I've been walking around carrying your babies and you refused to even see me. The only thing I got from you was a legal document saying that you'll pay child support. But now that you're giving me flowers you expect me to jump up and down with joy? It's not gonna happen," Aisha ranted, all the hurt and pain that she had been carrying around for the last eight months erupting from her like her morning sickness.

"I know. I'm sorry. I was overwhelmed. I had Darla, then you . . ."

"One thing has nothing to do with the other," Aisha spat.

"You're right. I see that now. And again, I'm sorry. That's why I'm here. I want to make it all up to you."

Aisha set down her spoon. "How do you plan on doing that?" she said, asking more out of curiosity than anything else.

"I don't know," he sheepishly admitted.

"That's stupid," Aisha snorted.

"I don't know because I want you to tell me what I have to do," Aisha gave him a sharp look. "I mean, I can tell you what I can do, but that might not be what you want. I want you to tell me."

The statement startled Aisha, but she stirred her ice cream and munched on chips while she studied his request. "Do you believe this baby is yours?"

"I do," Derrick answered softly.

Aisha tilted her head at him, then: "Why?"

"Because I know that you wouldn't lie about something as serious and life impacting as this."

"Why didn't you believe me before?"

"Oh I did," he said, laughing nervously. "I just didn't *want* to believe it. I never thought that I was that type of man."

"What type of man is that?"

"Like my father."

Aisha nodded but left that alone. "What are you going to do about Darla's baby?"

"Oh, that's my baby too, believe that. I'm his father and I'm going to take care of him just like I plan on taking care of yours—I mean ours."

"I'm glad," Aisha admitted. "I want our children to know their father. I want you three to have a relationship. I don't know how you plan on dividing your time between your three children but it should be equal. Just because these *babies* aren't your firstborn, I don't want them being short-changed."

"It won't," Derrick promised, then: "I-I-I—" he stuttered.

"What?"

"Did you say *babies?*" Derrick asked as he realized what Aisha had just told him.

"Yeah, two girls," she said softly.

"Oh my God!" Derrick said. His face went slack and he sunk onto the sofa next to Aisha.

"Do you need some water or . . . ice cream?" she asked, trying to be nice but not wanting to part with her food.

Derrick shook his head, then quickly changed his mind. "I need a shot of something, but water will do for now."

Aisha sighed. As much as she wanted to help him, getting up was an ordeal. She wished that there was a crane available to lift her. Moving to the edge of the couch, she rocked forward, then tried to propel herself up. After a couple of tries Derrick pulled himself out of his daze to notice her dilemma.

"What are you doing?"

"I'm trying to get up!" Aisha huffed.

"Well, it looks like you're trying to launch to the moon. Here, let me help you." He got up, stood between her legs, grabbed her hands and braced himself before tugging her up. If he hadn't been so shocked at the news of the twins, he would've been on the floor laughing.

"Whew! Thanks."

"How do you get up when no one's here?" Derrick asked as he followed Aisha into the kitchen.

"Sometimes if I remember I'll put a folding chair in front—that always gives me the support I need to pull myself up."

"Well, maybe you should call me when you need to get up."

Aisha rolled her eyes. "*Every time?*" she asked, handing him a glass of water. Then she turned on her heel to return to the living room and her food. "Do you know how many times a day that is? I'll have to call you when I go to the bathroom, get out of bed, get up from the couch. That's a hundred times a day."

"I'll be here for you and I promise to take care of you and the children."

"Is there anything else?" she asked, then gestured to her mini ice cream bar. "I've got to finish eating."

"There is something."

Aisha sighed. "What is it?"

"I would like for us to go out."

"What?"

"On a real date. We haven't done that. The few times we got together it was at my place. I want to take you out."

"What about Darla? Isn't that your girlfriend?" Aisha asked, then put her hand on her expanded waistline.

"*Was* my girlfriend. Our thing fell apart before I left Chicago. If it wasn't for D.J., I wouldn't even be seeing her."

"But you're screwing her!" Aisha protested. "I heard her at your door."

Derrick wanted to laugh, but he knew it would only piss Aisha off. "That was a mistake—"

"Why, because you got caught?"

"No. It was a mistake," Derrick patiently continued, "because I was so desperate to see my child that I would've done anything she wanted. People can't judge unless they've been in that situation. I got played, but that situation ended right before the baby was born. Something like that won't *ever* happen again," Derrick vowed.

"But why did I see her at your apartment with the baby?"

"Well, I'll be honest that wasn't the best decision. But when I saw my son being born all I wanted to do was protect and take care of him. I wanted him close by and I still do," he admitted. "But the only way that could happen at that time was to invite Darla to stay with me. Besides, she didn't have any friends or family here. I couldn't have let her go home by herself with a newborn."

"Well, you just have an excuse for everything, don't you?"

"They're not excuses. I'm telling you the truth. Think about it. I could have continued to ignore you and just paid child support."

"Then why didn't you?" Aisha asked.

"Because of my father," he admitted. "He made me look at Derrick. I didn't realize the path I was on until he backed up and stood beside me. I was following in his footsteps and didn't even know it," he said sadly. But then he suddenly brightened. "But not only that, I like you. I really like you."

"You do?"

Derrick nodded. "Now will you do me the honor of going out with me?"

"You want to go out with a fat cow?"

Derrick tenderly cupped her face and gazed into her eyes. "You're beautiful to me. So would you let the father of your child—I mean children, take you out?"

Chapter 47

Aisha glanced around the crowded restaurant and shook her head. The whole dating scene made her sad. Single men and women were scattered throughout the restaurant wearing their game faces, the men with the pathetic smiles and nods and the women trying not to let the men pick up their scent of desperation. They all pretended not to care about what the other thought of them, but they all were more aware of each other than a pimple on their butt. *That was me a year ago,* she mused. *Time sure does fly. Now I'm the mother of twins and living with the love of my life.*

"Okay, let's make a toast," Tiffany said, interrupting Aisha's thoughts.

"Don't you think you're toasted enough?" Felicia asked dryly. Tiffany had been drinking like she was a navy person just off a submarine after a two-month stint. Felicia knew that she was going to have to drive her home.

"Just having a good time!" Tiffany roared. "Let's toast my new jobs."

Aisha and Felicia grinned at each other before raising their glasses and clinking them together. "To your new jobs." Since Aisha's business was going so well, she had offered Tiffany a full-time position and Felicia had hired her on an as-needed basis.

"I still get to work with my two favorite ladies."

"Well, we couldn't let you go. We taught you too much."

"I really do appreciate you two helping a sistah out," Tiffany said suddenly, sounding very sober. "I don't know what would've happened if you guys hadn't rehired me."

"You would've gotten another job."

"Yeah, right, making no more than ten dollars an hour. I was doing some temp jobs right before you guys called me back. And I tell you the check wasn't even funny. I swore I even saw the teller smirk when I went into the bank to cash my check. At least Tyrone's father pays his child support on time—that's a big plus. But trust me, I truly appreciate you two."

"Have you considered going back to school? Your schedule is a little more flexible now," Aisha asked.

"I've been thinking about it."

"Well, don't think, girl, get off your butt and do. Now is the time to do it, while you're still young."

"I'll really think about it," Tiffany promised.

"I want to make a toast," Felicia announced.

"To what?" Tiffany asked.

"To my two beautiful nieces."

"Good choice."

They each held their glasses up and touched them. "To Morgan and Taylor, the two most beautiful babies in the world."

They were silent as they sipped their drinks.

"How do you think Derrick is doing?" Felicia asked her sister.

"I don't know, but I'm two seconds away from picking up the phone and calling him."

"But this isn't the first time he's been alone with them, is it?" Tiffany asked.

"No. He's watched them for a couple of hours at night, but this is the longest."

"I know we've been shopping and eating," Felicia laughed. "But you called him while we were in Bloomingdale's. You don't need to call him again."

"I think I will. I need to see how my babies are doing." Aisha whipped out her cell phone and called Derrick only to find out that the babies had been fed and were sleeping peacefully.

"See!" Felicia teased. "Told you everything was okay."

"Yeah. I'm a momma and those are my babies, and I won't be at peace until I know that they're doing okay."

"I totally understand," Tiffany chimed in. "So are you two getting married?"

"I haven't even been thinking about that. Don't get me wrong. Derrick has been awesome. He's my man now. You should see him with the girls and D.J. He's wonderful. We're wonderful. But I don't want to jump into something just because we have kids. I want to make sure it's right. Y'all know the divorce rate is crazy high. I'm not looking forward to that. Especially since my business is doing so well."

"I still can't believe you took that money from Lance," Felicia said.

"Believe, girl. Believe it hard. I had to think about it. But the price the dude was offering was too good to pass up. I had to ask myself whether or not I was being bought, but then I thought, Fuck it! I'm not ashamed to say that I needed the money and he was offering it. Now was that stupid?" she asked no one in particular. "I think not. I got a quarter of a mil out the deal, I got some phenomenal pics to add to my portfolio, and I made some once-in-a-lifetime contacts. Because of that job, I was able to get five more."

"I wasn't judging you, girl. I don't want you to think that," Felicia said, throwing in her disclaimer a little too late. "But it's not something I would've done."

Aisha smirked. "Yeah, you would. If sorry-ass Lawrence were to call you up tomorrow wanting you to cater his wedding for fifty thousand dollars, you would take it."

"His wedding?" Felicia hedged. "I don't know."

"You'd better, girl. Gotta separate your feelings from the job," she said while eyeing her sister and friend. "I had to learn that one. Money ain't got no pride. You'd be sitting home with light pockets and the person who did take the job would be planning their trip to Jamaica."

"I guess you're right."

"I wouldn't tell you nothing wrong," Aisha said confidently. "So what's going on with your wedding? What else do you need me to do?"

"Well, as my maid of honor," Felicia started, then giggled. Everything about the wedding made her giddy. Aisha and Tiffany rolled their eyes at each other. They had one more week of this. "You've gotten a reprieve for this weekend. But I want my maid of honor *and* my bridesmaid to go shopping with me. I need wedding favors."

Aisha groaned. "I think we've visited every wedding boutique in Atlanta."

"Nope. Just the Southside. We still have plenty left to visit."

Then: "Look at us all happily coupled up. We're almost like an episode of *Friends*," Felicia said.

"Eww!" Aisha groaned. "I would prefer to be compared to *Girlfriends*. And you're the anal, Joan," Aisha said while pointing at her sister.

"Hell no, I'm the fierce Maya. She kicks ass first and asks questions later."

"You're Maya?" Aisha and Tiffany asked at the same time, then looked at each other and burst out laughing.

"All of us aren't coupled up," Aisha said before sneaking a look at Tiffany.

"I saw that look!" Tiffany shouted.

"Would you calm your drunk behind down," Felicia hissed.

"I saw that look," Tiffany whispered. "And I'm not alone. Chauncey, Tyrone's father, and I have sorta been kicking it."

"You and Chauncey are back together?" Aisha asked. Tiffany had told her about him. She shuddered.

"He's changed," Tiffany reassured her, even in her semi-drunk state interpreting Aisha's reaction. "He's gotten a job, he's spending a lot more time with our child, and he's going to school to be a mechanic."

"Just be careful," Felicia said softly.

"Yeah, once an asshole always an asshole," Aisha quipped.

"Didn't you call Derrick an asshole once?" Felicia asked, her lips lifting into a smile.

"Oh, he's still an asshole. A cute asshole but definitely still an asshole."

Tiffany pushed away from the table and stood up. She swayed side to side as though she was in the middle of one of Atlanta's wind storms. "Well, Chauncey is no asshole!" she shouted before pitching forward and hitting the table face-first.

Chapter 48

"Why do I feel like I'm being taken advantage of?" Felicia asked Tarik, Derrick and Aisha.

"Don't worry about it, you're not. It's just that you're a great cook, baby. And you know what they say—you got to use it or you'll lose it," Tarik answered while spooning pasta on his plate.

"So we're really helping you," Aisha said around a mouthful of duck.

"Oh, so that's what y'all call it?" Felicia asked before sliding next to Tarik. "I keep busy enough. Since catering breakfast, lunch *and* dinner for that movie crew that was in town, I've gotten more clients than ever," she said. Then: "But I really loved cooking in that kitchen. Derrick, your house is off the chain!"

"Thanks," he said proudly. His six-bedroom house sported five full baths and a finished basement. It was four-sided brick and sat on three quarters of an acre. "I can't believe the fabulous price I paid for this. The house gods were smiling down on me."

"Wasn't it owned by that rapper who was arrested for murder?"

"Yep—he needed some cash pretty quick and I was glad to help him out."

"Too bad he still ended up in prison. I kinda liked his stuff," Tarik said.

"And," Derrick said, swaying the conversation back to his house, "my baby is decorating the whole thing." He gave Aisha a loving look.

"I can't wait, I have so many ideas.

"So how much is she charging you?" Felicia asked. "Now that she's big, you know that she's asking beaucoup bucks," she said, teasing.

Derrick grinned. "Man, she can haggle better than a welfare mom at a flea market. But we finally came to an agreement."

"Oh, what?"

"This," Aisha answered softly, then she held out her left hand and Felicia noticed a simple platinum band on her sister's ring finger.

"Oh, just a piece of jewelry. Cool, girl. It'll be a nice part of your collection."

"Not *just* a piece of jewelry," Aisha answered, then she twisted the ring around, exposing a 5-karat solitaire diamond.

Felicia's gaze flicked over the ring then quickly darted back as soon as her brain registered it. "Oh my God!" Felicia shrieked. "You're getting married," she cried before rushing over to her sister and pulling her in a bear hug.

"Congrats, man," Tarik said while giving his boy the black man hug. "Did you think that during our college days while we were out chasing broads we'd end up like this? Doing well financially, you a family man and both of us getting married? To twins?" Tarik asked while watching his fiancée and her sister with their heads bent together.

"I never would've guessed it. I'm so blessed," Derrick said, thinking of his two beautiful little girls sleeping upstairs, his son D.J. and Aisha.

"I'm so happy for you," Felicia said. "And I know you love him. He's the one who made you hang up your G-strings," she joked.

"He's a good man," Aisha whispered while glancing at her fiancé and Tarik.

Felicia wrapped her arms around her sister's shoulders. "This has been an interesting year and a half for us."

"I know, girl. When I had to fire Tiffany and work with just a handful of customers at FAACS I thought I had lost my world."

"Yeah, but I had to work for you when I really should've been catering full-time."

"Hey, I wasn't that bad to work with," Aisha protested.

"You were awesome. My heart wasn't in it. I think I could've been working for Earl Graves and still not enjoyed it."

"You know what?"

"What?"

"We did blossom after we separated," Aisha said.

"Hell, we soared," Felicia agreed.

"What do you think this means?"

"It doesn't mean that we're better off apart than together," Felicia answered, her brow wrinkled like a halved prune.

"But look at everything that happened," Aisha said, and

began ticking items off with her fingers. "I have two gorgeous babies, I'm getting married, and I own an up-and-coming interior design firm. And you are getting married and your catering firm is crazy successful."

"I can't disagree with that. But I think it was our argument that really forced us to go outside our comfort zone and do things that we wouldn't normally do. And the good thing is that we turned out to be like rosebushes. All the dead branches were pruned, which allowed us to blossom."

"Thanks, girl, I love you so much," Aisha said.

"I love you more," Felicia teased. "Now have you thought about where you're going to have *your* wedding?" Aisha shook her head. Felicia eyed Derrick's professionally maintained lawn. The grass was so green and lush that it looked fake. She knew from a previous trip to the backyard that there were peach, lemon and pear trees dotting the landscape. Flowers of every imaginable color decorated the house border and lined the driveway. "I think it would be nice to hold the wedding, if not the reception, here."

"Here?" Aisha asked as her eyes quickly retraced the route that her sister's had just taken. "Why not both? If we do it late spring or early summer we can set everything up outside."

"I like that idea," Felicia added. "And who are you planning on using as your caterer?"

"Who do you think?" Aisha teased, then: "Are you ready for your bachelorette party?"

"Whoa! I heard that," Tarik said, inching toward the ladies, then slid his arm around Felicia's waist. "You're having a bachelorette party?"

Felicia and Aisha shared a conspiratorial glance with each

other. "Yeah, but all we're going to do is finish the wedding favors."

"Yeah, and I want to make some miniature wedding cakes for the bridal party," Felicia chimed in.

Derrick looked at his fiancée, who looked like she had just found a whole closet full of Kate Spade shoes. "You two lie like a rug. Besides, I heard you on the phone ordering a stripper for next weekend."

"You were spying on me?" Aisha asked.

"I wasn't spying. I just happen to have overheard the conversation."

"I call that spying. Once someone realizes that they are privy to something they weren't invited to and they don't remove themselves from the situation, then I call that spying."

"You're having a stripper!" Tarik shouted.

"Baby, he's not really a stripper. I was told that he won't take off all his clothes, just his top."

Tarik pulled Felicia into his arms. "Just his top, eh?" he confirmed, and Felicia nodded. Tarik leaned down and breathed against Felicia's ear. "Just make sure all you do is look, don't touch."

Felicia giggled. Tarik was jealous. "Maybe or maybe not," she answered nonchalantly.

"What?"

"I won't touch if you promise to strip for me."

"For you, baby, I'll strip it down, flap it up and turn it around. I'll do anything for my baby," Tarik said before grazing his lips over Felicia's.

"That's so sweet," Aisha gushed.

"It is. Give me some sugar," Derrick said as he tried to pull Aisha to him, but she stepped out his reach.

"No sugar."

Derrick cocked an eyebrow. "Don't make me take it."

"You don't have the balls," Aisha teased.

"Oh really." And before Aisha knew what was happening Derrick scooped her up in his arms. "We'll be back in a couple hours," he called over his shoulder to Felicia and Tarik.

Printed in the United States
By Bookmasters